CW01509341

That's Why the Lady is a Tramp

MERRY FARMER

THAT'S WHY THE LADY IS A TRAMP

Copyright ©2022 by Merry Farmer

This ebook is licensed for your personal enjoyment only. This ebook may not be re-sold or given away to other people. If you would like to share this book with another person, please purchase an additional copy for each recipient. If you're reading this book and did not purchase it, or it was not purchased for your use only, then please return to your digital retailer and purchase your own copy. Thank you for respecting the hard work of this author.

This book is a work of fiction. Names, characters, places, and incidents are products of the author's imagination or are used fictitiously. Any resemblance to actual events or locales or persons, living or dead, is entirely coincidental.

Cover design by Erin Dameron-Hill (who is completely fabulous)

ASIN: B09KQ66NLR

Paperback: 9798797989950

Click here for a complete list of other works by Merry Farmer.

If you'd like to be the first to learn about when the next books in the series come out and more, please sign up for my newsletter here: http://eepurl.com/RQ-KX

 Created with Vellum

Chapter One

"I suppose you would all like to know why I called you here today," Lord Christopher Rathborne-Paxton, Marquess of Vegas, addressed his sons in the gravest manner Samuel had ever seen.

Samuel Rathborne-Paxton stood side by side with his brothers in their order of birth—Francis on his right, Dean on his left, and Joseph on Dean's other side—the way their father had required them to line up for military-like inspections all throughout their childhood. Sam sent Francis a wary, sideways look that was returned with an equal sense of foreboding. Nothing good had ever come out of their father calling all four of them to stand before him in the stiff and formal private parlor at the back of their family's London townhouse.

They all knew the drill, though. All four of them stood with their backs ramrod straight, their expressions schooled to seriousness and piety. Sam rushed through a list of his grosser indiscretions as though he were about to enter a confessional with a particularly harsh priest, even though the family was

1

not Catholic. No, their father was the staunchest, most vitri-olic Church of England man that had ever walked the face of the earth—pious, self-righteous, and merciless with his sons when it came to upholding morality and God's laws. Sam and his brothers had had virtue and dignity drilled into them—both through their father's rigid example and through a rod that was not spared so that they were not spoiled—from the time they were boys.

"Father, are you well?" Francis—the heir apparent and most commanding of the brothers—asked, his brow knit in concern when their father wavered rather than getting to the point. "You've gone positively pale."

"I...." Lord Vegas opened his mouth, but the sounds that issued forth were like words uttered from a particularly dusty tomb. That didn't surprise Sam at all. Their father's insistence on moral fortitude, thrift, godliness, and virtue was so devout that it was as though the man were already in the grave—and that he wished his sons to be there as well, what with the way he insisted on their absolute perfection and obedience as well.

Not that they followed that insistence. Not at all.

What Father didn't know couldn't hurt him.

"I am afraid...." Lord Vegas said, a pallor of actual fear spreading over his features.

Sam frowned. Fear was the one thing his father never showed.

"That is, I very much regret," Lord Vegas tried again. He let out a small moan, then gestured for Samuel's mother to come forward from the corner of the room—a corner that she'd been banished to for the past thirty years, since producing the heir. "Smelling salts," Lord Vegas groaned.

Sam was utterly unsurprised that his mother had the bottle on hand, tucked in a hidden pocket of her dowdy skirt. She produced it silently, handed it over without a word, then skittered back to her corner, like the mouse her husband had made her into.

Sam saw red every time he considered the way his father had snuffed the light out of his mother with his moralizing and insistence on womanly virtue. She had been young and vibrant, funny even, when he was a boy. Now she was a mere shell of a woman.

Lord Vegas took a long sniff from the bottle of smelling salts, coughed, winced, and groaned again. Then he pulled himself together to face the line of his sons.

He took a deep breath, seemed to focus on a point on the wall behind Sam's head, then said, "I very much regret to inform you that the Rathborne-Paxton family is utterly ruined."

There was a bone-deep silence as the statement sank in. Then Sam turned to his brothers, frowning, silently asking if any of them knew what this was about. They all ended up looking at Francis in the end.

Francis cleared his throat and got right to the point, as he always did. "Father, I do not understand. Ruined?"

Lord Vegas's face pinched, as though he might cry. That was enough to have Sam's back prickling with unease and his hands going numb with foreboding.

"It's gone," Lord Vegas admitted with a hopeless shrug. "All of it. It's gone. The money, the properties...everything."

"I beg your pardon, Father?" Joseph, the youngest and most serious of the sons, asked, looking genuinely worried.

"Surely, you cannot mean everything," Dean, the son between Sam and Joseph, said with a half laugh. For Dean, everything was a joke. Except perhaps this moment.

Lord Vegas squeezed his eyes shut, then let out a breath that seemed to drain all the sanctimonious, self-righteous life force that defined him. "For many years now, I have...I have engaged in...in speculation." He opened his eyes and addressed his sons.

Sam shrugged. "That is nothing. You know full well that I speculate on the markets as a hobby myself."

Lord Vegas's brow knit in a scowl, and he glared at Sam, demanding silence with his eyes and reminding Sam of the sort of all-powerful, tyrannical father he had been.

His expression melted to woe a moment later as he shook his head and said, "I have not speculated on the markets. I have...I have engaged in wagers and...and gaming, of sorts. Bad sorts. With...with Montrose."

Sam sucked in a breath. His brothers reacted with the same sort of horror. Montrose was infamous among the noblemen living in London. He was the very devil. He was the sort of man who only needed a single name, his reputation was so notorious. No one was quite certain where Montrose had come from or how wealthy he was, but it was well-known that he had grown that wealth through the systematic squashing of noblemen of good name. But perhaps not good character.

Montrose annihilated men. Once he fixed someone in his sights—something he did for reasons that only he knew—he pursued them until they were decimated. Sam could think of two men off the top of his head who had been driven to suicide by Montrose's dealings. And while it was true that Montrose only dealt with noblemen whose reputations were already besmirched through their own, vile actions, driving men to take their own lives was beyond cruel. Montrose considered himself a sort of vigilante, but that did not—

Sam's thoughts stopped cold. "You cannot mean that, Father," he said, taking a half step forward. "Montrose only goes after those nobles he deems to be villains themselves."

Lord Vegas's pale face splotched purple. He visibly shook as he dragged his eyes to meet Sam's. He was never satisfied speaking to Sam, or any of his younger sons, though, so he turned his gaze to Francis and said, "I have gambled shamelessly over the years, putting up various properties and assets as collateral for far too many loans. And...and there has been other behavior that I am not proud of. Behavior which—" He paused and swallowed, then gripped his hands in front of him to steady their shaking. "Behavior which Montrose is now using as blackmail to twist me into signing over the lease to all of my country homes, save Paxton Manor—which, as you know, is entailed and cannot be sold or transferred."

Sam and his brothers gaped at their father in utter disbelief.

"Are you saying that you have lost all of your money? All of *our* money?" Dean asked, his face a mask of shock.

"No, Father, wait one moment." Joseph held up his hand. "Are you saying that you have behaved in such a way that, if word of it should get out, you would be embarrassed, or worse?"

To Sam's utter surprise, his mother stepped forward from her corner. Her eyes were wide and she'd lost every bit of her color. "Say it isn't so," she demanded of him, her voice a hoarse whisper. "Say you did not—" She paused and gulped, pressing a hand to her stomach. "I asked you, years ago, if you...and you swore to me that you hadn't...but it's true, isn't it?"

Sam didn't have the first idea what she was talking about, but he noticed the cold fire in his mother's eyes and the sharp guilt in his father's. All he knew was that his heart was in shreds for his dear, long-suffering mother. She would be ruined and impoverished by Lord Vegas's dealings, which was a fate she most certainly did not deserve.

"Muriel, we will discuss this later," Lord Vegas said.

For the first time in his entire life, Sam watched his mother's back stiffen with rage. And unlike every other time his father had barked at her or put her down, this time she snapped back. "No, we will not," she said. She then promptly marched out of the room.

Sam's heart swelled with pride for his mother. He exchanged a wide-eyed look with Francis as Lord Vegas shouted, "Muriel! You will come back here at once!" That astounded look grew more exaggerated when Lord Vegas went on to hiss, "Dammit all to hell."

Lord Vegas never swore.

"Father, perhaps—" Joseph started, looking thoroughly out of his depth.

"Quiet, you!" Lord Vegas hissed. He growled wordlessly, grasped his hands into fists at his sides, then said, "What is done is done, but all is not lost yet. I am destitute, without a single penny left to my name or yours, but Paxton Hall is entailed. It will be gutted and the furniture and adornments sold. Some of the land as well. But the money from those sales will go straight to Montrose to settle the debt. This house is safe as well, because I had the foresight to transfer it to Francis's name. As Viscount Cathraiche, it belongs to him and therefore cannot be touched by Montrose. Yet. I would not put it past the bastard to go after you four, now that he has crushed me."

Sam had been aware of the transfer of ownership of Rathborne House six months ago. He'd asked Francis about it, since the move seemed incongruous on many levels, but Francis had been as baffled by the seeming act of charity as the rest of them were. Francis had his own estate in Hampshire that had come along with the viscountcy. Now they understood its intent.

"Fortunately, we have it within our means to restore the family fortune and repair our name and standing in society," Lord Vegas went on.

Sam exchanged another look with Francis, then with

Dean. "How can we do that, Father, particularly when you mentioned matters other than money?"

"Matters Mother seems to know about," Dean added in a low grumble.

Sam nodded, standing straighter at Dean's mention of their mother. Mother was his primary concern now. He would do anything to rescue her from the morass Lord Vegas had created.

Lord Vegas ignored Dean. His usual fury and indignation at anything his sons said that crossed him had returned. "You leave those things to me. They are none of your concern. What is your concern is infusing the Rathborne-Paxton family with cash, and lots of it."

"How do you propose we do that, Father?" Joseph asked, equal parts frustration and anxiety in his voice.

"By marrying," Lord Vegas said. "Marrying rich, and marrying swiftly."

Sam and his brothers were stunned to stillness. Of course, as noblemen from a prominent family, he'd always known the four of them would—or at least should—marry. Frankly, he and Francis were getting a bit long in the tooth at ages thirty and twenty-eight. Francis continually hinted that he would get around to finding a bride eventually, but "eventually" had yet to come.

Sam had envisioned other things for his life. Not every nobleman needed to marry, after all. Some merely enjoyed their family's wealth and status, going into some sort of business or playing the markets to increase their worth. To Sam, the term "idle rich" was not derisive, it was aspirational. If asked when he planned to take a wife two years ago, he would have given a similar answer to Francis's. But everything had changed after one blissful ferry journey from Belfast to Liverpool. Sam had one very good reason why he was in no hurry to rush into marital bliss—a reason with flame-red hair, emerald-green eyes, and a feisty sense of humor that kept him entertained in bed and out. As beautiful and delightful as that reason was to him, Alice Woodmont was as far from marriageable as it was possible for a woman to be.

"You want us to marry wealthy women?" Francis asked, restating the order and shaking Sam from his thoughts again.

"Yes," Lord Vegas said. "By Christmas at the very latest. Sooner, if you can manage it. Otherwise, we will all be out on the street, without help or solace. Surely, there are dozens of heiresses wandering the streets of London, looking for suitable husbands. Go out and find them." Before any of them could protest, Lord Vegas marched toward the door. "Now, you will excuse me while I deal with Lady Vegas."

"But, Father—" Joseph tried to snag Lord Vegas's attention, but failed.

The four of them were left alone in the parlor, stunned.

"What do we do?" Dean asked, pushing a hand through his hair. As always, the mood relaxed considerably once the four of them were alone.

"We marry, as Father ordered us," Joseph said, scowling at the floor.

Sam snorted. "You always were the dutiful one," he said, though not unkindly.

Joseph snapped a glare at Sam. "Just because Father stumbled somehow does not mean the rest of us should fall off the narrow path as well. He is our father. We must do as he says."

Sam winced slightly, moving to clap a hand on Joseph's shoulder. "I am sorry, Joe. I know that you have taken many of the things Father has thrown at us over the years to heart, but obeying that man now simply because he demands it is poppycock."

"You're still young," Dean added. "You'll learn the truth of things soon enough."

Joseph looked as though he would lash out at them for a

moment. Instead, he blew out a sigh and slumped, rubbing a hand over his face. Joseph was at the age where the structured ideals he'd adhered to as an adolescent were crumpling in the face of the temptations of the real world. They had all been there. Sam was grateful that enough of their father's moralizing had stuck with them that they'd each avoided serious vice. Although, it could be argued that keeping a mistress like Alice Woodmont made Sam as vice-ridden as his father apparently was.

"So, what do we do?" Dean asked, appealing to Francis.

Sam and Joseph turned to Francis as well. Francis straightened his back and rubbed his neck, wincing. "First and foremost, we investigate Father's finances and this Montrose person. If, in fact, Father truly did lose everything to the devil, then, to be honest, we might want to heed Father's demands and marry money."

"Francis, no!" Sam protested, stung by the thought of upsetting a life that he enjoyed just the way it was. "I will not sacrifice myself and my life to save a father that has proven himself to be the worst sort of hypocrite. And from what we've heard tonight, I am quite certain Father has committed a myriad of sins we've yet to uncover."

Francis fixed him with a flat stare. "I agree, but you are forgetting Mother's lot in all of this."

Sam deflated, knowing where Francis's argument would go before his brother continued.

"Father can go to hell, but Mother does not deserve to go along with him," Francis said. "I have a very bad feeling that she will feel the devastation of this blow more keenly than the rest of us. Her reputation and her comfort are in danger. I believe she knows it as well, thus her reaction to Father's announcement."

"Mama knows more than we do," Joseph said, his expression deeply troubled.

"We must protect Mother at all costs," Francis continued. "If it takes marriage to a quartet of wealthy brides to have the money to establish her in a comfortable home of her own, we must do it. If respectable brides from lofty families are what is required for her to continue in society without being laughed at or denigrated, we must find those brides."

Sam's heart squeezed hard in his chest at the thought of old friends and strangers turning their backs on his mother or causing her the least bit of embarrassment or harm. "We must," he sighed.

"There is nothing for it, then," Francis said with a nod. "We should seek out as many invitations to social events where we might meet suitable heiresses as we can secure."

"It's a shame the season is nearly at its end," Dean grumbled.

"You cannot be suggesting that we actually marry women we barely know simply for their money, can you?" Joseph spat.

"What's wrong, Joe?" Dean asked with a grin. "Does the idea of a wife terrify you?"

"I did not say that," Joseph stammered, taking a half step back. "I do believe we should honor Father's demands, but...." He swallowed. "I did not think it would happen so immediately."

Dean clapped Joseph on the shoulder. "The time has come, Joe. Prepare to kiss your sweet virginity farewell."

Joseph blanched and whimpered. Dean and Francis laughed.

Sam enjoyed the interplay between his brothers. They all got along splendidly with each other, even if their father was a tyrant and their mother a withered martyr. If marrying well was what it took for his mother to be redeemed and for his brothers to be happy and to remain financially secure, then Sam would do whatever was necessary for them.

Alice wouldn't be pleased at all.

But if anyone would know who the eligible heiresses of the season were and whether they were inclined to marry into the Rathborne-Paxton family, it would be Alice.

"*Fratres*, I think we know what we need to do," Sam said, resting his hands on both Francis's and Dean's shoulders. "And as such, I hope you will excuse me. I believe I must consult with the lovely and talented Mrs. Woodmont on this matter at once." He started for the door.

"Tell Alice I say hello," Dean laughed as Sam departed.

Of course, all four of his brothers knew about Alice. They'd known almost from the moment his and Alice's acquaintance began—on the ferry from Belfast two years before, when Alice had begun her new life after a spot of trouble in her homeland. His brothers knew the two of them were fast friends. They knew Alice had discreetly offered her services as a courtesan after moving out of the house of her close friends, the Earl and Countess of Carnlough, six months after arriving in London. And they had certainly put two and two together when it came to the nature of his relationship to Alice. It didn't matter to Sam. Alice was delightful, and his brothers thought so too. If anyone knew what he should do about the predicament they were all in now, it would be Alice.

Hyde Park was glorious in the warm light of April as Alice Woodmont walked along the Serpentine, arm in arm with her dearest friend, Maeve O'Shea, Countess of Carnlough.

"I would feel much better about my investments if I could travel to South Africa to take a look at the mine myself," Alice was in the middle of telling Maeve as the two of them enjoyed the afternoon.

Maeve laughed. "I can imagine. And in truth, an adventure to South Africa would be terribly exciting."

"Wouldn't it?" Alice grinned. "I'm certain Ryan would

love it." She glanced ahead, toward the edge of the water, where her six-year-old son was tugging on the string of the small, wooden boat Alice had bought him the week before, making it sail through the Serpentine's waters. "Ryan loves a good adventure."

Maeve laughed. "He most certainly does. So much of his life has been an adventure already. I dare say he will be quite the role model for little Alonzo." She glanced to the pram that her nanny pushed several yards ahead of them.

Maeve and Avery had welcomed their son, Alonzo, into the world a year ago, and the boy was the apple of Maeve's eye. Maeve had also found the very best nanny in London, Mrs. Cottrell, who adored Alonzo as though he were her very own. The care Mrs. Cottrell showed Alonzo made Maeve feel secure enough to spend an afternoon with her wayward friend now and then.

Not that Maeve had any idea just how wayward Alice had become. That was a secret Alice had done a very good job of keeping from her friend, if she did say so herself.

"The trouble is that I've heard nothing from Mr. Kalman for weeks now," Alice went on, lamenting about her investment. "The last deposit to my bank account was made over two months ago, and I'm afraid I'm spread a bit thin at the moment."

"Oh?" Maeve's face lit up, and Alice instantly regretted the topic of conversation. Because she knew Maeve would go on to say, "If you need a bit of pin money to see you through until Mr. Kalman and his diamonds come through, Avery and I would be more than amenable to giving you whatever you need."

Alice kept a smile on her face, but inwardly she winced. Maeve and Avery were the dearest friends she could possibly have, but accepting their charity came with strings that she wasn't certain she wanted to be attached to.

"It's nothing to worry about yet," she said, focusing on her son as Ryan found a playmate by the water's edge. "I have many resources yet to tap." Though not all of those resources were the sort she wanted to dip into at all.

"Just know that Avery and I are at your disposal," Maeve said with a smile.

Alice was gladder than she could express for the friendship Maeve had shown her since they were girls. Maeve had been there when the nefarious Michael Feeney had spun her head, stolen her heart, and left her unmarried and with child before rushing off to America. She'd been loyal when Michael returned and tried to kidnap Ryan and use her darling to extort money from his own brother, Mr. Rory Feeney. And when Ryan's parentage was revealed and Alice's reputation ruined in Ireland, Maeve and Avery had graciously offered to bring Alice to London with them so that she could escape her ruin there.

Of course, she'd leapt from one form of ruin to another within months of landing in London. She could have stayed as a ward of Maeve and Avery indefinitely, but to do so would have reduced her to the role of a child in someone else's house. At first, Alice had looked for gainful employment in various shops or offices in London. But after receiving a shocking proposal from a charming gentleman at the theater one night, she'd realized there was a great deal of money to be made by doing something she'd already done for Michael.

It had been surprisingly easy to slip into that sort of life, and without Maeve or Avery knowing it. As it turned out, her particular skills and ability to do whatever was necessary to give Ryan the life he deserved was quite lucrative. Particularly when one of her early lovers endowed her with shares in a diamond mine run by Mr. Kalman.

But none of that would have succeeded or meant a thing to Alice were it not for Sam.

She'd met Samuel Rathborne-Paxton on the ferry from Belfast to Liverpool at the very beginning of her new life. They'd formed a fast friendship during the journey to London, and once established there, the two of them had remained friends. More than friends, as it turned out. Once Alice's scruples about how she spent her evenings were shed, Samuel was one of the first men she'd rushed to take to her bed. With Sam, it wasn't entirely business. They were too good of friends for their interactions to be so callous. They enjoyed each other in every way. Sam had taught her about investing and speculation, and although she didn't consider herself very good at it, his encouragement kept her hoping.

And after the diamond mine had started producing enough profits, Alice had promptly bid goodbye to all of her lovers, except Sam. She considered the year in which she'd done what was necessary to support Ryan a lost year of her life, but now, with just Sam, she was back on the straight and narrow.

The rest of the world did not see things as she did.

"Gerald, no!" a harsh woman's voice snapped Alice out of her thoughts. "Get away from that boy this instant."

"But nanny," the boy playing with Ryan whined, "he's my friend."

"A boy like that is most certainly not your friend," the nanny huffed. She sent a narrow-eyed glance straight to Alice. "He is rubbish, and we do not play with rubbish."

"But, nanny," young Gerald protested as his nanny marched down to the Serpentine and snatched him away.

"Stay away from filth," the nanny said, shaking poor Gerald.

Alice's heart sank as Ryan sadly collected his boat, then rushed up the slope to bury his face against Alice's skirts.

"I say," Maeve gasped in horror. "I have never seen anything so rude in my life."

14

"It's all right," Alice sighed, petting Ryan's head.

The fact was, she had seen rudeness like that before. She saw it all the time, every day, from everyone who had heard the rumors about her reputation. They were rumors she couldn't deny, because each and every one of them was true. She was a fallen woman with a soiled reputation, and she was treated as such.

"I should speak to someone about that sort of behavior," Maeve blustered on. "Perhaps Mrs. Cottrell knows what family that horrible woman is employed with." Maeve marched off toward her own nanny.

"No, Maeve, truly, you mustn't," Alice tried to stop her.

A moment later, her heart caught in her chest and her depressed spirits improved drastically as she glanced past Maeve to the figure of Sam approaching along the path. Sam smiled broadly when their eyes met, and Alice knew that her day was about to get much brighter.

Chapter Two

Sam burst into a smile at the sight of Alice. At last, something bright in his otherwise miserable day. Alice was the most beautiful woman he'd ever known. Her flame-red hair caught the afternoon sunlight, even though it was styled fashionably and hidden by a pert hat with pheasant feathers in it. He liked the way Alice's silky hair looked spread across the pillow when the two of them made love. He liked the alabaster glow of her skin and all of the perfect curves of her body as well. Even dressed in a conservative walking outfit of the sort she wore now, there was something undeniably sensual about Alice's form. Sam supposed that was what made her such a devilishly good courtesan.

Although as far as he knew, Alice wasn't entertaining anyone other than him at the moment—a thought which sent a thrill through his heart, and lower, to organs he was a fool to relish.

"Good afternoon, Mrs. Woodmont," he greeted Alice with a tip of his hat. "And to you, Master Ryan."

"Good afternoon, Mr. Rathborne-Paxton," Alice returned the formal greeting with just as much formality.

Ryan, on the other hand, continued to hide against Alice's skirt, though he peeked up at Sam as he did.

Alice laughed. "You'll have to excuse Ryan," she said, petting the smart young lad's head affectionately. "We've just had a bit of an upsetting moment, I'm afraid."

"Oh?" Sam suddenly forgot all of his own concerns. He only cared whether Alice and Ryan were happy.

His question was answered in the unlikely form of Lady Carnlough storming over to them from the side of the path, where her nanny minded the future Lord Carnlough. "Mrs. Cottrell says that the woman in question is named Agnes, and she's nanny for Lord Manchester. I've half a mind to write to Lady Manchester and—oh! Hello, Mr. Rathborne-Paxton." Lady Carnlough's countenance went from horribly vexed to rosy and knowing as she glanced to Alice.

"Good afternoon, Lady Carnlough," Sam greeted Alice's friend with another formal tip of his hat. He liked Lady Carnlough. Lord Carnlough too. The couple had been the very best of friends to Alice under extraordinary circumstances. That made them the very best of people in Sam's eyes. "Out for a stroll on this lovely afternoon?" he asked.

"Yes," Lady Carnlough answered, her smile growing. She peeked to Alice. "It is a fine afternoon for it. Although I think perhaps it is time that Mrs. Cottrell and I take young Alonzo home."

"Oh, Maeve, truly, you don't need to leave," Alice said. Though when she stole another glance at Sam and likely saw how eager he was to speak with her, she changed her mind and said, "Though if it is getting on toward tea time...."

"I will call on you tomorrow morning," Lady Carnlough whispered, sending Alice the sort of look that only lifelong bosom friends shared with each other. "Good day, Mr. Rathborne-Paxton."

"Good day, Lady Carnlough." Sam bowed to the woman,

17

then waited with Alice as they watched the woman return to her nanny to gather her child.

Once Sam and Alice were alone, Sam relaxed his posture a bit and bent over to address Ryan. "Now, my boy. What seems to be the trouble this afternoon?"

Ryan peeled away from his mother's skirts enough to say, "I was playing with my boat, and another boy came to play with me, but his nanny told him not to speak to me and that I was rubbish." Ryan's lower lip turned down in a pout.

Sam instantly wanted to find the nanny in question and ask how she dared to speak of such a sweet child in that manner. Alice wasn't the only one Sam had grown fond of in the last two years. He'd watched Ryan grow as well, and he quite enjoyed the young chap's company.

"What sort of a nanny is that?" he asked with real indignation that he tried to temper into something humorous for Ryan's sake. "It sounds to me as though she doesn't know much."

"I don't think she does," Ryan said.

"Certainly not," Sam agreed. "I think we should ignore her thoroughly and go home for tea." He sent a questioning glance Alice's way, hoping he could communicate with a look that he wished to speak with her about other matters, and he wished to do it in private.

"Can we take the omnibus?" Ryan asked, his eyes lighting up.

Sam broke into a smile. "Of course we can, my boy. Come along."

There were elements of London society who most likely thought it was scandalous of him to do something like taking the hand of a young boy who had been born under dubious circumstances to a woman of questionable character, but Sam had a suggestion of where anyone who would say that could go. He grasped one of Ryan's hands and picked up the lad's toy boat while Alice took Ryan's other hand. Together, they headed for the closest omnibus stop that would take them to Marylebone. Alice had a charming set of flats on Dorset Square that looked out over a beautifully kept garden. If ever there were a place to make Sam feel at ease while discussing one of the gravest matters of his life, Alice's flat would be that place.

"The way some people conduct themselves these days is reprehensible," Sam complained on Alice and Ryan's behalf as they took their seats on the omnibus. "That nanny should be sacked for her rudeness."

Alice sent Sam a sweet, though quelling, look. "You know full well why any woman who considers herself respectable would feel at liberty to say those sorts of things," she told him. "Ryan, do be careful," she cautioned her son as he turned to kneel on the seat between them so that he could watch London go by outside the omnibus's window.

"I understand," Sam said with a sigh, "but I am scandalized all the same."

Alice laughed. "Others would be scandalized for an entirely opposite set of reasons," she told him, one ginger eyebrow raised.

"Then they would be wrong," Sam insisted. "They do not know how lovely you are."

Alice blushed beautifully, which was half the point of Sam's compliment. She truly was the most delightful creature in the world.

But they were on a public conveyance, and more than a few people were watching them with interest, even though they hadn't the slightest idea who they were.

"How fares the diamond mine these days?" Sam asked instead of addressing the point of his visit. Alice enjoyed investing and speculation as much as he did, and from what he understood, she was a great deal more skilled at it than he was.

"I haven't heard from Mr. Kalman in months," Alice answered with a frown. "I must confess, I've been too busy with my volunteer work at the Clerkenwell Ladies Home to seek out news of goings on in South Africa. Though I was just telling Lady Carnlough this morning that it would be such an adventure to travel to South Africa myself."

"That would be an adventure," Sam said, his smile broadening. That was one of the things he loved about Alice. She did not restrict herself to thinking the sort of things that well-bred ladies of society thought they should think. She had much broader interests and tastes. "And the other investments?" he asked. "That shop you wanted to fund, for example."

Alice sighed and let her shoulders droop a bit. "I was hoping for more of a return on those investments," she said.

"Mama, look." Ryan took that moment to point to something of interest outside of the omnibus.

That was the end of the adult conversation for the moment. Sam wasn't terribly keen on asking Alice for more details of her investments while there were so many ears around them that might get it into their heads that one or both of them were ripe for robbing once they departed the bus. He would wait to ask her more once they were at Dorset Square.

Once they reached Dorset Square, however, Sam was distracted by other things.

"Oh, Mrs. Woodmont," Harriett, the maid of all work who also served as Ryan's nursemaid greeted them when they stepped into the first of Alice's two flats, "Mrs. Knox would like a word with you, when you have a moment."

"Thank you, Harriett," Alice said with a smile, removing her hat and handing it near the door while Sam waited just inside the room. "We've had a bit of an upset at the park," she went on, "so perhaps a bit of extra sugar in Ryan's tea this evening."

"Yes, Mrs. Woodmont," Harriett said with a smile for Alice and a look of deep sympathy for Ryan. "What seems to be the trouble, then, dearest?" Harriett went straight to Ryan, relieving Sam of the toy boat with a kind smile and a nod of deference for him. Harriett knew which way the wind blew when it came to Sam's association with Alice.

"A nanny called me rubbish," Ryan reported as Harriett helped him off with his coat and ushered him over to the small table at one end of the flat's main room.

"What a horrible nanny," Harriett said.

"That's what I told him," Sam added.

"You're a good man, Mr. Rathborne-Paxton." Harriett nodded to him.

Sam was tempted to laugh. Things were quite different in Marylebone than they were in Mayfair, just a short distance away. The high and mighty lived in Mayfair, and more often than not, their mistresses and lovers lived in Marylebone. Sam rather liked being part of a place where people were more practical about the goings on of men and women, and where they took everything with a grain of salt instead of expecting everyone to live up to an impossible standard—his father's standard.

Although, as it turned out, his father's standard wasn't what he'd thought it was.

Alice was gazing at Ryan with the tense sort of fondness in her eyes that hinted her love for the boy only barely outweighed her fear for his future. Sam found her to be a thousand times more beautiful for the way she worried about her son than any free and unencumbered society beauty. Alas, one of those unencumbered society ladies was exactly the sort he needed to engage himself to now.

"I should probably tell you what I've come about," he said

in a quiet voice, cupping Alice's elbow in a signal that he was ready to draw her away.

Alice turned her anxious smile to him, slipping her hand into his. "Yes, of course." To Harriett she said, "We're just going down the hall."

"Yes, Mrs. Woodmont," Harriett nodded to her.

Alice led Sam out of the cozy, domestic little flat and out into the hall. To Sam's mind, Alice had come up with the most ingenious living arrangement he could think of. The flat where she lived with Ryan was modest and respectably decorated. It had a bedroom for her, one for Ryan, a kitchen and a main parlor, and not much else. By all appearances, it was exactly the sort of place a widow—as Alice necessarily pretended to be—and her son should live.

Across the hall and down one door, however, Alice kept another flat. Sam had the key to that one, and he unlocked it for them both and drew Alice inside. The second flat was entirely different and much more exotic. It was decorated in rich velvets and silks of red and burgundy. The furnishings were designed for reclining and entertaining of a different sort, and the artwork was certainly not suitable for children like Ryan. That flat was smaller, with one opulent main room, a small kitchen off to the side, and a large bedroom that looked out on the mews instead of the square. Where the other flat had a feeling of domesticity about it, this one sizzled with sin.

Sam felt it through every part of him, and as soon as he had the door shut and locked behind him, he tugged Alice into his arms.

"I am terribly sorry that you met with so much prejudice today," he said in a low growl, smoothing his hands over Alice's sides and bringing his mouth close to hers. "Anyone who doesn't see you as a treasure is a fool."

Alice hummed in response, but Sam didn't give her time to say anything more. He slanted his mouth over hers, kissing

Alice with every bit of hunger he'd been saving up since the last time he'd come to see her, the day before yesterday.

Kissing Alice was one of his favorite activities, right alongside hearing the news that one of his investments had borne fruit. Everything about Alice was marvelous, from the taste of her on his lips to the warmth of her curves as he stroked and traced the outline of her body. He'd wanted her almost from the moment they'd met, and when she gave herself over to him so joyfully a year and half ago, he'd accepted her as she was and never looked back.

"Oh, this is lovely," she sighed as Sam undid the buttons at the top of her high collar so that he could kiss his way down her neck. "This is precisely what I need after a morning like that."

"I am so terribly sorry you have to endure that sort of behavior," Sam said, unbuttoning more of her bodice so that he could taste more of her skin. "You are far too good for them."

Alice laughed, the vibrations meeting his lips and traveling straight to his cock. "A great many people would disagree with you on that score," she said, one eyebrow raised.

"They aren't worth my attention," he said, pulling back enough so that he could focus seriously on undressing her.

Thankfully, Alice set to work undoing his buttons and pushing his jacket off his shoulders as he went. She even removed his hat and tossed it halfway across the room, as though they hadn't a care in the world.

The problem was that they did have cares.

"Before we proceed," he said, more than a little bit of a sigh in his voice, "I have to share with you my reason for seeking you out today."

Alice grinned and tugged his shirt up over his head, tossing it aside and spreading her hands across his naked chest. "You came to me for a reason other than this?" She punctuated her question by leaning forward to tongue one of his nipples.

Desire that always surprised Sam, no matter how many times he and Alice had been together, zipped through him. He growled and threaded his fingers through Alice's hair, pulling and sending hairpins scattering as he did.

"Yes," he said with a laugh that turned into a groan of pleasure. "In fact, there was a reason other than this. And Alice, I'm afraid it's serious."

Alice straightened, gazing at him as though they were back in Hyde Park, having a normal conversation, instead of half dressed and on their way to bed. "Not too serious, I hope," she said, resting a hand on the side of his face.

Sam winced. He truly did care for Alice, and he knew she cared for him. He felt more than a little sheepish when he blurted, "I have to find a socially suitable woman to marry."

Alice tensed and blinked. "Oh."

Sam sighed, stepping away enough to take her hand and lead her on to the bedroom. He hated the fact that she might feel hurt by the consequences of his father's actions.

"Believe me, this is *not* what I want," he said, swinging her back into his arms once they were in the bedroom. "If I had my way, nothing at all would change." He smiled and kissed Alice softly as if to prove his point. "I enjoy my life just as it is, with you in it. But such are the ways of the bloody aristocracy," he went on, feeling more morose than he thought he would.

"What happened to bring this all about?" Alice asked, unfastening her skirt and petticoats and stepping aside so that she could remove them.

Sam shrugged and finished undressing himself. "My father has been caught in the web of that beast, Montrose. His reputation and Mother's have been severely compromised in ways that he has been uncommonly cagey about. If you know anything at all about Montrose, then you know that once a man becomes his target, he is doomed."

"I am aware," Alice said, her eyes wide with wariness.

"Everything is gone," Sam went on. "Father is demanding that his sons marry well to restore the family's standing. My brothers and I do not give a damn what Father thinks, but we would do anything for Mother. I do not think I could stand it if she were ostracized and laughed at for my father's sins."

Alice turned to him as she unhooked her corset, biting her lip as she did. "How did your father end up tangled with a man like Montrose?"

Sam tilted his head to the side as he slipped out of his trousers and socks, then moved to pull the covers back on the bed. "To be honest, we didn't ask for details. I'm not certain he would have given them in any case. He said something about wagers and speculation and blackmail. We think Mother knows more than we do."

"Good heavens." Alice's eyes were wide with wariness, but that didn't stop Sam from drinking in the sight of her as she removed the rest of her clothes, revealing her angelic body. It didn't matter how many times he'd seen them, the sight of Alice's perfect, round breasts always stirred his blood and made him want her.

Alice knew it as well. She took her time coming to bed, taking a moment to light a lamp that limned her features in warm light, then moving to shut the curtains on the off chance that someone across the mews might try to spy on them. Only then did she slink her way to bed, climbing over him to straddle his lap as he pumped pillows up behind him.

"Do you think it's fair of your father to demand his sons marry for status so that his mistakes can be corrected?" she asked as she brushed her hands over his shoulders and chest, then leaned down to kiss him.

Her kiss was so intoxicating that Sam nearly forgot what

they were talking about. He swept his hands down to grab the curves of her backside, nudging her sex closer to his already hard prick. She was already hot and wet, and he couldn't resist slipping his fingers between her thighs to slick them in her sex. That earned a gasp from Alice that he answered with a groan.

The only way he could remember he was there to have a serious conversation with her at all was when she straightened, giving him a sly look that said she knew his mind had wandered, and reached up to pluck the remaining pins from her hair. Although, the sight of that cascade of orange falling around her shoulders and back didn't help him concentrate.

"Whether it's fair or not," he answered a moment too late, "it is what he demands."

"I see," Alice said, shifting so that she could rain kisses across his chest.

"And I've come to you today because, well, because I was hoping you might be able to advise me as to young heiresses in need of a desperate husband," he went on, his breath coming in shorter and shorter pants as she kissed her way lower.

She'd nearly reached his enthusiastically hard cock when she glanced up at him. "Does she have to be young?" Alice asked, mischief in her eyes.

Sam laughed, then gasped as she closed her hand gently around the base of his cock. "I don't know," he sighed. "Father didn't specify."

"No, I don't suppose he would," Alice said with an arch of one brow.

She returned to her task, closing her mouth around the head of his cock and brushing her tongue across his tip. Sam jerked his hips forward before he could stop himself, burying himself deeper in her mouth. All other thoughts were completely impossible from that point on. Alice was the most wonderful woman on God's green earth. No wife, no matter how wealthy, would consider doing the things that the two of them loved to do together.

And as Alice had repeatedly insisted, she loved pleasuring him. She was extraordinarily good at it too. Her lips and tongue were magical as they teased and caressed the head of his prick, and her hand was bliss as it stroked his length. When she combined the two and bore down to draw him deep into her mouth, Sam groaned in ecstasy and had to grip the headboard to stop himself from forcing her to take more of him than she was ready for. He was careful to always do things Alice's way and to never push her further than she wanted to go.

"Oh, God, darling, I'm close already. I just needed you so much today that—"

Alice cut off his desperate blabbering by pulling up and shifting so that she could kiss him. She laughed as she did, then positioned herself over him so that she could sink down on him, sheathing him tightly inside of her.

They both made delicious sounds of pleasure as their bodies joined. Sam grasped her hips tightly and thrust into her while Alice bounced on him, giving herself all the pleasure she needed. They worked so well together, brought each other such excitement. It was a damn shame that the son of a marquess couldn't possibly marry his mistress, a known courtesan. If society would allow him that, he would have Alice at the altar by day's end.

He was more than ready to burst, but he waited, biting his lip and forcing himself to hold off with everything he had, until Alice's cries grew high-pitched, then switched into a deep, pleasured gasp as she came. The second Sam felt the first squeeze, he let go, spilling himself inside of her with a shout that was so loud it was unseemly. They probably should have been more careful, but Sam knew her rhythms now as surely as he knew the chimes of Big Ben, and Alice insisted she knew how to avoid pregnancy. He trusted her, which was more than he could say about most people.

As they both relaxed, panting, and slumped against each other, he drew Alice into his arms.

"All right," she said between wispy pants. "I will help you. Somewhere out there in London, a wealthy woman is just waiting for you. I will help you find her."

Chapter Three

There were decided benefits and definite drawbacks to being the sort of woman that Alice had become in the two years since she'd arrived in London. She wouldn't have traded the freedom of the life she lived, a freedom that few women born in her class would ever be able to enjoy, for the world. Life as a courtesan enabled her to live as she pleased, to dress in fabulously garish clothing—like the aubergine gown and glittering faux diamonds and amethysts she donned for tonight's outing—and to attend the theater boldly whenever she wanted.

After fastening her sparkling earrings, she stood back and admired herself in one of the many full-length mirrors—which had been a gift from a past lover with a penchant for observing himself in the act—in her professional boudoir. She grinned at her image, turning this way and that to gauge the full effect. Her looks—particularly her startlingly Irish hair—were just one of the features that had made her so popular with a certain set of gentlemen the year before, when she was as much on the market as any carrot on a costermonger's cart. She sincerely hoped that those days were behind her, but regardless, she knew Sam liked the way she looked, and that was all that mattered.

Sam.

Alice let out a breath, her shoulders dropping, and turned away from the mirror. There was the principle and most painful drawback to her brief profession and current reputation. It was pointless for her to deny the fact that Samuel Rathborne-Paxton held a deliciously special place in her heart. He had been there to assist her in a very real way when she'd fled Ireland, and he'd been there for her countless times in the past two years. As she crossed from her boudoir to the front room of her professional flat, she snatched up the elaborate fan and opera glasses that he'd gifted her for Christmas the year before, pausing for a moment to handle them as though they were jewels.

Sam needed to marry. She'd known that day would come from the very start. Single sons of a well-regarded marquess did not remain single for long. And unfortunately for her, they did not marry their mistresses. They couldn't. To do so would have been horrifically scandalous at the very least. And even if Sam were able to look past her middle-class birth, her professional dalliances with other men, and Ryan—although Sam and Ryan got on splendidly, which only exacerbated the problem in Alice's heart—society would never, ever accept her as his bride.

Alice ran her hands over the delicate silk of the fan Sam had given her, opening it to reveal a garish, painted scene of some booby's idea of what Ireland looked like. The ridiculous greens and rainbows and mythical creatures had made her and Sam laugh uproariously when they'd spotted it in a shop window while strolling on Oxford Street. They'd turned heads and garnered disapproving looks for their outburst, but it had been worth it. And then Sam, ridiculous darling that he was, had gone back and purchased the hideous thing for her.

Alice blinked rapidly, surprised that the memory could bring her close to tears now. But why wouldn't it? Her darling, sweet, considerate lover had asked for her help in finding him the sort of woman that would make him a respectable wife while she'd been pulsating on his cock the afternoon before, and glutton for punishment that she was, she'd said yes.

Would that she could have said yes to an entirely different question.

A knock on the flat's door jolted her out of her increasingly morose thoughts. Alice sniffed wetly, patted her face to make certain she hadn't smeared any of her cosmetics in her fit of melancholy, and went to answer the door.

"Oh, good evening, Mrs. Knox." Alice did her best to smile as though she hadn't a care in the world as she opened the door to her landlady. "You are looking quite lovely this evening."

Mrs. Knox—a woman well past her prime who was likely never told she was lovely—met Alice's compliment with a strained smile. Alice's heart quivered anxiously.

"This came for you earlier, Mrs. Woodmont, but I haven't had the chance to bring it up," Mrs. Knox said, presenting Alice with a battered envelope.

"Thank you so much, Mrs. Knox," she said with genuine gratitude, taking the letter. "You are a godsend. I do not know what I would do without you."

Alice's smile faltered as she glanced at the envelope to see it was covered in stamps and post marks from South Africa. Her stomach tightened.

"Yes, well," Mrs. Knox went on, more hesitant than before, her face pinched awkwardly, "there is also the matter of the rent, you see."

Alice swallowed, feeling sick. "I have instructed my man of business to forward you the payment as soon as possible, Mrs.

Knox, though I believe there is some delay at the moment," she said.

Mrs. Knox smiled—or perhaps winced. "Yes, Mrs. Woodmont," she said. For a moment she hovered there, as though she would say more, then she closed her mouth, shook her head and stepped back. "Have a lovely evening, Mrs. Woodmont."

"And you as well, dear."

Alice smiled at the woman, then stepped back into her flat and shut the door. Her smile dropped as she tore into the letter.

Sure enough, it contained bad news.

"*Dear Mrs. Woodmont. I regret to inform you—and, indeed, all of the investors in Niemeer Mines—that all diamond mining operations have been suspended as of this time, as per special agreement with De Beers Consolidated Mines. As such, all payments of profits have been suspended until such a time as Niemeer Mines can reorganize and consider our future options. Your patience in this matter is appreciated. Sincerely, Randulph Kalman.*"

Alice let out a breath and dropped the letter on the nearest table as though it were made of fire. Worry and anger warred within her. Mr. Kalman did not specify that the mine was devoid of diamonds or that the supply had been exhausted, only that they would no longer be mining. She clenched her jaw and walked back to the table beside her sofa, where she'd left her purse for the night's outing. Damn that Cecil Rhodes and his wretched De Beers Consolidated Mines. The more she learned about the man and his business dealings, the more she cursed his name. No matter how ridiculously wealthy he'd become.

A moment later, her anger turned into a sense of hopelessness as he snatched up her purse and headed into the hall. There was no point in fighting against the likes of Cecil

Rhodes, or any of the great titans of commerce, just as there was no point in resisting the truth that aristocrats did not marry whores. Her entire life seemed to be all about putting on a brave face and carving out the best possible path through the thorns, so that was what she would do.

In light of the letter, hiring a cab to take her to the Concord Theater didn't seem like a particularly wise idea. But dressed as she was, taking a public conveyance would only position her for trouble.

She felt that trouble around her all the same when she arrived in the theater's brightly-lit, overcrowded lobby and immediately garnered more stares than she was in the mood for. It wasn't the first time she'd arrived unaccompanied in a public place and drawn attention. She did her best to ignore the creeping feeling of intrusion as she moved deeper into the lobby, searching for Sam. They'd made arrangements to meet there so that they could discuss which of London's finest debutantes might be amenable to marrying a desperate man in a rush—and to see the latest Niall Cristofori play starring the incomparable Everett Jewell, of course.

Sam wasn't immediately apparent as Alice stood on her toes to glance out over the crowd in the lobby, but unfortunately, another man was.

"Good evening, Mrs. Woodmont." Alice was approached by the looming figure of Montrose. The man seemed to single her out as soon as he spotted her, and the waiting crowd opened a path for him to reach her as though he were the sort of man one stepped out of the way for. "You look stunning as usual."

"Thank you, Mr. Montrose," Alice smiled, holding out her hand when Montrose gestured for it. She let him kiss her gloved knuckles, shivering a little as he did.

"How encouraging to see you in attendance tonight after suffering such a difficult blow," Montrose went on with his owlish smile, straightening to his full, considerable height.

Alice's gut clenched. How could Montrose possibly know about Sam? Then again, he was the one who had landed the Rathborne-Paxton family in the mess they were in now. And she and Sam had never been particularly subtle about their relationship when they were in certain circles.

"These things happen," she answered him, pretending nonchalance.

"Yes," Montrose said, dripping with sympathy that felt as false as the jewels Alice wore. "The monopoly that De Beers has created in South Africa is scandalous and decidedly unfair to investors such as yourself."

Alice blinked, her blood running cold. If Montrose had come to her to gloat about her loss of Sam, she might have understood. That he knew about her investment in Niemeer Mines and the losses the company had suffered was a deeper intrusion than knowing about her romantic woes.

"I am certain Mr. Kalman will compensate his investors fairly," she said, her voice hoarse.

"Yes, indeed," Montrose said with a nod. "But, of course, Mrs. Woodmont, if you should ever need any help...." He left his statement open-ended.

Alice tried to keep her smile in place, but Montrose was far and away the most disturbing person she'd ever met. Even more so because she did not sense a lick of lasciviousness from him. He did not stare down the front of her dress, he did not gaze at her with overt fondness, and he had not once propositioned her, even when she would have accepted his offer quickly because of the money it would have brought in. Stranger still, she hadn't observed him lusting after anyone else either, woman or man. He simply wasn't interested in those things. And nothing was more disconcerting than a man who had no interest in bedsports.

"Yes, well," Alice stammered, no idea how to answer his offer for help. "I am not certain—"

"Ah, there you are, Mrs. Woodmont."

Alice breathed a sigh of relief as she was rescued by the unlikely person of Mr. Dean Rathborne-Paxton. Sam's brother cut through the crowd, making a direct line to her. His mouth wore a smile, but his eyes were steely with hate as he glanced to Montrose.

"We've been waiting for you up in the box," Dean said, slipping deftly between Alice and Montrose and offering himself as a sort of shield, even though it represented a direct cut to Montrose.

Montrose didn't seem to care. He merely huffed a small laugh, one corner of his mouth tilted up, glanced to Alice as though restating his offer for help, then walked away.

Alice rested her hand in the crook of Dean's arm when he offered. "Thank you," she breathed. "That man is entirely too disconcerting for his own good."

"He's the very devil," Dean agreed. He paused, then asked, "I trust Sam informed you of our family's woes?"

"He did," Alice admitted with a weary sigh. "And I am terribly sorry for your misfortune."

Dean snorted. "My esteemed father is the one who should be sorry," he said as they made their way past the young man taking tickets and up a private stairway to the boxes. "All four of his sons and his wife have turned against him. Mother packed up and departed for my Aunt Marion's estate in Shropshire this morning, and I do not believe she will ever return."

"Am I sorry for that?" Alice asked as they proceeded down the hall toward the Rathborne-Paxton's family box.

Dean shook his head. "Not at all. It is long past time Mother got herself away from the tyrant."

There wasn't time to say more. They arrived at the box,

and the moment Alice saw Sam—sitting near the front edge of the box with Francis, the two of their heads together in conversation as they surveyed the audience below—her heart sang and felt happy for the first time that day.

As if he could sense she was there, Sam turned, then stopped what he was saying to Francis in mid-sentence. His whole, gorgeous face lit with joy and appreciation at the sight of Alice, and he leapt out of his seat to greet her.

"I swear, Alice," he said, taking her hand and bringing it to his lips in one fluid motion, "you grow more beautiful every time I see you. Is this a new gown?"

Alice laughed, her heart light. "No, silly. It's the same gown I wore to the theater last week."

"Oh." Sam swept her body with a look, his eyes resting on the low cut of her bodice for a moment. "Perhaps I will recognize it more when it is crushed into a ball by the side of the bed."

Alice giggled, ridiculously happy with even Sam's worst behavior.

"Easy now," Francis said with a mock disapproving scowl. "We are in public."

"In a private box located in the middle of a noisy theater," Sam told him, grasping Alice's hand and leading her down to the seats at the very front of the box. "And I dare say there isn't a patron in this entire establishment who doesn't know the way of things."

"Probably not," Dean laughed, shooing the two of them to the side so he could slide in and take a seat at the front of the box as well, "but Cristofori and Selby are in the next box over, and they've brought their gaggle of children with them tonight."

Alice brightened, leaning forward to see past the partition separating the boxes. Indeed, Niall Cristofori and Blake Williamson—the Duke of Selby to those who did not know him and his entire, tragic tale personally, as Alice did—were seated with Selby's three children, and one girl that Alice did not recognize. Selby's valet, Mr. Lawrence, was with them—which was highly unusual, but made Alice like Selby all the more.

When Selby caught her staring, Alice burst into a smile and waved. "Your Grace, you have returned from America I see."

They were on friendly terms, so Selby smiled back at her. "Just last week," he said. "The mission was a success."

He rested a hand on his young son's head. Those who were in the know within the circles of London society that the high and mighty tended to turn their nose up at were aware of the entire story of how Lady Selby absconded with Selby's son, Alan, whisking him off to her family's residence in New York when she discovered that Niall Cristofori had been Selby's lover ten years before. Her horror over discovering her husband's inclinations and her subsequent actions had the paradoxical effect of driving Selby back into Cristofori's arms...where he appeared to be deliciously happy now. Alice approved of the match, as wildly unconventional and outside of the bounds of propriety as it was. Her time in the less than savory circles of society had taught her that love came in all guises, and what the moralizing ladies and gentlemen of the acceptable set did not know—or were willing to turn a blind eye to—would not hurt them.

"How dare you spend the evening lavishing your attention on other men?" Sam asked playfully, swatting her hand in jest. "I need you to help me scan the audience for an heiress."

Alice laughed and shifted to give Sam her full attention, but her heart broke a little as she did. There was nothing for it but to give Sam all the help he required. As uncomfortable as it made her, she would have done anything for Sam.

"What precisely are you searching for?" she asked,

pretending as though she were a broker searching out just the right investment for her client as they leaned forward to watch the audience funneling in for the show.

"I don't care," Sam sighed, leaning against her arm and peering into some of the boxes closer to them. "Someone wealthy? That seems to be the entire point of this endeavor."

Alice's heart bled for him. Whoever they decided on, Sam would be bound to the woman for the rest of his life. "Is money the foremost necessity?" she asked.

"In Father's eyes, yes," Sam said, gazing out across the theater instead of at her. "I'm not so certain myself," he went on in a quiet voice.

Alice nodded, taking that to mean that the marriage itself would be far more important than the bank account that came with it, whatever Lord Vegas's dictate had been. Sam wanted to marry. It was time.

Heart heavier than ever, she glanced through the crowd. On a usual night, there was no telling who would be at the theater. As this was the premier performance of Cristofori's latest play, everyone who was anyone was in attendance.

"What about Miss Nelson?" Alice asked, nodding to the industrial heiress in a box across the way.

Sam hummed and scrunched his face. "She's a bit young for me."

Alice hummed. Indeed, the woman was barely past twenty and only just out. "Lady Heloise, then?" she asked, gesturing to a box at the back of the theater.

Sam tilted his head to the side, considering. "Her father is an earl. They have an estate near Lancaster, and one in Cornwall too, if I remember correctly." He shifted restlessly. "There must be an American in the audience somewhere."

"You would choose to marry an American, then?" Alice asked, hoping she sounded amused when actually the idea made her quiver in fear. If she was exotic as an Irishwoman, an American would be ten times more exotic.

Sam pinched his face, as if all he saw before him was secondary goods. "No, I suppose it must be Lady Heloise."

Alice's brows inched up. "You think so?"

Sam let out a sigh and sat back in his chair, angling himself toward her. "What do you think?" he asked, picking up her hand and threading his fingers through hers.

What Alice thought was that Lord Vegas was ten times crueler than Montrose for forcing his sons to marry when they did not want to. What she thought was that the standards of society that forbid a man from marrying a woman he might actually love and be happy with were bitterly unfair. What she thought was that a girl like Lady Heloise wouldn't know what sort of a gem she'd found if Sam turned his attentions toward her and seriously sought her hand in marriage.

"I think Lady Heloise is precisely the sort of young woman your father would approve of you marrying," she said judiciously.

Sam laughed, then shook his head. "God help me, I think you're right." The theater staff began the process of dimming the house lights as the orchestra struck up the opening notes of the overture, and Sam went on, "I suppose I'll introduce myself during intermission and arrange to walk out with the girl sometime soon. Until then—"

He slipped off his shoe and moved his stockinged foot under the hem of Alice's gown. It was all Alice could do to keep a straight face as he teased her in a way that anyone observing them from elsewhere in the theater wouldn't have the first idea what was going on.

As diverting as it was to misbehave with Sam, Alice couldn't help but feel as though their time for amusement was swiftly coming to an end. And once that ended, she had no idea what the rest of her life would look like.

Chapter Four

I t was all moving entirely too fast for Sam's liking. One moment, his father was telling them all the family was in ruins and he and his brothers had to marry to make things right again, and the next, he was strolling through Hyde Park with Lady Heloise Barrington. Barely four days had passed between the two events, but it felt as though it had been a lifetime—a lifetime he hadn't chosen at all.

"Did you enjoy the performance the other night, Lady Heloise?" he asked as he steered Lady Heloise along the path toward the small café where Alice was waiting. He wasn't going to be able to accomplish anything without Alice.

Lady Heloise's face pinched into a strained smile. "I found the performance too bombastic, the acting second-rate, and the musical numbers grating."

Sam's smile dropped. The woman couldn't be serious. "Then why were you there?" he asked before he could temper himself.

Lady Heloise tilted her chin up and kept her gaze straight forward. She had barely looked at him the entire time they'd been walking together. "Mama forced me to go," she said with an air of doom.

"One hardly needs to force oneself to attend the theater," Sam said trying to sound light and jovial.

Lady Heloise sent him a sidelong look, as though he'd been boorish and crass instead. "I enjoy the works of Shakespeare and other performances which display taste and forbearance, and that contain a moral lesson. I am not fond of the works of Mr. Cristofori, and I do not understand why such a scandalous person has been allowed to display himself and his ideas in public spaces."

"I...er...oh," Sam said. So Lady Heloise was that sort, was she? He scrambled to find a way to go on that wouldn't offend her. "I've been very pleased with the weather we'd have so far this week," he said.

Again, Lady Heloise wrinkled her nose and touched the brim of her hat as if to adjust the way it shaded her face. "I have found it too bright of late myself. So much sunlight is not healthy for one's complexion."

"How true, my lady." If Sam couldn't find a bit of common ground with the woman, at least he could agree with whatever she said. "Would you care for a spot of tea?" he asked as they came to within sight of the café.

Lady Heloise seemed to consider for far longer than necessary before saying, "Yes, that would be acceptable."

Sam did his best to hold in his relief that the woman had finally agreed to something. In theory, Lady Heloise was exactly the sort of woman his father would have been pleased for him to marry. She was from a good family, she brought a considerable dowery with her, and she was not difficult to look at. She had striking features, porcelain skin, and masses of chestnut brown hair that was currently piled in a fashionable style under a hat. There was nothing wrong with her shape or her bearing—aside from the fact that she was painfully formal at the moment—and she seemed as intelligent as any young woman who had been blessed with a first-rate governess. As an added advantage, she was past twenty-five, which meant she might be in as much of a hurry to wed as he was.

And Sam found her utterly, painfully uninteresting.

He nearly shouted for joy when he spotted Alice sitting quietly by herself at an outdoor café table facing the Serpentine. For all intents and purposes, she appeared to be reading a book while enjoying an afternoon treat on a lovely day. Sam knew it was her in an instant, but anyone passing by who was not already acquainted with Alice wouldn't have known her at all, for she wore an enormous hat with the widest brim Sam had ever seen. The monstrosity was festooned with ostrich feathers and a wide ribbon, and it was roughly the size of a serving platter. Not only did it serve to conceal Alice's face entirely, it most likely blocked out every ray the sun could throw at her.

Doing his best not to laugh, Sam led Lady Heloise to the table directly behind Alice's and helped her to sit. He then took up the chair immediately to Alice's back, so close he could smell the flowery scent of Alice's perfume.

"Please feel at liberty to order anything at all that strikes your fancy, Lady Heloise," Sam said once a waiter had come over to attend to them. "And I do hope that some of the things that are not on the menu will strike your fancy as well." He winked at her for good measure.

Lady Heloise stared at him with utter incomprehension. "I beg your pardon?" she asked, eyes vacant.

"I was merely suggesting that you might find something else to your liking as well," Sam said, smiling.

Still, Lady Heloise stared. "Such as?"

Sam cleared his throat and squirmed. "A treat of a non-culinary nature?"

Lady Heloise blinked. "Why on earth would a café serve

something that was not of a culinary nature?"

Behind him, Sam heard Alice snort with laughter. That nearly set him off as well.

"Would a cream tea suffice?" he asked Lady Heloise, still grasping for good cheer.

"Yes, that would be adequate," Lady Heloise answered.

Alice choked on another laugh.

"Right away, sir, ma'am," the waiter told them with a nod.

"It's 'my lady'," Lady Heloise corrected him.

"Of course, my lady. Very sorry, my lady." The waiter bowed, then ran off.

Sam rather wanted to run off with him. He kept his smile in place and studied Lady Heloise—who had turned to narrow her eyes at a group of ducks that had wondered up from the Serpentine, hoping for a few crumbs.

"So if you do not enjoy the theater, Lady Heloise, what entertainments do you enjoy?" Sam asked, hoping there would be some common ground between them.

"I did not say I did not enjoy the theater," Lady Heloise snapped, her voice a whip crack.

Sam flinched. "Er...right. Aside from the theater, what entertainments do you enjoy?" he rephrased his question.

Lady Heloise sat straighter and tilted her head. "I enjoy Sunday sermons and lectures by the Christian Ladies' Society."

"Naturally," Alice murmured behind him, too low for Lady Heloise to hear.

Sam snorted, then hid his laugh with a feigned cough.

"Are you well, Mr. Rathborne-Paxton?" Lady Heloise asked. "I despise illness of all sorts."

Her comment did not make it easier for Sam to recover himself. "Quite well," he said. "I believe I may have breathed in some sort of insect."

"I see," Lady Heloise said, as though men of good breeding never did such a thing.

That left Sam at a complete loss. He opened his mouth, but no further topic of conversation spilled out. He tried again, but his brain continued to draw a blank.

That was when he felt something tapping at his thigh. With a start, he glanced down and found, Alice's hand stretched out behind her. She held a small piece of paper that she seemed intent on him taking.

"Is that Prince Albert?" Sam asked, pointing off in the opposite direction.

"Is it?"

When Lady Heloise turned away, Sam grabbed the slip of paper from Alice and opened it under the table.

"*Ask her about her mother and sister*," the tiny slip read.

"I must have been mistaken," Sam said, crushing the paper in his hand.

"Yes, you must have," Lady Heloise said, looking put out over being made to turn around.

"How is your mother?" Sam asked, showing a great deal of concern, though he had no idea how much would be appropriate. "And your sister."

Lady Heloise looked suddenly pleased. "They are recovering adequately," she said. "Of course, it was a shock to us all, but they are brave soldiers and always have been."

Blast. The least the woman could do was give him more to go on than that. "Are they...are they in town at present?" he asked.

Lady Heloise frowned. "Of course not. The accident was in Italy. They have not been able to return to England as of yet."

"Oh," Sam said, squirming awkwardly. "And...and was there much damage? In the accident?"

He felt another tap against his bum and reached down to find Alice's hand there with another scrap of paper.

At the same time, Lady Heloise's frown deepened, and she shook her head slightly, "Damage, sir?"

Sam was saved by the waiter bringing their tea. As he served two cups from the silver teapot, Sam quickly read Alice's newest note.

"They fell down a hillside when stones dislodged."

"Ah!" Sam made a triumphant sound of understanding. When he glanced up to find Lady Heloise gawking at him, he picked up his teacup and said, "Ah, there's nothing like a fresh cup of tea on a beautiful day."

"Indeed," Lady Heloise said, eyeing him suspiciously.

Sam took a fortifying gulp of his tea, then said, "What I meant was, did the surrounding area sustain any damage? You know, when the stones dislodged."

Lady Heloise nodded, as though his line of questioning finally made sense. "It did, I suppose," she said. "Though one does not particularly care about damage sustained to the Italian countryside."

Sam's brow flew up, and he nearly choked on the tea he was in the process of swallowing. "I see," he said in a rough voice. "And have you been to Italy yourself?"

"Good heavens, no!" Lady Heloise said. "I cannot abide the Italians."

"Then why did your mother and sister go?"

Lady Heloise gasped, her face flushing. She did not answer, though, she merely pressed her lips together.

Blessedly, there was another tap on Sam's bum at just the moment when the waiter brought them a plate of scones with jam and cream.

"Her sister ended up in the family way. Change the subject. Ask about horses."

As soon as Sam had an opportunity, he blurted, "Who do you favor at Sandown Park this year?"

Lady Heloise nearly dropped her teacup, tea and all. "How dare you ask me such a thing, sir?"

Sam scrambled, at a complete loss. "I thought...that is...I was told to ask you about horses?" He winced as soon as the words were out of his mouth, particularly when he heard Alice stifle a groan behind him. Within moments, she was frantically tapping at his bum again.

"How dare you rub my brother's disgrace in my face, sir? A great many gentlemen take interest in breeding and raising horses. That does not mean my brother's interests were purely in wagering away his inheritance—which he did not do, I might add, despite rumors and gossip."

"I didn't mean...that is to say...I had no idea—"

"Perhaps this outing was ill-advised," Lady Heloise said, making as though she would stand.

"No, my lady, please," Sam said, rising with her.

Unfortunately for Sam, not only did his motion spill all of Alice's previously written messages from his lap to the grass, he managed to catch her hand as he moved, tugging her sideways enough for Alice to squeak.

At first, Lady Heloise's eyes fell to the bits of paper in the grass. Then she leaned to the side and noticed that Alice wasn't as innocent an observer in the tea shop as she might have appeared to be.

"Is something the matter, miss?" she asked, enunciating each word, as though Alice were either a child or a foreigner who could not understand her.

"No, nothing at all," Alice said, turning her head so that her ridiculous hat served as a shield.

"Let me just—" Sam began, bending to snatch up the bits of paper.

Lady Heloise was suspicious enough to jerk forward and

grab one of the bits of paper that had fallen. "What is this?" As soon as she opened it, she gasped and her face went red. "In the family way?" Her voice reached a high-pitched shriek.

Of all the slips of paper for the woman to retrieve, it had to be that one.

"I can explain," Sam said, stepping forward, his hands outstretched as if to placate her. When no words came to his lips, he backtracked and said, "Er, or not."

Lady Heloise dodged him, narrowing her eyes at Alice's hat. "Who is this woman?" she demanded. "Who are you? Do you have something to do with this slanderous note? This is a woman's handwriting, and you clearly have a pencil and paper."

"Oh, dear," Alice said, turning her head so that her hat continued to block her identity as Lady Heloise shifted to the side to get a good look at her.

"You!" Lady Heloise demanded. "Reveal yourself."

She stepped to one side then the other, attempting to dodge around Sam, who was doing his level best to protect Alice's identity.

"Really, Lady Heloise, there is nothing important to see here," he insisted, countering each of Lady Heloise's movements, his hands still outstretched. "Please sit down and enjoy this lovely tea."

"Not when this horrid woman, whoever she is, is spreading such despicable rumors about my sister," Lady Heloise growled. "Not when—oh!" She shouted as Sam grabbed her around the waist to prevent her from lunging at Alice.

That was the very last straw, as far as Lady Heloise was concerned. She beat Sam away, continuing to smack and thrash him for laying his hands on her. Her blows were surprisingly sharp for a woman who pretended to be so delicate.

Alice apparently did not like the attack. She leapt up from her chair, no longer intent on hiding her identity, and shouted, "How dare you strike this man?"

As soon as Lady Heloise realized who the woman in the enormous hat was, she gasped so loudly Sam was certain the gesture would tear her throat, then hissed, "You!"

Alice stood straighter, tilting her head in such a way that the fluffy feathers on her hat waved brazenly. "Yes, me," she said with a proud grin.

"Bloody hell," Sam grumbled, his shoulders dropping.

Lady Heloise glanced between Sam and Alice, her eyes going wide. "I have heard the rumors, but I never would have imagined…." She stiffened, balling her hands into fists at her sides. "Mr. Rathborne-Paxton, how dare you arrange to meet with your *whore* under the pretenses of walking out with me?"

Alice flinched at the particularly virulent intonation of the word "whore". That was enough to have Sam seeing red.

"I would thank you not to insult my friend, Lady Heloise," he said, shifting to stand by Alice's side—though the show of solidarity was marred by the brim of Alice's hat stabbing him in the eye as he moved too close.

Sam slapped a hand to his eye, and Alice sidestepped away from him, clapping a hand to her mouth to stifle a laugh.

"This is no laughing matter," Lady Heloise growled. "I have never been so insulted in all my life. Women like you should be banned from public venues."

"At least I am honest about who and what I am," Alice fired back.

"And just what is that supposed to mean?" Lady Heloise said, thumping a hand to her heart as though Alice had shot an arrow at her.

They were quickly gathering an audience of amused onlookers from every class, but that did nothing to stop Alice from saying, "How is your sister, by the by? Is Italy treating her well? Do they have good doctors there? And what about your brother and his horses?"

Lady Heloise's face turned puce and splotchy. "I...I will not stand here and allow myself to be insulted by...by the likes of you."

"And what will you do about it, hmm?" Alice asked. "Run to share your grievances with your chaperone?" She tilted her head to one side, causing Sam to dodge her hat once more. "What is this? You walked out in Hyde Park alone with a man, without a chaperone? Good heavens, Lady Heloise, is that quite right?"

"I will not stand for this," Lady Heloise said, closer to weeping than shouting now. She snapped to face Sam. "Do not ever call on me again, Mr. Rathborne-Paxton. If we encounter one another in public, I will not acknowledge you, and I ask you to do to the same with me. Good day."

With that, Lady Heloise turned and marched off, hands still balled into fists at her sides.

A pair of young lads who looked as though they'd skipped out on school applauded as though they'd just seen a theatrical performance. They were swiftly shuffled away by a gentleman who seemed like the sort who abhorred all public displays. He glared at Sam as he shoved the boys off and got the crowd moving.

Sam turned to Alice and sighed. "Perhaps not Lady Heloise after all," he said.

"No," Alice agreed, one eyebrow arched.

They stared at each other for a few, tense seconds, and then both of them burst into laughter.

"Did you see the way she sat?" he asked through laughter that nearly had him in tears, reaching for Alice's arm. "Like there was a poker fastened to her chair?"

"Something tells me the esteemed lady could use a poker

in just the right place," Alice laughed in return, wiping the corners of her eyes.

"What in God's name did you mean by telling me to ask her about horses?" he asked, gesturing for her to take Lady Heloise's vacated seat at the table.

"Her father breeds and raises them, you idiot," Alice laughed. She collected her book, paper, and pencil, then moved to Sam's table. "Everyone knows that."

"Did I know it?" he asked, sitting and gesturing for the waiter to bring a new teacup for Alice.

"I'm certain you did, darling," Alice told him with a flat look.

The combination of that endearment and the frank, intimate way Alice looked at him had Sam's chest seizing with longing. The two of them got on so well together. They had from the start. With Alice, there was no worry about getting to know someone, no introductory period. They had the sort of rapport that a married couple already had. He relied on Alice for things he couldn't imagine himself relying on anyone else for.

If only....

"I supposed we shall have to try again," Alice said once she had a fresh cup of tea in one hand and a scone slathered with jam and cream in the other. "Who else is out there in London that you might feel inclined to marry?" she asked, then proceeded to lick the cream off her scone in the obscenest manner imaginable.

Sam went immediately hard at the sight, remembering the way her talented tongue could wrap around his prick and drive him to the most glorious heights of pleasure. Alice was brilliant and talented in so many ways. As far as he was concerned, she put women like Lady Heloise to shame.

"Sam, are you paying the slightest bit of attention to me?" Alice asked, alerting Sam to the fact that she'd gone on talking while he was imagining the taste of her lips with raspberry jam glossing them. Or perhaps other parts of her slathered in raspberry jam. "Sam? Samuel."

Sam blinked and sat straighter. "I do beg your pardon," he said with overstated formality. "I was lost in fantasies of licking raspberry jam off your—" he coughed and reached for his teacup to cover the word, "cunny."

Alice snorted with laughter, spraying crumbs from her scone across the table. A pair of ladies at a table near their shook their heads in disgust, but Sam thought Alice was the most beautiful thing he'd ever seen.

"Perhaps we should finish this tea as swiftly as possible so that we can return to my flat to finish the discussion there," Alice said, her voice a low purr.

"That would be perfect," Sam said, arching his eyebrow, his heart bursting with affection.

Chapter Five

For a ploy that was designed to throw her lover into the matrimonial arms of another woman, Alice certainly did enjoy the interlude in Hyde Park. Women like Lady Heloise were an endless source of amusement to Alice. They followed every social convention demanded of them and deported themselves like perfect angels while in public, but as Alice had swiftly come to learn in her life, what happened behind closed doors was the same whether someone was a paragon of virtue or a trollop.

"I thought I might expire with laughter when the woman attempted to dodge around you and you matched her every move," Alice laughed as she and Sam walked up the stairs in her building to her flats. She removed her hat, handing it off to Sam. "For a moment, I had a vision of an organ grinder and a monkey dancing."

Sam chuckled so hard he snorted. He offered her his elbow so that he could escort her up the stairs. "Good heavens, don't tell Lady Heloise you thought she resembled a monkey."

It was Alice's turn to snort with laughter. "Who said it was Lady Heloise I envisioned as the monkey?"

Sam looked momentarily shocked, pausing on the stairs to send her a look of comical offense and using the hat and all of its feathers to block his mouth, then the two of them doubled over with laughter as they continued up to the second floor.

"You really ought to have seen your own face," Sam said between hiccups as they started down the hall. "You looked like—"

He stopped abruptly as they were met by the anxious figure of Mrs. Knox heading down the hall toward them. Mrs. Knox must have heard their laughter, as she didn't look the least bit surprised to see the two of them.

"Mrs. Woodmont, I need a word with you," she said, her voice a bit wispy and worried. She glanced to Sam, then cleared her throat and said, "Alone, if you do not mind, sir."

"Not at all," Sam said, his spirits still sailing high. He let Alice's arm go, brought her hand to his mouth to kiss her knuckles, then stepped away, saying, "I'll just go inside and put the kettle on." He ducked in to kiss Mrs. Knox's cheek as he passed her, earning a startled yelp from the woman.

Alice's heart blossomed with the deepest sort of affections she could imagine as she watched Sam stride down the hall to the door of her private flat. He made a show of bending over enough as he fit the key in the lock to give her a clear outline of his bum under the hem of his jacket, waving her hat above his rear as though it were tailfeathers. Alice clapped a hand to her mouth and shook her head at his antics as he straightened, sent her a lascivious wiggle of his eyebrows, then ducked into the apartment.

She loved him so desperately that it made every part of her throb with pain.

Mrs. Knox could apparently read her like a book. "My poor dearie," she said, clasping her hands in front of her and sending Alice a pitying look. "The charming ones are always the ones we cannot have, and yet we fall in love with them all the same."

Alice sucked in a breath, contemplating correcting Mrs. Knox, but there didn't seem to be any point, considering the woman was right.

"He's asked me to find him a wife," she admitted in a shaking voice.

"Oh, no." Mrs. Knox reached a hand to rest on Alice's arm. "I am sorry. But he is the son of a marquess, and that sort must marry women of their own social standing eventually."

"His father demands it," Alice said. "He has demanded that all of his sons marry so that the family might save face in the wake of...of something unsavory that has happened."

"I understand," Mrs. Knox said with a sage nod. "Marriage is a sign of respectability."

"It is indeed," Alice agreed.

"Which is why your sort can never marry."

Alice flinched. The words felt like a dagger driven into her back just when she'd fallen over. Mrs. Knox was kind and far more accommodating than other landladies might be, but every now and then, like at that very moment, Alice was reminded that prejudice, when covered in silk and lace, was still prejudice.

Alice cleared her throat, stood taller, and faced Mrs. Knox with as much of a smile as she could manage. "Did you have something you wished to discuss with me?"

"Yes," Mrs. Knox said hesitantly. She rubbed her hands in front of her, then said, "The payment for your rent has failed again. I...I pursued all of the proper channels, but when I made inquiries of your man of business, he said...he said you're skint, ma'am."

A large, acidic rock formed instantly in Alice's gut, and her hands went numb. She felt the color drain from her face as well. "He said that?" she asked in a shaking voice, knowing it was true.

"He did." At least Mrs. Knox looked sympathetic. "And as much as I enjoy your company, Mrs. Woodmont, I cannot allow you to keep two flats when you cannot even pay for one. I am afraid...I am afraid I must give you notice that if the rent is not brought up to date by the end of the month, then...then I will have to ask you to leave both flats."

Alice's spirits sank heavily. "I will do what I can, Mrs. Knox," she said. She managed a weak smile for the woman, then started down the hall toward her flat.

"If I may be so bold," Mrs. Knox called after her. Alice paused to turn back to her. "I know how fond you are of Mr. Rathborne-Paxton, but I recall that you had a few other gentlemen callers who were generous with you. Perhaps you could renew your acquaintance with them?"

Tears pricked at the back of Alice's eyes. The fact that her landlady would suggest she whore herself out to pay the rent without so much as batting an eyelash was all the proof Alice needed that the woman saw her as nothing but a strumpet who had come into a little luck.

"I shall consider it, Mrs. Knox," she said, managing a smile. "Thank you for your kindness."

She headed on to her door, sucking in a breath before entering so that she could face Sam with a smile. The trouble was, Mrs. Knox was right on all counts. Alice did have a source of ready income at her fingertips. Or rather, between her legs. She could earn enough money to pay her rent simply by attending the theater that night and going to a hotel with any one of a dozen gentlemen who already knew she was willing, and that she was skilled. She'd always selected her clients carefully, and the gentlemen in question would be perfectly understanding about her needs and necessities. They would not judge her for needing to pay the rent...just for being a whore.

She shook her head and cleared her throat, forcing herself to smile and think of Sam before she pushed open the door.

The moment she stepped into the room and saw Sam, she burst into laughter. Sam had undressed entirely and draped himself across the chaise lounge in the center of the room in an astoundingly suggestive pose. He'd primed himself as well so that his magnificent prick stood at attention, ready to play. And on his head, he wore her hat in all its ostrich feather glory.

"Madame, I am at your disposal," he declared in a mock serious voice, stroking himself a few more times for show.

As quickly as Alice's laughter had struck her, the horrifying urge to weep until she was dry flew in and gripped her a moment later. It was so powerful that she had to clap her hands to her face to keep from sobbing.

Sam's ridiculousness vanished in a moment, and he leapt up from the sofa and ran to her, the feathers on her hat fluttering as he did.

"My darling, what is wrong?" he asked, swiftly gathering her into his arms and kissing her. Her hat got in the way, so he tore it off, tossed it across the room, then kissed her again.

"Nothing," Alice lied, sniffing. "Nothing at all. It is just that...." She gulped, unable to bring herself to admit the situation she was in.

"My heart, it is most definitely not nothing," Sam said, pulling her tighter against him and stroking the side of her face with one hand. "Has Mrs. Knox said something to upset you?"

Alice's heart roiled in her chest. Mrs. Knox had said a great many things, but the thing that upset her the most was the tenderness of Sam's embrace and the warmth of his repeated, soft kisses as he did whatever he thought he could to make her feel better. She would have given up anything—well, except Ryan, of course—to have Sam and to keep him. Sam was glorious and amorous and kind. He had saved her in so many ways and made her life bright and enjoyable for the last two years.

And now she had to choose between remaining loyal to him and ending up on the street or betraying him by taking other men to her bed. All while watching him waltz off with some fresh, young debutante from an aristocratic family who could restore the Rathborne-Paxton fortunes.

Of course, the situation was not quite as bleak as that. She and Ryan wouldn't truly end up on the street if Mrs. Knox evicted them. Maeve would never let that happen, for one. Sam wouldn't either. But Alice was loath to ask for more money than Sam already gave her in support, and life with Maeve carried strings of behavior and humility with it that she wasn't willing to attach herself to.

"Alice, dearest, say something, please," Sam said, kissing her forehead. "This protracted silence is wreaking havoc on my erection."

Alice laughed, knowing full well Sam had only said something so outlandish to make her laugh. She sighed, wriggled away from him, and took his hand, leading him toward the bedroom. Once there, she began to undress.

"There is a problem with the payment of my rent," she said, not looking at Sam as she admitted it. She was lucky that Sam stepped up behind her to undo the fastenings of her skirt and petticoat so that she could continue not to look at him, though their reflections were apparent in all of the room's mirrors. "It is nothing to worry about," she lied, "just an administrative hiccup." She drew in a shaky breath. "But Mrs. Knox also said a few things that reminded me just what she thinks of me."

"That you are beautiful and intelligent and delightfully droll?" Sam asked, pushing her skirts down once they'd loosened enough to slide over her hips.

Alice stepped out of the cloud of fabric, then turned to

face him. "That I am a shameless strumpet," she admitted, her head tilted down, glancing wistfully up at him.

Sam took one, large step to her, slipping his fingers under her chin and tilting her face up to meet his eyes. "You are my strumpet," he said, his eyes glittering with affection.

That only caused Alice to burst into tears in earnest. "Oh, Sam," she said, her voice a squeak.

Sam silenced anything else she might have said with a kiss. That kiss turned into another, deeper one. The sparks of desire flickered through Alice, urging her to forget her troubles and to simply be with Sam, enjoying him in the best of ways while she could. Sam seemed to have similar ideas. He undressed her with deft hands, tossing her clothes aside carelessly and stealing kisses between all of her innumerable layers until he was able to carry her to bed and slip between the sheets with her.

"We are in a pickle, aren't we," he said once he had spread his firm, fit body atop her, nestling his reenergized prick between her legs in a delicious manner.

Alice made a sound that was half weeping, half laughter and reached between them to stroke his erection. "I rather enjoy your pickle," she said with a mournful groan.

Sam laughed, thrusting playfully into her hand, and bent to kiss her. "Then said vegetable is at your disposal," he said.

"Is a pickle truly a vegetable?" Alice asked, then gasped in surprise as Sam buried the article in question deep within her.

They'd done little to tease and arouse each other to lead up to that moment of penetration, but Alice found she didn't mind at all. Sam wasn't searching for completion or his own pleasure. She sensed that, like her, he just wanted the two of them to be intimately joined. It felt so good and so right that Alice let herself relax as she wrapped her arms and legs around him.

Sam used her gesture to sink deeper. He hummed in

contentment, kissing her mouth, her cheeks, her neck, and all the other parts of her within easy reach as he rocked gently in her.

"You did not choose this life," he murmured against her ear. "You had it thrust upon you." He accented his point by plunging into her with more force. "And to me, that makes you the farthest thing from a strumpet. You are strong and merciless, even with yourself, in your pursuit of independence, and for that, I admire you more than I can say."

His words were so beautiful that they were like a thousand kisses and passionate caresses. Her body responded to them and to his touch and invasion, building the fire of need within her.

"You are precious, Sam," she sighed. "So very precious. Whichever lofty lady ends up as your bride will be the luckiest woman in all of Europe, all of the world."

Sam stopped nuzzling her neck and rocking with her to raise himself above her. "Alice, you know that I have no intention of giving you up, even if I do marry," he said with a look of utter seriousness.

Hot and cold prickles of desire and guilt raced through Alice. Of all the wicked, teasing things Sam had ever said to her, that was perhaps the wickedest. And while it was true that some of her former gentlemen callers were married, the prospect of being an adulteress with Sam chilled Alice to her bones. But at the same time, part of her sang with relief that he wouldn't abandon her. It was the other part that believed it to be so, so wrong that she wasn't certain she could manage.

"Are...are you certain you could do that?" she asked in a weak voice, gripping his upper arms tightly and gazing up at him.

Sam let out a long breath, moved within her a few times while thinking, then stared straight into her eyes and confessed, "I don't think I could give you up, even if I tried."

It was such a beautifully bittersweet sentiment, and it made Alice burn from the inside out. Sam increased the pace of his thrusts, making love to her with intent, and she allowed herself to close her eyes and just feel him. Sam was her rock and her compass. He was the lighthouse on the shore that always showed her the way home when she feared she was lost. He made her feel so uncommonly good, even when the situation she found herself in was as bad as could be.

The pleasure that radiated from her as he thrust in her was wonderful. She could feel an orgasm tightening within her, desperate to unfurl like a flag of victory after a hard-fought battle. Sam groaned and sighed, his body tensing as though he, too, were ready to spill himself into her, connecting them on the deepest level. It should have taken more than his thrusts and a heart full of conflicted emotions to make her come, but with surprising strength, her body throbbed into ecstasy, gripping around him and making her feel as though she were in heaven.

"Oh, Sam," she cried out. "Marry me."

Sam let out a strangled cry in reply and burst into her. The motion of his body intensified, then slowly ebbed until he held himself above her on unsteady arms, panting, with a sheen of sweat glittering on his face and upper body.

"What?" he asked, post-coital confusion seeming to envelop him.

Perhaps it was Alice's own pleasure haze that made her bold, but she said, "Marry *me*. Not some blushing nob or industrial heiress. Me. We love each other. We always have. The two of us are perfect together in every way. And if you intend to keep me even after whatever sham of a marriage your father wishes you to engage in for his own ends, why not simply make me your bride? We would be so happy together."

As fast as the words had gushed out of her, they stopped. She couldn't think of anything more to say, for one, but for another, Sam simply stared down at her with wide, almost frightened eyes.

Alice sucked in a breath, instantly regretting everything she'd said. It was wrong. Somehow, she knew that what she'd said was wrong.

As if to prove that, Sam pulled out and scooted back, kneeling between her legs. His body glistened with sweat and his softening cock bore the evidence of what they'd just done. Alice found him to be the most amazing sight she'd ever seen, but for the startled look in his eyes.

"Sam," she panted, unable to catch her breath for a variety of reasons. "I'm sorry. I spoke out of turn. I shouldn't have—"

"I must go," Sam said, his face bright red and his gaze unfocused. He climbed swiftly out from between her legs and off the bed.

"I didn't mean to offend you or to...to suggest anything untoward," Alice insisted, increasingly desperate as she rolled to her side and watched him lunge for his clothes—which he must have piled on the bureau in her room when he'd undressed, knowing where he would need them when the time came.

"I am not offended at all," Sam insisted, not looking at her. "It is just...."

Alice waited, but he failed to elaborate. "Just?" she prompted when he remained silent.

He finished donning his trousers, socks, shirt, and waist-coat—though the only thing he'd buttoned was his trousers—then stepped over to the side of the bed. "It is just that I must go," he said, then bent to kiss her lips.

His kiss was too hurried, too frantic. It pulled at Alice like iron filings drawn to a magnet, but it left her aching when he moved away, marching for the door.

"I will call or send a note when I've...." He let that sentence drop as well, pausing in the doorway. He blew out a heavy breath, then pushed a hand through his hair. "I will contact you," he said, then marched off into the front parlor, shutting the bedroom door behind her.

Alice lay where she was on her side for a moment, utterly stunned. She could still feel the slight ache in her body from where she had been stretched and wrapped around him. She could still taste him on her lips. And yet, she didn't have the first idea what he was thinking or what he had meant by his words and his speedy departure.

All she could do was collapse on her stomach and let herself burst into weeping on her pillow—a pillow that still smelled of him and their love. She'd been far too hasty in speaking her heart and suggesting the impossible, but it was too late now. She could no more change who and what she was than she could stop loving Sam.

Chapter Six

S am shivered as he tore down the stairs of Alice's building and out to the street. His thoughts were scattered in a thousand pieces, and his body still thrummed with passion and fear, hope and anxiety. Alice's impassioned suggestion that he marry her had derailed every thought process he had in an instant. He was lucky that he'd managed to button his jacket correctly and fit his shoes properly on his feet before stepping out into public. He was equally lucky to be able to find his way to the nearest omnibus stop and to secure a seat on the crowded conveyance so that it would take him home.

Marry Alice. The thought inspired him with a dozen conflicting emotions. Nothing in the entire, wide world would have made him happier than doing just that. Alice was his sun and his moon. He loved everything about her, even the things that he was supposed to abhor about a woman of low moral character. The thing was, as he'd told Alice, he didn't consider her moral character to be low at all. She'd been a woman in a difficult spot and she'd found her way out of that spot. And to be perfectly honest, he himself had reaped the benefits of her boldness, even if he wasn't the only one.

Though he was the only one now, as he knew full well. Alice had never explicitly said she'd dropped her other lovers and he'd never asked, but he'd gleaned as much from a few obvious clues. He hadn't stumbled across masculine articles left behind in her flat for many months. Alice hadn't needed to consult her calendar before agreeing to spend an evening with him, even when the evenings he claimed were frequent. And there was that moment at the Concord Theater two months prior when Lord Farthingale had congratulated him on pipping the rest of them at the post. He'd been reasonably certain Farthingale hadn't been speaking about horses.

Thoughts of horses drew him on to remembering his disastrous encounter with Lady Heloise. Those memories had him laughing despite the turmoil gripping his heart. That laughter and the memory of Alice's part in the fiasco, the sound of her laughter as she'd teased him for conducting himself all wrong, circled Sam right back into a sort of panicked melancholy and painful hope as he walked from the omnibus stop to his family home in Mayfair. How could something so lovely and so perfect also be so impossible and so wrong?

But was it impossible? Was it truly?

"You look like something the cat toyed with and grew tired of," Dean greeted him as Sam wandered into the private parlor at the back of the house that the two of them and their brothers had adopted as their own since moving back into the family house. One of the first things to go after their father's announcement were the flats that Sam and Dean had been renting for the past few years. Francis had his own townhouse associated with his title a street over, and Joseph had yet to leave their parent's house.

"I've had a bit of a rocky afternoon," Sam grumbled,

walking straight to the small table that held a selection of decanters of brandy and port and the like. Without noticing which decanter he had grabbed, he poured himself a large drink.

Joseph—who sat in the stiffest chair in the room, reading a book that was, no doubt, meant to improve him—sniffed and wrinkled his nose. "By the smell of things, I question how difficult your afternoon was."

Sam huffed a laugh and downed a large gulp of alcohol. "What would you know of the way I smell, Joe? Have you ever been within six feet of a naked woman before?"

Joseph turned beet red and hunched in on himself, deliberately not answering.

"Don't tease Joseph," Francis sighed, leaving the window he'd been looking out and walking over to flop onto the sofa where Dean had just taken a seat. He rubbed his eyes as he did. "It's not his fault he's a virgin."

"Francis!" Joseph hissed, hunching deeper into the chair and raising his book to hide his face.

"If Father has his way, that won't last long," Dean laughed. "I think it's rather quaint that our baby brother will be deflowered on his wedding night."

"Sometimes it happens," Francis said in a tone that might have been defending Joseph, but with a grin that suggested he was teasing Joe too.

"Well, it won't happen to me," Dean said. "It's already much too late for—"

"I have a terrible problem on my hands," Sam burst out before his brothers could descend into some sort of ribald, teasing conversation.

All three of them glanced up at him. Even Joseph lowered his book and glanced at Sam curiously.

"Go on," Francis said. "Perhaps we can help."

Sam downed the last of his drink, hoping its effects would

kick in quickly. "I know we're all supposed to be on the search for wealthy brides of good standing to protect Mother and restore the family name," he blurted, trying to get it all out as quickly as possible so that it could become a fraternal problem and not just his own, "but I've just come from Alice."

"Don't you mean you've just come *in* Alice," Dean muttered, then snorted.

Francis and Joseph both sent him scathing looks, causing Dean to press his mouth shut.

Sam ignored his brother's outburst and rushed on. "I love her," he said with a hopeless sigh, setting his tumbler back on the tray with the decanters. "There's no other way to put it. I love Alice more than I thought my heart could bear, and I have for some time. And the very idea of seeking out someone else to marry, and for such mercenary reasons too, breaks my heart."

"I warned you not to attach yourself to a courtesan in such a way," Joseph said.

This time, it was Joe who earned three starkly disapproving scowls from his brothers.

"Perhaps you should reserve your opinion on matters of the heart until you grow a heart of your own, dear brother," Dean said, one eyebrow arched.

"I have a heart," Joseph protested. "I very much have a heart. In fact, I—"

Joseph fell silent when Francis cleared his throat. Francis then glanced to Sam and said, "Do go on."

Sam let out a breath and sank into the chair opposite Joseph's. "Alice proposed to me," he said.

"She did?" Dean looked both fascinated and delighted by the prospect.

"We were—" he cleared his throat and felt his face heat, "—in an intimate moment, and she burst forth with an offer of marriage, saying that the two of us are the perfect pairing, that we love each other, and that we would be happy."

Sam's hopes for immediate advice were thwarted when his brothers merely stared at him and at each other.

"She isn't wrong," Dean said, tilting his head to the side and rubbing his chin thoughtfully. "The two of you are a good match."

"Aside from the fact that she is a courtesan," Joseph mumbled.

Francis sent him a quelling look, but Sam said, "He's right. I could never marry Alice." He hadn't intended his words to come out in such tones of despair, but they did.

"Let's examine the facts of the matter," Francis said in his most responsible manner. "Alice is special to you. The two of you already have a fast bond." Sam nodded at both statements. "And you have mentioned before that she is quite adept at investing."

"She is brilliant," Sam said. "She owns stocks in a diamond mine that are worth a small fortune. And she has other investments that have done well, I'm certain."

"You know this for a fact?" Francis asked.

Sam shrugged consideringly. He hadn't actually perused Alice's portfolio or even asked for specifics about her financial status for some time, but he was certain that she was flush with cash. Why, she occupied two expansive flats in a respectable neighborhood of Marylebone. She employed a nanny for Ryan and a man of business for herself. The furnishings in her flats were lovely, and she had more diamonds than the Queen, likely thanks to her investments. What other conclusion could he draw about her monetary worth from those things?

"Yes," he answered at length.

"Interesting," Francis said, his mind clearly at work. "So aside from her unfortunate reputation, she is precisely the sort of woman all of us should be seeking to engage ourselves to."

Sam tilted his head to the side. He hadn't thought of it that way.

He was about to comment on the matter when a commotion from the hall interrupted.

"...no right to invade my home in such a way," their father's voice railed from the hall. "You are not welcome here, sir, and I demand you depart at once."

"I am not here to call upon you, Lord Vegas," the deep, menacing voice of Montrose sounded from the hall. A moment later, the man himself rounded the corner and entered the parlor, followed by Lord Vegas and the family's harried-looking butler, Flynn. "I am here to call upon Lord Cathraiche."

Francis wasn't the only one who practically jumped out of his seat and stood to face the gaunt figure of Montrose with a look of defiance. Sam and the others stood as well, forming a rank against the man almost without thinking.

"Montrose," Francis said, narrowing his eyes as he stepped forward. "What is the meaning of this?" He glanced briefly to Lord Vegas, who seemed equally offended that Francis would take the lead as he did that Montrose would barge into a private, family parlor.

"Good evening, Lord Cathraiche," Montrose said with a deep, respectful bow to Francis. "I am pleased to see that you and your brothers are looking well." He grinned like a weasel about to devour its prey.

"State your reason for intruding, Montrose, and then get out," Francis said, his back going stiff.

Sam sent his older brother a sidelong look. He hated Montrose as much as the rest of them, but he questioned the wisdom of treating the devil as anything less than a venomous spider set loose in their midst. Indeed, the length of the man's arms and legs was somewhat spider-ish.

Montrose smiled as placidly as if Francis had invited him

to stay for supper. "I have no wish to occupy more of your time than is necessary, Lord Cathraiche," he said. He cleared his throat, clasped his hands behind his back, and went on with, "I am under the impression that felicitations are in order for the four of you."

"I beg your pardon?" Dean asked, inching closer to Francis's side and standing just as stalwartly.

"I understand that the four of you are intending to marry," Montrose said, fixing his gaze on Sam. He smiled and went on with, "I approve of this intention."

"I do not care if you approve or not," Lord Vegas cut in, crossing so that he stood in front of his sons, facing Montrose as though he were still the primary authority in the house. "It has nothing to do with you."

"Oh, but you see, it does," Montrose said. "For it has come to my attention that, in spite of the payments that have already been made to me, Lord Vegas, there is the matter of interest on that money to consider."

"Interest? Nonsense," Lord Vegas huffed. "You've extracted your pound of flesh. More than a pound, I daresay. There is nothing left to give you."

"There is always more to give," Montrose said with a toothy smile. "Even stones can have water squeezed from them if one squeezes hard enough."

"That is preposterous, I—"

Francis cut Lord Vegas off by raising one hand and stepping slightly in front of him. "Let us be clear, Montrose," he addressed Montrose directly. "Are you extorting more money from us?"

"Thank you for your clarity, Lord Cathraiche," Montrose said with a mock respectful half bow. "In fact, I am."

"You cannot do this, sir," Lord Vegas protested. "You cannot."

"In fact, Lord Vegas, I believe you will discover that I can,"

Montrose said, his smile as pleasant as if they were at a garden party. "Because, you see, I am quite certain that you and your sons would be willing to pay a great deal of money for your greatest and most egregious misstep to remain a secret."

Lord Vegas made a strangled noise. "You wouldn't dare."

Montrose laughed. "How could you have a single doubt in your mind about the fact that I would most certainly dare? You've seen how the mighty have fallen by my hand in the past."

Sam had to admit Montrose had a point. The man was shameless, and he had no scruples at all when it came to destroying aristocratic families, and all of London knew it.

"Can we assume that this further secret is the sort that would annihilate the Rathborne-Paxton family's respectability once and for all?" Sam asked.

Montrose nodded as though conceding a point. "You would be correct to assume that," he said. He glanced to Lord Vegas, then Francis. "It is my experience that the reputation of families such as yours do not recover from the sort of revelation I have yet to make. A revelation that I will never make, should my demands be met."

"Never," Lord Vegas grumbled. "You will never thwart me. You may think you have means and weapons, but you will never bring me down. My reputation is pristine. No one would believe you if you claimed I was anything less than moral and pious."

Sam exchanged a sideways glance with Dean that was returned with similar wariness. Their father was too defensive, too vocal. The were all thoroughly fucked.

"Would you be willing to send me a written request for the amount you require?" Francis answered with as much wariness as there was firmness in his voice.

"I would be," Montrose said hesitantly, "Provided you are willing to destroy the paper once my demands are made."

That made sense to Sam. Montrose was thorough and he was smart.

"I agree to those terms," Francis said. "Now, will you get out of our house?"

"How dare you assume the role of master of this house, whelp?" Lord Vegas snapped at Francis.

Sam shook his head. Their father couldn't recognize the only allies he might have had when they were standing in a half-circle around him.

"I will," Montrose answered Francis, ignoring Lord Vegas. "Good evening to you all."

He promptly turned and left the room, escorted by Flynn.

Lord Vegas spun to face his sons. "That was utterly beyond the—"

"Father, the time has come for you to be quiet," Francis nearly shouted.

For a moment, Lord Vegas was so stunned he could only stand there, his mouth flapping in shock. Finally, he managed to say, "How dare you—"

"What sort of dire secret is Montrose holding over your head, over all of our heads, now?" Francis cut him off.

Lord Vegas went rigid. "Nothing," he said, clearly lying. "Nothing at all." He snapped his mouth shut, whimpered for a half second while looking terrified, then made a whining sound that solidified into, "The four of you need to stick to the task I've given you. Marry money and marry it fast. That is the only part you need to play in this matter. I will take my supper in my room tonight," he finished, then turned and stormed out of the room.

"Do you know," Dean said with just a hint of humor in his voice, "I am beginning to believe that our father is an unforgivable prick."

Sam snorted a laugh despite himself. "I've known that for years."

Dean started to laugh with him, but Francis wheeled around and glared at them.

"This is a serious problem," Francis said. "Montrose has us by the balls, and in spite of what he said, I do not believe he ever intends to let go."

The analogy was painful, and Sam adjusted the way he stood with a wince because of it.

"What are we supposed to do?" Joseph asked, looking and sounding younger than he was.

Sam felt deeply sorry for his youngest brother. "What can we do?"

He intended it as a rhetorical question, but Francis answered, "We can discover what sort of evil is hanging over Father's head and we can reveal it before Montrose does."

Sam blinked. So did Dean and Joseph. Sam exchanged another look with Dean, but this time Dean merely shrugged.

"Don't you see?" Francis said. "Montrose has Father in his grip. There will never be a time when he does not wield his power over the entire family. He will continue to extort money and favors and God only knows what else from us as long as he thinks he has that control."

"So how do we wrestle that control back from him?" Sam asked with a hopeless shrug. Everything in his life was turning bitterly hopeless, even the very best of things, like Alice.

Francis paced across the room, rubbing the bottom half of his face, his brow knit in thought. Sam watched him. He had the feeling that Francis wasn't mulling over the answer to the problem. He already knew the answer, he was just debating how to explain it.

His suspicions were proven right when he turned to the other three and said, "What is the best way to strangle a fire?"

"Throw water on it?" Dean suggested.

"Starve it of fuel so that it has nothing to burn," Joseph answered a moment later.

"Precisely," Francis said, grinning at Joseph. "The only way we will ever stop Montrose from ruining this family's reputation is if we completely and utterly destroy it ourselves.

Sam blinked in shock. "How will that do any of us a lick of good?" he asked. "We'll be ruined one way or another. And won't that hurt Mother?"

"That is what we are trying to avoid above all else, is it not?" Dean asked.

"It is, and Mother should continue to be our primary concern, but I have the horrible feeling that, thanks to Montrose, the family is already destroyed," Francis said. "At least, if we choose the weapons of our destruction for ourselves, we will control the conflagration. And with money, we could establish Mother in a situation in the country or send her to Europe on a grand tour."

"I am still not certain what you mean," Dean said.

Francis glanced to Sam. "Samuel just gave me the idea."

When both Dean and Joseph stared at Sam in confusion, Sam shrugged and asked, "What idea? I am as much in the dark as the rest of you."

Francis resumed pacing. "Father has demanded that we marry money and status in order to restore the family. Montrose is demanding that money or else he will further destroy us. But if we destroy ourselves by marrying brides with money but without stellar reputations, we will gain the tools to protect and shield mother and to buy back some of what we've lost while also robbing Montrose of the ability to black-mail us."

"Sam gave you that idea?" Dean asked, eyeing Sam as though he were a wolf in sheep's clothing.

"He did." Francis finished his pacing by standing directly in front of Sam. He grinned. "Go marry Alice," he said.

A shiver of excitement zipped down Sam's spine. "I beg your pardon?"

"Go marry the woman you love," Francis said, his smile widening. "You love her, she loves you, she is wealthy, and marrying her will set the scandal pages alight and bring shame and ruination down on our family in a manner which *we* control, not Montrose."

"Would that not hurt Mother more than it would help her?" Joseph asked.

Twin emotions of joy and fury swirled through Sam, and instead of answering Joseph's astute question, he said, "Francis, it is unforgivably rude of you to suggest that marrying Alice would cause a scandal that would—" He didn't even bother to finish his sentence. Francis was right. The gossip rags would fall all over themselves to print every kind of malicious venom about the Rathborne-Paxton family over his choice of bride. He would become an instant pariah, and it would reflect badly on the entire family.

But he and Alice would be happy. And Montrose's threats would be neutered. They would be social outcasts, but they would be wealthy social outcasts.

"Furthermore," Francis went on, "I suggest that all of us seek out and marry the most unsuitable brides possible. London is filled with wealthy heiresses of dubious honor and no reputation whatsoever. The more shocking the match, the better."

"But Mother," Joseph argued with more passion. "This could devastate her."

"It could," Francis said with a grimace. "But it could also console her as well. She would have the protection of wealth, not to mention the prospect of grandchildren to dote on."

"Grandchildren?" Joseph asked in a strangled voice, sinking into the nearest chair, his eyes wide.

Sam grinned. "Mother has been hinting for years that we'd better hurry up and provide her with grandchildren."

"And who is to say she wouldn't fully comprehend our

actions and condone them?" Francis argued on. "Mother has a rebellious spirit—one that Father has smothered for decades. You observed her reaction to Father's revelation. She was as furious as all of us. I believe that she would encourage us in this endeavor."

"I would be more comfortable if you would write to her or speak to her directly to make certain of that," Joseph said, his eyes still wide.

"I will," Francis said with a nod.

There was a heavy pause before Dean asked, "Do you...do you really think we could do this?" His eyes were alight with inspiration.

Sam would have wagered everything he had that Dean already had a lady in mind.

"I do not like this plan," Joseph grumbled, sinking deeper into his chair.

"No doubt you'd intended to marry someone straight from the convent," Dean laughed.

Joseph looked offended. "Not all of us are heathens," he said.

Francis crossed to him, resting a hand on his shoulder. "I never said you had to marry a woman of dubious virtue, Joe. There are plenty of heiresses out there who are as pure as the driven snow, but also utterly unacceptable for whatever reason —industrial heiresses, foreigners...Americans."

Joseph made a face, but he seemed placated.

Sam would have laughed, as Dean did, but his mind and his heart were already churning with ideas. "I could marry Alice," he said, brightening as if the idea had just come to him instead of Francis more or less feeding it to him moments ago. "I could marry her, and we would be happy."

"That is the general idea, yes," Francis said wryly.

That was all Sam needed to hear. "By Jove, I could marry Alice!" He burst into laughter that bubbled up from his very soul, then lunged forward. He grabbed Francis's shoulders, then kissed his cheek soundly. "I can marry Alice."

"Yes, yes, of course." Francis wiped his face with a look of mock disgust as Sam peeled away. "Go and claim your lover," he said.

"I most certain will," Sam told his brothers as he fled the room. He had wheels to set in motion and plans to make. Happiness of the sort he never expected had just been handed to him, and he intended to make the very most of it.

Chapter Seven

"It was the most beautiful and the most tragic moment of my life," Alice sighed to Maeve late the next morning, as she served her dear friend tea in her domestic flat. Maeve had never visited Alice's professional flat before. Indeed, Alice had never so much as mentioned the existence of the second flat to her. "One moment, everything was lighthearted and gay between me and Sam, and the next, I suggested that the two of us marry and he ran."

Alice's shoulders slumped as she sipped her tea. All the sugar in the world couldn't sweeten the predicament she'd found herself in.

Maeve—who looked as proper as a good countess should look as she sat on the other side of the sofa from Alice—frowned. "You say that Mr. Rathborne-Paxton feels compelled to marry?"

"Yes," Alice said, putting her teacup down. Her stomach was in knots, and she didn't think she could manage more than a few swallows of tea, let alone any of the lovely sandwiches Harriett had made for them before taking Ryan out to the park so she and Maeve could talk in peace. "It seems that Lord Vegas has done something unforgiveable, and he has demanded that his sons all marry women of good breeding and high social standing to make up for it."

"He has?" Maeve's frown deepened as she took another sip of her tea before setting her cup down. "Why would Lord Vegas feel that his sons marrying well would provide a solution to his indiscretions?"

Alice tilted her head to the side. She had the distinct feeling she'd forgotten the entire scope of the demands being placed on Sam and his brothers, but those details didn't really matter. Sam had to marry, and she wasn't the sort he could offer for.

"I suppose the connections and social standing that good marriages would provide would be enough to counteract Lord Vegas's indiscretions," she said, folding her hands in her lap and staring at the plate of tea sandwiches, debating whether she should try one. "The point of it all is that I love him, and it will tear my poor, battered heart to shreds to watch him marry another."

Never mind the fact that Sam had made it clear he intended to carry on their affair after his marriage. That idea still had her moral compass spinning. She didn't think she could stoop so low, no matter how much she loved Sam. She was loath to see him debase himself in such a way either.

But how long would she continue to feel that way without Sam? How long could she keep her scruples intact with Sam just a breath away, pining for her?

"And you say there is also the problem of your rent being in arrears?" Maeve asked, pushing Alice out of her increasingly melancholy thoughts.

"Yes," Alice sighed. "Mrs. Knox is a fair and good landlady, and she has let me carry on with far more things than any other landlady would, but she does not run a charity house. She can only accommodate me for so long."

Maeve nodded, still frowning. "This is because of the diamond mine, is it not? I understand that you have lived off the profits of that mine, and your other investments, for some time, but I never did quite understand how you found yourself in possession of such a valuable investment. When you left my and Avery's house, you barely had enough for trolley fare."

A creeping feeling that perhaps the game was up slithered its way down Alice's spine. The way Maeve furrowed her brow and stared at Alice had Alice thinking that perhaps, after all this time, Maeve was piecing together everything that she knew, but perhaps hadn't wanted to see.

"My current situation is a result of the failure of the mine, yes," Alice said slowly. "My other investments have disappointed me as well. And...and my greatest fear is that their failures will mean that I must return to the manner in which I earned all of the money and favors that I had last year."

Maeve blinked, her face a mask of confusion. "But how did you—" She stopped, staring hard at Alice.

Alice felt herself blush up a storm. "Women have been earning money in such a manner since the dawn of time," she mumbled, unable to look her friend in the eye.

Maeve's eyes suddenly went wide. Then her mouth dropped open. "Oh, Alice, no. You didn't."

Alice lowered her head with a wince, peeking up at her friend hesitantly. "It isn't as bad as you might think," she said. "I was lucky to find a few generous and kind patrons. Their gifts and advice have helped me to establish myself."

"But you...you couldn't have...with more than one man... you didn't—" Maeve dropped her hands to her lap and abruptly sat straighter, looking indignant. "In the same flat with your son?"

Alice flinched. "No, not precisely." She stood, gesturing for Maeve to come with her.

They left the flat and headed down the hallway to Alice's second flat. There weren't words to describe what Maeve was about to see, so Alice simply unlocked the door and pushed it open, showing her friend the other half of her life inside.

Maeve stepped into the flat with her mouth dropped open and her eyes wide. She took only a few steps in, then surveyed the lurid decorations and sumptuous furnishings as though she were in a museum. The door to the bedroom was open, but thankfully Maeve didn't go in to have a look. Alice was not inclined to explain to her the presence of so many mirrors in the room to her.

Finally, Maeve cleared her throat. "Well, I must say, it does look rather jolly in here."

Alice's brow shot up. That wasn't at all the reaction she had expected. "It is a bit garish, but that is all part of the show."

Maeve nodded, then blinked as though a thought had just occurred to her. "What does Mr. Rathborne-Paxton think of all this?"

Alice worked her mouth, but no words came out. Maeve would figure it out in a moment.

As soon as she did, Maeve gasped and clapped a hand to her mouth. "He already knows," she said. "He was...*is* one of your...patrons."

"One of the very first," Alice admitted with a sigh. "And the most steadfast. In fact, I threw the others off six months ago, when the diamond mine looked as though it would be profitable. And yes, Sam does give me a bit of money." She cleared her throat, her face going red, but forced herself to go on with, "Most men pay their mistresses a stipend of sorts to help them along."

Maeve gasped, a light of deeper understanding coming to

her eyes. "You're his mistress, and gentlemen of Mr. Rathborne-Paxton's standing cannot marry their mistresses."

"And therein lies the problem," Alice said with a helpless gesture. "I crossed that uncrossable boundary yesterday when I suggested he marry me, and he dashed out of the room as though there were a fire."

"You weren't—" Maeve started, glancing to the bedroom.

Alice's face heated even more. "We were, in fact. He didn't just leave in the middle of the conversation, he left in the middle of—" She nodded to the bed.

"Oh, dear." Maeve clasped a hand to her mouth. She took another look around the room, seeing it in a different way, no doubt.

"So you see the predicament I'm in," Alice said, gesturing for Maeve to leave the flat with her. Such a garish setting wasn't where Maeve belonged, and they were far more likely to be able to finish their conversation in peace in a more domestic setting.

"We are in love, if that eases your mind at all," she told Maeve once they were seated in the other flat once more. "It is not as sordid as it could be."

"But you must admit the situation is still fraught on many levels," Maeve said, taking up her teacup as though she needed the tea to fortify herself after what she'd seen.

"It is an unforgivable muddle," Alice admitted with a sigh. "Particularly with my rent situation and Sam's determination to marry. I...I don't know what I will do." She flopped back into the sofa, raising a hand to rub her forehead. "I don't want to take other men to my bed again, but if I have to...."

Maeve was silent for a long time, her eyes unfocused with deep thought. Alice was increasingly afraid that after all this time, after everything the two of them had been through together and after all the ways Maeve had stood up for her when no one else would, she had finally done something so outrageous that even her best friend couldn't forgive her. It was agony to wait for the swirl of thoughts Maeve was caught in to resolve itself and for Maeve to speak.

When, at last, she did, Alice was so relieved she immediately sat up straighter.

"I will tell you what you are going to do," Maeve said with sudden determination. "The first thing you are going to do is let these flats go, as you can no longer afford the rent."

Alice glanced at her warily. "Where will I live, then?"

"With me and Avery, of course." Maeve burst into a smile. "You know you are always welcome under our roof, no matter...." Her sentence trailed off as her cheeks turned pink. Maeve shook her head and went on. "Most of London knows that we are friends. I think I understand now why you have been hesitant to attend my and Avery's social functions or to be seen with us on public occasions, but all of that is done now."

"I never intended to hurt you," Alice said. "In fact, I have kept my distance in public to save you."

"And I would expect nothing less from you," Maeve said, reaching out and resting a hand on Alice's as it rested on her knee. "That is why we will implement a program of moral reform that will expunge every untoward rumor or mark on your reputation that might exist."

"We...we will?" Alice asked, suddenly uncertain whether she liked Maeve's plan.

"Absolutely," Maeve said, brightening. "We will start with your wardrobe, throwing out everything that carries even a hint of suggestion to it. We will purchase you a whole new wardrobe of simple, modest clothes. Then we will be certain to attend church every Sunday. Perhaps more than one service, just to be certain. We will attach ourselves to a good, solid Christian women's association that will enable us to engage in charity work."

"I already volunteer at the Clerkenwell Ladies Home," Alice said as she reached for her teacup, desperate to drink something sweet to cover up the sense of foreboding that was turning her gut. Maeve was a darling, and she meant well, but her idea of moral reform was Alice's idea of hell.

Maeve shook her head. "It is not enough," she went on. "As lovely as Lady Clerkenwell is, her reputation is not of the spotless variety. You will have to find a more upright institution to attach yourself to. And you will *have* to keep your distance from men, of course," she said, striking another, horrific blow. "Especially Mr. Rathborne-Paxton. But then, if he is to marry, you would have to disassociate yourself from him anyhow. And you should not attend the theater on any score."

Alice set her teacup down with shaking hands. The cure Maeve was suggesting was far worse than the disease.

She was about to suggest that perhaps there were other ways to go about reforming her reputation when the incongruous sound of music drifted in through the flat's windows. Not just any music either. A brass band of some sort was playing in the street, and it sounded as though they were drawing closer. The jolly sound they made was at complete odds with the way Alice felt inside.

"It may be best for us to return to Ireland for a time," Maeve went on as the band drew so close that they were a strong interference. They seemed to stop in the street just outside Alice's building. "Perhaps for a year, or even two. I know Avery has estate business to attend to, and I do so want Alonzo to experience his homeland. And—good heavens, why is that band so loud?"

As soon as Maeve asked the question, a shout of, "Alice! Alice Woodmont!" in Sam's voice sounded above the noise of the band.

Alice's heart was in her throat in an instant, and she

dashed to the window as fast as her legs would carry her, sticking her head out.

The sight in the street below had her laughing out loud. Somehow, Sam had commandeered an eight-piece band that was playing a rousing version of a popular love song. The band wasn't the only thing he'd commandeered. A dozen children of various ages were with him, all of them carrying massive bouquets of hothouse flowers of every sort. A few others had bright pink streamers on sticks that they waved madly. It appeared that half the neighborhood had come out to witness the spectacle as well.

"Sam, what is this?" Alice laughed, shaking her head.

"Come down, my love, and I will explain," he said.

Alice's heart caught in her throat at his use of the endearment. Something had changed with him, she could tell. Hope instantly suggested what it was, but she dared not foster that hope, not after everything she'd just said to Maeve.

She pulled her head back into the flat, sent Maeve a wide-eyed look of excitement, then turned to rush across the apartment and out to the hall. Several other tenants of the building were on their way out to see what the fuss was as well, and as Alice burst onto the street, Maeve on her heels, she brought an entire entourage of her neighbors with her.

"Samuel Rathborne-Paxton, what are you doing?" she laughed as she slowed her pace and approached Sam.

"What I should have done a long time ago," Sam said in a voice loud enough to include the massive gathering on the street in his exhibition. "I should never have let the fear of social stigma keep me from what, from *whom* I love. You are everything I need and more, my dearest Alice. You have beauty, grace, humor, a tidy investment portfolio, and above all else, you have my heart."

Alice's breath caught as Sam took a step toward her, reaching for her hands. As mad as it was with everyone surrounding them, Alice gave him her hands, grinning and shaking her head. "You do beat all, Sam," she said.

"I will beat whatever you want me to, my love," he said, lowering his voice to the level of a private conversation between the two of them. He drew her close. "I am so sorry for dashing out on you yesterday the way I did. Your suggestion took me by surprise is all. It had never occurred to me that I might actually be able to have the thing that would make me happier than anything else on this earth. But why not?" he asked with a shrug.

"I can think of several reasons why not," Alice said, arching one eyebrow.

"Those reasons do not matter," Sam said. "The only thing that matters is that I love you. And after discussing the matter with my brothers, after gaining their approval, mind you, because they are all very fond of you, I knew that there is only one woman in all of London whom I wish to marry. There is only one woman in the entire world I could see as my wife and the partner of my life, and that is you."

Alice blinked rapidly, tears flooding her eyes. Sam was saying everything she'd ever wanted to hear, and in the most beautiful way.

And then he dropped to one knee.

"Alice Woodmont, would you marry me?" he asked.

Alice opened her mouth, but before she could say anything, one of the members of the brass band shouted, "Go on, love! Say yes!"

That sent the rest of the band, the children carrying flowers, and the neighbors who had come out to see the show into loud shouts of, "Yes! Say yes!" and a few, "Blimey, it's romantic."

Underneath those shouts of assent and well-wishes, Alice vaguely heard one voice mutter, "That's the luckiest whore I've ever seen."

A twist of anxiety pulled Alice away from the pure joy of the moment. She wondered if Sam knew what he was asking. She wondered if he would regret his impetuosity if they went through with marrying. It wouldn't be all brass bands and flowers if they did.

She refused to let that mar her happiness, though. All that mattered was that she loved Sam and Sam loved her, and the two of them would be able to spend the rest of their lives together.

"Yes," she breathed out at last. "Yes, my dearest, darlingest Sam. I will marry you."

The crowd burst into loud shouts of huzzah and well-wishes. Sam rose quickly and pulled Alice into his arms, kissing her thoroughly. One of the mothers of a young girl who had come out to see what was going on clapped her hand over her daughter's eyes, but that only made Alice laugh as she and Sam continued to kiss.

"You've made me the happiest man in the world," Sam said once he was finished kissing her.

"You cannot be as happy as you've made me," Alice laughed. Not only happy, but relieved too. Now she didn't have to worry about flats and rent and reputations. Sam would likely want to move them into a townhouse of some sort. In spite of their recent troubles, she was certain Sam's family had the money to provide that. Her financial woes were solved. And the Rathborne-Paxton family was well-respected. As tarnished as her reputation was, she would be able to secure a place in respectable society with such an esteemed name behind her. It was all a dream come true.

"We have so much to plan for," Sam said, taking her hand and leading her back toward the door to Alice's building. "Lady Carnlough, we will, of course, require your expertise and support in planning a wedding. The wedding should happen soon as well. I'll obtain a special license. I simply cannot wait another moment to marry this woman whom I love."

"I will give you any help you require," Maeve said, looking genuinely pleased. She beamed at Alice and said, "It seems as though all will be well after all."

Chapter Eight

Sam could not have been more pleased with the way his proposal to Alice had transpired. He'd thought it was a bit much to hire a full brass band and to purchase the entire stock of a florist's shop to bring to Alice, but a momentous proposal required extravagance. And with any luck, the sheer exuberance of the whole thing would cause the gossip columnists to take notice and begin printing stories that would aid with his brother's plan to destroy the family's reputation before Montrose could.

The only thing left was to announce his engagement to his family, and the dinner party his father was throwing for a selection of his most distinguished friends—friends whom he was hoping he could rely on for support when news of Montrose's deeds against him became public, but who would likely abandon him in an instant.

Sam had covertly asked Flynn to see that an extra place was set by his side at the supper table for Alice, and when Alice arrived—looking resplendent in a gown of emerald green that matched her eyes, her fiery hair caught up with a single, green ostrich feather as an accent—Sam was so overjoyed at the way his and his brothers' plan was working out that he could hardly keep still.

"You look positively divine, my love," he told Alice as Flynn took her coat. He grabbed both of her hands and kissed her knuckles before planting a kiss on her ruby lips.

"I am not too proud to admit that I am a bit terrified," Alice answered breathlessly as Sam took her arm and led her deeper into the house, to the formal parlor where his brothers and father and the night's guests were waiting.

"Nonsense, darling," Sam said, happy to be able to address her by terms of endearment with impunity. "You know my brothers already, and they adore you. Well, Joseph is a bit of a stick in the mud, but even he likes you on the sly, whether he will admit to it or not."

Alice laughed, but Sam could hear the tension and uncertainty in the sound. He stopped them just before they reached the entrance to the parlor and turned her to face him.

"Truly, my dearest, you have nothing to worry about," he said, brushing his fingertips over the side of her face. "You are beauty and liveliness personified. My father will hate you, and he will be a right arse about it, to be sure, but you have far more supporters in this house than you have detractors."

Alice drew in a deep breath, her hand tight to her belly. "If you say so."

"I do," Sam insisted, then leaned in to steal one last kiss on her lips. "And now, let us go beard the lion in his den."

Alice put on a beautiful smile and took Sam's arm. They turned the corner, entering the parlor, Sam feeling as though he owned the world and everything in it.

"Ah, Samuel, I see your friend has arrived," Francis said, rising from the chair near the fire, where he'd been fretting about something. Francis put on a kind smile for Alice as he crossed the room to greet her. Sam let her go so that Francis could take her hand and kiss her knuckles. "You have my deepest admiration for accepting my brother's hand," he said in a low voice.

"How could I possibly have said no?" Alice asked, beaming from Francis to Sam.

"What is the meaning of this?" Lord Vegas snapped, cutting off the sweetness of the moment. The man struggled to rise from his chair, but then did no more than stand and glare at Alice. "You would bring this kind of a woman into my house?"

"Forgive me, Father," Sam said, knowing he could beat his father at his own game, "but what do you mean 'this kind of woman'?"

Lord Vegas opened his mouth, then thought better of commenting. He glanced to the esteemed figures of Lord Shaftsbury and Lord Abingdon and their wives, shaking as he was torn between his favorite pastime of berating his sons and saving face with fellow peers.

Finally, he settled on saying, "Who is her family? What sort of standing does she have?"

To her credit, Alice kept a perfectly amiable disposition and said, "My family are the Woodmonts of County Antrim, my lord," as though that were something extraordinary.

"Is that so?" Lady Shaftsbury said, seemingly impressed.

Sam exchanged a look with Francis. Already, their plan was off to a brilliant start. The look of approval in Francis's eyes said as much.

"Woodmont," Lady Abingdon said with a sage nod, as though she were in the know. "Yes, I do believe I know the family."

"Mrs. Woodmont is great friends with Lord and Lady Carnlough as well," Sam added, singing Alice's praises.

"Carnlough, you say?" Lord Abingdon said, impressed.

"*Mrs.* Woodmont?" Lady Shaftsbury asked, her eyes slightly narrowed.

"I am very sorry to say that my husband was killed in service to his country in South Africa," Alice lied with all of the convincing smoothness of an actual war widow.

She received sounds of sympathy and kindly looks from Lady Shaftsbury and Lady Abingdon.

Lord Vegas was nearly beside himself with rage. He held his body rigidly, his hands balled into fists at his sides. Sam had to work exceedingly hard not to laugh. His father knew precisely who Alice was, of course, and knew that her story was as false as his moral compass, but to acknowledge so in front of his guests would damage his reputation as much as Alice's.

Which was precisely the point.

"Dinner is served, my lord," Flynn announced from the doorway, saving them from further danger or questions Alice might have a harder time answering.

Sam took Alice's arm, and the other guests lined up in order of precedence to walk down the short hall to the dining room. Sam noticed with a smirk that his father had spared no expense in both decorating and planning the meal for his guests, even though he barely had two farthings to rub together anymore. It was all just a further part of the hypocrisy that they had all lived under without knowing it for so long. Sam was glad that as soon as he married Alice and her investing fortune, he, at least, wouldn't have to worry about paying the butcher.

"The situation in South Africa is alarming," Lord Shaftsbury began the conversation as they were all seated and the footmen began serving the first course. "Mark my words, there is conflict coming between our good, British colonists and the Orange Free State and South African Republic."

"There has already been conflict between them, has there not, Lord Shaftsbury?" Alice asked as she started on her soup.

Lord Vegas appeared livid that Alice would address an earl like Lord Shaftsbury without being spoken to first.

"I suppose you are right, my dear," Lord Shaftsbury said with just a hint of condescension. "There was that little war last decade."

If Alice noticed the man's condescension or minded, she didn't let it show.

"Mrs. Woodmont is invested in South Africa," Sam explained, beaming with pride. "In diamond mines. She does quite well with her investments at that."

"You don't say," Lord Abingdon said with a smile. "Are you an investor in De Beers, then?"

"No." Alice lowered her head slightly, looking suddenly anxious. "In a separate company."

Lord Abingdon frowned. "Strange," he said. "I was under the impression that Rhodes and his company had accomplished something of a monopoly in the South African diamond mining industry."

Alice suddenly seemed out of her depths. Her beautiful face flushed an alluring shade of pink. Sam instantly felt compelled to step up and rescue her.

"Mrs. Woodmont is one of the most talented investors I know," he complimented her, smiling fondly at her and likely leaving no one at the table in any doubt of his feelings for her. "One of the things that brought us together was our interest in investments and speculation. I have done passingly well myself over the years, but Mrs. Woodmont is the one who has truly made a place for herself in the financial world."

"How unusual for a woman to be involved in investing," Lady Shaftsbury said. The way she studied Alice almost had Sam thinking she might like to take up investing as well.

"You should have Mrs. Woodmont call someday to share her secrets with you," Sam said, speaking the idea as soon as it came to him. How lovely would it be for Alice to gain friends amongst the very highest and most well-respected of the aristocracy? Then it wouldn't matter what her past was or where she'd come from. She could be accepted wherever she went.

To Sam's surprise, Dean was staring at him across the table as though he'd gone mad. A second too late, Sam remembered that the point of his association with Alice was to ruin reputations, not repair them.

"Lord Abingdon," Lord Vegas began in a brittle voice, fidgeting with his spoon as it balanced above his soup bowl, "what do you think of the latest information gathered in this year's census? It seems to me as though the Church of England has much work to do to return its members to the fold."

As the conversation veered toward Lord Vegas's favorite topic, the salvation of souls—which was outlandishly hypocritical—Sam reached under the table to squeeze Alice's leg in congratulations for a conversation well-managed.

He was only slightly alarmed by the vaguely panicked look she sent him in return, though she was still doing her best to keep her smile in place and to be as amiable as possible. Whatever had her worried, he would get to the bottom of it as soon as he could. Surely, Alice had nothing at all to concern herself with.

Except, perhaps, the moment when he announced their engagement.

That moment came right about the time when the footmen began to circle, keeping an eye on when the main course was finished. Lord Vegas was in the middle of a painfully dull conversation with Lord Shaftsbury and Lord Abingdon about some bill that had recently been set before the House of Lords that was of no consequence to Sam whatsoever.

"Father," he interrupted the drone of the conversation, "I

suppose you would like to know why I invited Mrs. Wood-mont to supper this evening."

Not only did Lord Vegas appear livid at being interrupted when he had the attention of his guests, he narrowed his eyes at Alice, as though it were her fault. "Yes," he grumbled, "I was wondering why you would bring...your *friend* into my house."

The mood in the dining room instantly tensed. Francis sent a look of approval to Sam. Sam took that and stood with a proud smile.

"Father, esteemed guests, brothers," he said with all the formality he could muster and just as much showmanship as he had used to propose to Alice the day before. "I am exceedingly pleased to tell you all that I have asked for Mrs. Wood-mont's hand in marriage, and the delightful woman has agreed to give it to me."

The response Sam received to the announcement from the people around the table wasn't half as rousing as that of the people who had been in the street to witness the proposal.

"Oh?" Lady Abingdon said, blinking rapidly. "How lovely." She didn't sound particularly certain about whether it was lovely or not.

"Congratulations, brother," Francis said, playing his part well. "We are all very happy for you."

"We most certainly are not," Lord Vegas snapped. He grabbed his serviette, wiped his mouth as he stood, then threw the cloth down on his plate. "You cannot marry this woman, this...this *whore*."

Lady Shaftsbury gasped, then began to cough so hard she needed her husband to thump her back. Lady Abingdon looked suddenly faint. All of Sam's brothers glared at Lord Vegas.

Alice merely rested her fork on the table and glanced implacably toward Lord Vegas, indicating without words that she would not be bullied by him.

"How dare you speak in such a manner to my fiancée?" Sam demanded.

"You will not marry this woman, boy," his father snapped in return. "She is a filthy strumpet, not to mention Irish. Why, I doubt there isn't a bed in London that she hasn't gone to with legs spread."

Lady Shaftsbury coughed even more furiously, and Lady Abingdon pushed her chair back as though she would leave the table, but swooned before she could go anywhere.

"Have a care, Father." Francis stood and addressed Lord Vegas with a scowl. "You are upsetting your guests."

That seemed to have a slightly steadying effect on Lord Vegas, but it did nothing to quell his anger. "Do not worry," he addressed his guests. "Whatever farce this is, whatever prank my son is playing on me, it will not continue. This woman is no war widow, she is my son's mistress, a notorious courtesan. He only brought the woman here tonight to torment me."

"Is this...is this true?" Lord Shaftsbury asked. The frown he sent Alice was like night to day from the kind but condescending way he'd addressed her thus far.

Alice remained silent, her eyes downcast. Instead of looking cowed or ashamed of herself, however, she appeared to be lost in thought.

"Alice and I have been intimate friends for quite some time," Sam said, resting a hand on her shoulder as he defended her. "And yes, Father, we *will* marry, regardless of what you have to say about it. Is that not what you demanded all four of your sons do? Marry well?"

"I did not—" Lord Vegas began to shout, but held himself back. He sent a worried glance to his guests. Lord Abingdon was helping his wife out of her chair. Lord Shaftsbury rose to excuse himself and his wife from the table as well. "Please." Lord Vegas turned anxious when he saw his guests were about to leave. "Pay no mind to my miscreant son and his jokes. This is nothing, I can assure you."

"This strikes me as a family matter that should be resolved with family alone," Lord Shaftsbury said, signaling to Flynn.

It was the swiftest end to a supper party that Sam had ever seen. At least the meal had been delicious and they'd eaten most of it. Perhaps the footmen would bring the pudding to his and his brothers' private parlor later.

"I must apologize profusely for this upset." Lord Vegas followed his guests out of the room, looking as though he might resort to grabbing hold of them and dragging them back into the dining room to get them to stay. It was a hopeless cause, though.

"Good day, Lord Vegas," Lord Abingdon said in a grave voice, still mostly supporting his wife. "We will call on you again when we are ready."

Sam, Alice, and the others followed Lord Vegas and the guests into the hall, watching with varying degrees of shock and humor as Lord Vegas took his first steps along the path to ruin all on his own.

"This will be easier than I would have thought," Dean commented to Francis as the four brothers stood in a line.

"Has there been some grander scheme at play this evening?" Alice asked, gazing down the line at all of their profiles.

The brothers all turned to her in unison.

"It is nothing you need to concern yourself with, Alice," Francis said with a smile.

"We've all just been waiting for Father to stuff things up," Dean added with a laugh. "And he's gone and done it without us having to push at all."

Alice smiled at them, but there was a hint of uneasiness in her smile.

Sam didn't like to see his lover upset at all, so he took her hand. "Never you mind, dearest. Come into the back parlor with us and we'll have pudding brought around."

"Perhaps I should leave as well," Alice said instead with a judicious look.

Lord Vegas had finished with the guests, and as he marched back down the hall with a look of fury, he glared at her and said, "Yes, you should. And never set foot in this house again, do you hear me? You will end your wicked association with my son at once."

"Father, you cannot speak to my fiancée in such a manner," Sam said, stepping between his father and Alice as a shield.

"This is my house and you are my son. You will do as I say, or you will—" Lord Vegas cut himself off with a strangled cry, doubling over and clutching his stomach.

The brothers all suddenly looked anxious, but it was Joseph who stepped forward to take their father in hand. "You need to sit down and calm yourself, Father. These attacks of dyspepsia cannot be good for you."

"As if you care," Lord Vegas growled, yanking away from him. "Go and plot ruin with the rest of your brothers, you little imp." He shoved Joseph away.

Sam's heart bled for Joe and the look of hurt he wore at Lord Vegas's rejection. The blackguard should have stopped to see that he might have had one final ally in the form of Joseph —who had sought after his father's love for so long and so desperately that it hurt Sam to think about—but Lord Vegas seemed intent on burning even that bridge.

Once Lord Vegas had marched up the stairs, likely to retire to his own room, the brothers all let out sighs of relief.

"I think that went about as well as could be expected," Dean said with a smile.

"You expected worse?" Alice asked, pressing a hand to her stomach.

"With Father, you can never tell," Sam said. He leaned in and brushed a kiss across Alice's cheek. "You did magnificently, my darling."

"And you have done very well for yourself, brother," Francis said, thumping Sam's arm. He glanced to Alice and said, "In spite of the impression my father might have given, you are a welcome addition to this family, Alice."

Alice managed an exhausted smile. "Thank you, Lord Cathraiche. It is good to know I have at least some support."

"You have a great deal of it," Dean said with a smile. "I look forward to the wedding."

"As do I," Sam said, sliding his arm around Alice's waist and drawing her close. "I've already applied for the special license, so we should be able to be wed as soon as next weekend."

"Are you certain that is enough time?" Joseph asked, looking stung by Lord Vegas's comments, but still eager for the approval of his brothers.

"It will be more than enough time," Sam said. "In fact, the quicker we are able to marry, the better, as far as I'm concerned. What a sensation it will cause! And in the end, I will be wed to the woman I love more than any other for the rest of our lives."

Chapter Nine

I n spite of the cruelty of the words Alice had heard whispered when Sam proposed to her, she truly did feel like the luckiest whore in the world throughout the next week as lightning-fast preparations were made for her and Sam's wedding.

"I must admit, it feels very much as though you are the heroine of some sort of romantic story," Maeve said as she helped Alice don her wedding gown in a side room at the small church in Mayfair Sam had secured on short notice for the ceremony. "Especially considering the circumstances."

Alice winced slightly at Maeve's last comment as she wriggled into the fine, lace gown she'd purchased only the day before. Maeve was still shocked and most likely appalled by the behavior Alice had engaged in without telling her. Even though Maeve had supported her through the entire ordeal surrounding Ryan's birth, Alice's friend had more of a traditional, conservative viewpoint about how women should behave themselves.

"Circumstances be damned," Alice said, adjusting the bodice of her gown then turning her back to Maeve so that she could do up the impossible row of pearl buttons. "I am marrying the man I love today. More than that, Sam has proven his love to me by defying his father's expectations and marrying the person he loves instead of who he is told to."

"And that is why it feels like the conclusion of a romantic novel," Maeve said. Alice could hear the smile in her voice.

"I must admit, I am exceedingly proud of Sam for defying convention on my behalf," Alice said. "Not many men would so publicly marry their mistress."

"Mama, what is a mistress?" Ryan asked from the corner, where he sat playing with his menagerie of wooden animals.

Alice flushed, then twisted to send Maeve a wary look. When she turned back to her son, she said, "It is a particular kind of friend, dear," she said. "That is all."

"I am friends with Sam too," Ryan said, sitting straighter and smiling. "Does that mean I'm a mistress too?"

Alice laughed, though there was a great deal of anxiety in that laugh. "No, dear. Mistresses are women." Although she wouldn't have been surprised if there were kept men out there as well.

"If you are marrying Sam, does that make him my papa now?" Ryan asked, tilting his head to the side.

Alice's heart warmed and swelled in her chest. "I suppose that is entirely up to Sam, darling. It is something the two of you should discuss."

Ryan nodded, then turned his attention back to the cows in his hands. Alice watched him for a moment with a wide, tender smile, even after Maeve finished with her buttons. Of course, Sam could never claim Ryan as his own in any formal capacity. He could not make Ryan his heir. But so far, Sam truly had been a good friend to Ryan and a surrogate father of sorts. It warmed Alice's heart to think that Sam could be in Ryan's life to a greater degree. And with any luck, sometime in the near future, perhaps she and Sam could give Ryan brothers and sisters to play with.

Alice pressed a hand to her stomach and sighed with happiness. "I have a feeling that everything is about to be so wonderful," she said, turning and smiling at Maeve.

"As do I." Maeve took Alice's hands, and the two of them shared the sort of giggle that only life-long friends could manage.

From there, Alice sat so that Maeve could style her hair for the day. The wedding wasn't going to be a particularly showy or overdone affair. They'd invited Sam's family and a few of Alice's friends. There were other friends and acquaintances that Alice would have loved to invite, but to do so would have drawn far too much attention to her former profession. As it stood, they would have a small circle of dear friends around them, which was all Alice required.

At least, that was what Alice thought was in store.

A knock sounded at the door shortly before the ceremony was supposed to begin, and a moment later, Avery popped his head around the door. The look of concern he wore flattened Alice's smile entirely.

"Er," he began slowly, "you might want to come have a look at the church."

Alice frowned and stood from where Maeve had just affixed her veil to her hairstyle. "What do you mean by that?" she asked.

Avery hesitated, then rubbed a hand over his face. "Come and see."

Alice exchanged a curious look with Maeve, then gestured for Ryan to come to her. As soon as he did, still holding one of his cows, she took his free hand, and their small group left the side room to investigate.

Alice could hear what Avery meant by his cryptic comment even before she saw the chapel. A great, buzzing drone of conversation drifted from the main part of the church. It was far more noise than could be made by just the guests they'd invited. Alice tried to keep somewhat out of view as she gazed into the chapel, but gasped at the sight she saw there.

The tiny chapel was packed to the gills. Men and women of all sorts squeezed into the pews, shoulder to shoulder, whispering as though some sort of marvelous show were about to begin. Alice recognized a few of them as prominent journalists from some of the more widely read newspapers. Others were notable members of the aristocracy, but also people associated with the Concord Theater. The feeling of excitement that filled the chapel was an eerie combination of hope and well-wishes and pure scandalmongering.

"Oh, dear," Alice said, pressing a hand to her stomach. "It seems as though word of the wedding has gotten out."

"Why would all of these people be the slightest bit interested in your wedding?" Maeve asked, shaking her head with genuine perplexity.

Alice sent her friend a look, wondering if she truly was that naïve. She then glanced to the very front of the chapel, where Sam was already standing up with Francis by his side. Sam and Francis had their heads together, both wearing frowns as they appeared to debate something. When Sam caught Alice watching him from the back of the chapel, he burst into a bright, confident smile.

That single smile set Alice completely at ease. Whatever was happening with the congregation that had come to watch the wedding, Sam would make certain all was well in the end.

Sam gestured to the organ loft, and within moments, the polite strains of the prelude changed to the more formal wedding march.

"Are you ready for this?" Avery asked as he took Alice's arm.

"As much as I'll ever be," Alice answered as they started up the aisle.

The ceremony was designed to be as simple as possible. Maeve was Alice's only attendant, but she had the double task of accompanying Ryan. The two of them were seated in the front pew, and Avery joined them, as Alice continued on to join Sam at the altar.

"Who is that boy?" Alice heard someone ask without even bothering to whisper.

"I think that's her son," someone else answered.

An echo of gasps and sounds of surprise and understanding followed. Alice pushed them out of her mind, walking straight to Sam and taking his hands as they positioned themselves in front of the minister.

"Courage," Sam whispered to her, then winked.

Alice grinned back. The joy she felt over marrying the man she loved was far greater than any anxiety she might have felt for the oddities of the ceremony. She would not let anything touch her as long as Sam was by her side.

Or so she thought until the minister cleared his throat and asked, "Are you most certain you wish to proceed, Mr. Rathborne-Paxton?"

A tiny part of Alice's heart withered. If even the minister disapproved of the match, how could they possibly proceed with grace to a happy ending?

"I most certainly wish to proceed," Sam told the minister, indignation snapping in his voice.

The minister frowned, then sighed. "Very well then. Let us begin."

That would have been the end of things if Ryan hadn't suddenly blurted, "Mama is Sam's mistress," just as there was a hush. More gasps and sounds of shock followed the statement.

"Ignore them," Sam said, squeezing Alice's hands to reassure her. "What do those people matter to us?"

They did not matter one bit. Alice smiled at Sam, more grateful than she could say for his support in all things.

The ceremony proceeded quickly from there. The minister didn't seem any more inclined to prolong things than Alice or Sam did. Alice had the impression that he used the shortest version of the wedding ceremony from the Book of Common Prayer as possible to speed things along. In no time at all, they were exchanging their vows and pledging to join their lives to each other for all eternity. When the minister pronounced them man and wife, a bit of a reluctant sigh in his voice, the congregation let out a collective breath, as though they couldn't believe the two of them had gone through with things.

From there, all that was necessary was to flee the church as fast as possible to avoid what turned into an unexpected flurry of questions from the journalists in attendance.

"Mr. Rathborne-Paxton, what possessed you to marry your mistress?"

"Is it true that your father disapproves of the marriage? He was not present at the ceremony."

"Do you plan to leave the country to avoid the scandal?"

"Mrs. Rathborne-Paxton, what are the origins of your son?"

Neither Alice nor Sam answered any of the questions. They leapt straight into the carriage that was waiting by the church door to take them to the Rathborne-Paxton house for what Alice hoped would be a small reception attended only by family and invited guests.

"I never would have imagined anyone showing the slightest bit of interest in our marriage," she said, peering out the window as the carriage lurched forward. "Why all the attention?"

"I suppose people are interested in unusual matches," Sam said, a bit distractedly. He reached for Alice's hand, smiling broadly at her. "None of it matters, though, darling. All that matters is that we two love each other, and we will be the happiest married couple in London."

Alice let her worries go and burst into a smile. "We most certainly will be."

She leaned in to kiss Sam. His arms went around her in an instant, and the ardor of their kiss grew swiftly. She truly did love Sam, and she was more grateful to him than she could express for his courage in marrying her when he could easily have just cast her aside.

Before their kiss could turn into anything more, they arrived at the Rathborne-Paxton house. Flynn greeted them and helped Alice down from the carriage, wishing her and Sam every joy.

That was an auspicious beginning, but once they made it into the house, things took a turn almost immediately.

"Good God, you've actually done it," Lord Vegas said, greeting them in the hall with a deep scowl. "You've actually married the bitch."

"Father!" Sam protested, his temper flaring. "How dare you speak to my bride in such a manner?"

"I dare because you have married a whore," Lord Vegas said, then immediately turned and marched off toward his study, muttering.

Alice couldn't say she was surprised by the reaction, but she'd hoped things would be different. "Never mind him," she told Sam, taking his hand. "Let's investigate what sort of treats your family's cook has devised for us."

They headed into the larger of the two parlors at the front of the house, where a long table had been set at one end with refreshments. The rest of the Rathborne-Paxton brothers were only moments behind Alice and Sam, and Maeve, Avery, and Ryan came with them. Several others joined them as guests who had actually been invited walked or drove from the church. Flynn must have done a good job of keeping out those who were not invited, since Alice didn't see anyone she didn't know within the house. More than once, however, she caught sight of heads at the corners of the windows and eyes peering in to see what was going on.

The disconcerting feeling of being observed grew stronger as the reception continued, particularly when she and Sam were separated in the natural course of things. Something wasn't right, but Alice couldn't put her finger on what was amiss.

"Alice, you must come meet Mr. Phineas Mercer and his wife, Lenore," Maeve grabbed her hand to draw Alice away from a conversation with one of Sam's old school friends. "And Mrs. Mercer's sister, Ellen, is visiting from America. As it happens, we have a connection."

"Oh?" Alice let herself be drawn to the side of the parlor and the trio that was standing there as if waiting for her. She knew Mr. and Mrs. Mercer indirectly, as they had connections to some of Maeve and Avery's more well-bred friends, but she'd never been introduced to them formally. She didn't know Mrs. Mercer's sister at all, though one glance at the garish American woman hinted that she would stand out in any crowd, though perhaps not for the best reasons.

"Congratulations on your happy day," Mrs. Mercer said in her broad, American accent. She seemed genuinely pleased for Alice, as if there were nothing unusual about marrying one's mistress.

"Thank you so much," Alice returned the well-wishes. "I am beginning to see that any support Sam and I receive for our union will be a blessing."

"We know a thing or two about unusual matches ourselves," Mr. Mercer said, resting a hand on the small of his wife's back. He sent her a smile that said the two of them were very much in love.

"I never did understand why British people are so all-fired determined to hold the littlest things against people," Mrs. Mercer's sister said with an expression that hinted she held the rules of society in the greatest contempt. She shrugged one shoulder, drawing attention to her bright purple gown. "Why, back home in Haskell, if two people like each other, they marry, and that's that."

Mrs. Mercer cleared her throat and sent her sister a long-suffering look. "This is my sister, Ellen Garrett, Mrs. Rathborne-Paxton. As you can see, she has very strong opinions of things."

A thrill shot through Alice, not so much because of the introduction, but because she had been called by her married name. She didn't suppose she would ever get tired of that, or the air of respectability it gave her.

"I do have strong opinions," Miss Garrett said. "Particularly when it comes to the rights of women. Did you know that in my home state of Wyoming, women have been able to vote for years? And yet, here in England, they cannot."

"Women do not need to vote if their husband votes." The statement came from Joseph, who happened to be passing at just that moment and evidently could not let Miss Garrett's comment go unanswered.

Miss Garrett looked offended. "And who are you when you're at home?" she asked, rather cheekily.

"Joseph Rathborne-Paxton," Joseph said, standing a bit taller.

Alice might have been amused to watch the two young people cross swords, but her gaze drifted past Joseph to the parlor's doorway. There she spotted Sam deep in conversation with someone who might possibly be the most uninvited of all uninvited guests—Montrose.

Alice was immediately on the alert, particularly as though it appeared Sam did not like whatever Montrose was saying to him. She longed to break away from the conversation she found herself trapped in, but it felt impossible, particularly when Miss Garrett asked, "Don't you agree, Mrs. Rathborne-Paxton?"

Alice didn't have the faintest idea what the young woman was talking about, but she said, "Yes, of course," all the same, then glanced back to Sam and Montrose.

Her heart dropped to her stomach when whatever Montrose said caused Sam to snap his head toward her and to stare at her with a look of shock and alarm. What was worse, as soon as Montrose said one other thing, Sam jerked away from him and turned to march off, as though she, not Montrose, were the one who had offended him.

"Excuse me, there is something I must see to," Alice said, excusing herself from the conversation just as Miss Garrett and Joseph had begun to argue about something else.

"Alice, is something the matter?" Maeve asked.

Alice didn't answer her. She marched straight to the hall, intending to go after Sam. Instead, Montrose stepped into her path.

"Mrs. Rathborne-Paxton, I wish I could congratulate you on your nuptials, but I fear I have a matter of great importance that I must discuss with you instead."

Alice glared up at him. "I do not have time for your mischief, Montrose," she said, attempting to edge past him.

"It is not *my* mischief that you should concern yourself with, madam." He stepped into her path again.

Alice huffed an impatient breath. She was not going to get to Sam until she let Montrose say his bit. "What are you on about, sir?" she asked.

Montrose sent her a smile that Alice supposed was meant to be sympathetic. "Mrs. Rathborne-Paxton, I will not waste your time by drawing this matter out, and I promise you, I say these things as a friend, because I fear a great wrong has been done to you."

Dread trickled its way down Alice's spine. "Say what you need to say, sir," she said.

Montrose cleared his throat. "I trust you noticed the rather large crowd at your wedding this morning," he began.

"I did," Alice said, frustrated that she had to admit to it. She didn't want to hand this odious man a single victory.

"And I also trust that you observed several of them were journalists?" he went on.

"Yes," Alice said.

"I regret to inform you, Mrs. Rathborne-Paxton, that Mr. Samuel Rathborne-Paxton has married you deliberately to stir up controversy and to humiliate his father in the press."

Alice blinked at the man. "I beg your pardon?"

"The press," he repeated, as though that were explanation enough. "Particularly the gossip pages. Mr. Rathborne-Paxton married you with the sole purpose of humiliating his family and driving his father's social fortunes even lower than they already are."

Alice's heart all but stopped. "I do not believe you," she said, though the pieces quickly fit together in her mind. Sam had said he was marrying because his father had demanded he do so. It seemed unfortunately plausible that he might marry his mistress to spite his father.

"There is a bit more to the situation than that, I fear," Montrose went on. "You see, Mr. Rathborne-Paxton is under the impression that you are wealthy. The Rathborne-Paxton family is bankrupt, you see. Mr. Rathborne-Paxton mistakenly believed you would bring an infusion of cash into the family coffers. I have just informed him that you are as poor as he is, if not more so. He was displeased."

Real fear gripped Alice's stomach. "What have you done?"

she asked Montrose in a rough voice, then searched the hall to see if she could determine which way Sam had gone.

"I am your friend, Mrs. Rathborne-Paxton," Montrose insisted. "I have told the truth, as any friend would have done."

Alice wasn't certain she believed that for a moment. The only thing she was certain of as she turned and rushed down the hall was that she had to find Sam as quickly as possible and find out what was truly going on.

Chapter Ten

S am wasn't certain there would ever be a time in his life when he became used to things that appeared to be going so well crashing suddenly and spectacularly. His father's announcement of the family's poverty and disgrace had felt like a cannonball shattering his hull, but that was nothing to the revelation that Montrose made when he managed to corner Sam during the reception.

"So you see," Montrose explained as though he were a dispassionate solicitor, "your lady wife has no fortune to speak of after all."

"That is a lie," Sam growled at him, hands balled into fists at his sides. "Alice has a magnificent head for business. She has an entire portfolio of successful investments, not to mention shares in a lucrative diamond mine."

Montrose smiled indulgently at him. Sam wouldn't have been surprised if the man had reached out and patted his head as though he were a child. "Have you perused her portfolio of late? If you had, I think you would find it lacking."

"But Alice is—"

"And the lauded diamond mine has closed," Montrose

spoke right over him, "due to the monopoly Cecil Rhodes and his company have established in the South African diamond industry."

"But I've seen the share papers," Sam said, his outrage at Montrose's accusations quickly turning to panic. "I've seen the value of those shares."

"I am afraid that the value of those shares is as insignificant as the value of the paper they are printed on now," Montrose said. He stood a bit taller, smiled gloatingly, and said, "You have married your mistress for naught, Mr. Rathborne-Paxton. "Unless your purpose in marrying a woman of such questionable character was to humiliate your father. In which case, I applaud your choice."

Sam snapped his gaze up from where he'd been staring at the floor in shock to meet Montrose's eyes. A shiver of fear twined with the fury within him. How could Montrose know that part of his motivation for marrying Alice was to hurt his father?

Montrose had turned his attention to something across the hall in the other parlor. When Sam craned his neck to see what the bastard was looking at, he found Alice watching the two of them, her face a mask of anxiety. Alice was still the most beautiful thing Sam had ever seen, but it was as though he were observing her for the first time. She wasn't what he'd thought she was.

"Yes," Montrose said, his tone gloating, "you have indeed made a perfect match, if ruination was your intention."

That was the final straw, as far as Sam was concerned. Fury overcame him, leaking into his expression, before he fully turned away from Alice to glare at Montrose. "Get out of my sight and out of my home," he growled at the blackguard, then turned and marched swiftly down the hall.

Sam didn't glance back to see whether Montrose obeyed his demand, but after a few steps, he sensed he was being followed. He made it most of the way to his and his brothers' private parlor before the two sets of footsteps following him caught up and a hand rested on his shoulder.

"I say, Sammy, what is the matter?" Dean asked.

Sam pivoted to face Dean and Francis, who was with him, still fuming and bristling. "Montrose," he muttered, so livid he could have spit on the floor.

"He arrived uninvited," Francis said with equal anger. "Flynn notified me as soon as he was made aware. We've no idea how he made his way into the house."

"That bastard will pay for whatever mischief he is attempting to cause," Dean added.

Sam shook his head and rubbed a hand over his face. His anger swiftly drained into gnawing anxiety. "It isn't only Montrose," he said with a wary breath. "It's Alice as well."

"Alice?" Dean blinked, flinching at the unexpected statement. "What has Alice done?"

"She hasn't done anything," Sam said uneasily. "Montrose has just informed me that she is not who I thought she was. She has no money at all."

"What about the diamond mine?" Francis asked.

Sam shrugged and shook his head. "It closed. It's worthless, thanks to Rhodes's monopoly. And apparently her other investments have failed as well."

"Did she inform you of as much?" Francis asked, one eyebrow raised. "When was the last time you spoke to her specifically about her finances?"

Sam's mouth dropped open, but no words were forthcoming. When was the last time they'd spoken specifically about money? Certainly not between his proposal and the wedding. Not for a while before that either.

A creeping feeling spilled down Sam's back. If he were honest with himself, he'd made quite a few assumptions about

Alice's finances without actually asking her bluntly what her situation was.

He was about to confess as much to his brothers when Alice stormed out of the parlor, Montrose a few steps behind her. Montrose headed for the front door, but the moment Alice spotted Sam in conversation with his brothers, she balled her hands into angry fists at her sides and stormed toward him, looking as though she had something to avenge.

"Alice," Sam started to greet her, no idea whatsoever how he felt about her in that moment. "Are you—"

"Is it true?" Alice demanded, her voice shaking and her face pale. She didn't just look to Sam, she glared at Dean and Francis as well. "Is it true that you have married me in order to make me a laughing stock?" Her voice quavered with the question.

"It was never my intention to make you a laughing stock," Sam said. Between everything Montrose had revealed and the pure, venomous emotion Alice was hurling at him, he felt as stunned as a rabbit caught by a fox.

"But it was your intention to make your father the subject of ridicule and gossip, was it not?" Alice asked, her chest heaving with the force of her anger and hurt. "Because what would humiliate a man who has always prided himself on piety and morality more than his son marrying his mistress?"

"Alice," Sam tried again, but still, no words came to him.

He exchanged a look with Francis, as if begging for help. Francis scowled, but even though he glanced to Alice, Sam had the feeling his brother was more upset with him.

"I fear there may have been a few matters that should have been discussed before this wedding proceeded," Francis said in a grave tone. "It would appear that all parties involved were not fully honest with each other."

Alice barked an ironic laugh and crossed her arms. "I'll say."

Dean cleared his throat. "Perhaps we should just leave the two of you to sort things out," he said in a stage whisper, then grabbed Francis's sleeve, tugging him back to the heart of the party.

Sam wasn't certain whether he was grateful with his brothers for leaving him and Alice alone or furious. "We should talk in there," he said, gesturing over his shoulder to his and his brothers' parlor.

"I am not certain we have much to talk about," Alice said in clipped tones.

"No?" Sam's temper flared anew. "That seems to be your modus operandi," he went on. "Not talking about things which should very much be talked about. Money, perhaps?"

It was absolutely the wrong thing to say. Alice's eyes flared wide. She pursed her lips in fury for a moment before bursting out with, "You tried to marry me for money. That was all you wanted, wasn't it? Money and a way to drive a dagger into your father's back by causing a scandal."

"It wasn't like that," Sam tried to defend himself. Although, if he paused to think about it too much, that was precisely what it was like. "I do love you, Alice."

"Ha!" Alice laughed.

Sam's precarious anger found something else to grab hold of. "If you had just been honest with me about your financial situation, we could have resolved the matter. And it wasn't as though I was entirely deceptive about those aims."

"Weren't you?" Her back went straighter, and she arched one eyebrow.

"I told you that Father demanded his sons marry money," Sam said.

Alice blinked, her arms dropping to her sides. "You told me that your father insisted the lot of you marry well."

Sam blinked. "Precisely. What does that mean to you?"

He could practically see Alice shaking as she put the pieces together in her mind. It gave Sam no joy at all, though, to see her realize that she hadn't been completely deceived.

"Well," Alice said after a long and uncomfortable silence between the two of them, "I think it is safe to say that this entire, overly-hasty marriage was a terrible idea. Neither of us are the person who the other believed us to be. I am not wealthy, and you are not the man of heart and honor that I believed you to be." She was so hurt that her pain leaked through to her words and pinched her expression.

"Alice." Sam took a step toward her, his own heart twisting in his chest to match her misery. "I never—"

"No, you never did." Alice took a step back from him, her vigor melting into deep sorrow that was painted across her face. "And neither did I," she said. She took another step back, sniffed, brushed a small tear from one of her eyes, then went on with, "I don't want to see you again, Sam."

"I beg your pardon?" Sam gasped, worry lashing him.

Alice stepped farther away from him. "This entire thing was a terrible, terrible mistake that I never should have let myself make. I am through with you and your deceptions, your avarice disguised as cheer and good humor. I thought you were wonderful, Sam, but it turns out that you have as little heart as any of the men who have used me for their own pleasure then cast me aside."

"Alice, how can you say that?" Sam took another step after her.

She went rigid and glared at him before saying, "Because you married me for money and for gossip. In fact—" She blinked as though a new thought had just occurred to her. "Did you or your brothers have anything to do with the journalists that were in attendance at our wedding this morning?"

Sam winced. The journalists had been Dean's idea. Sam had begged his brother not to invite them. Dean had said the invitations had already been sent and that he would contact each journalist personally to rescind them. So much for his brother following through on a promise.

He didn't need to speak a word for Alice to know the truth. Her expression crumpled in misery and humiliation. "Oh, Sam, how could you?" she said, on the verge of a sob. "I loved you and I trusted you, and you have laid me far lower than I ever could have done myself."

"Alice, I'm sorry," Sam began.

Alice held up a hand and continued down the hall. "I do not want to hear it. I am leaving, Sam. Do not come after me, and do not come to call. I am through with you. Forever."

Sam called out, "Alice!" one last time, but it was too late. Lord and Lady Carnlough had entered the hallway from the reception at some point during the fight, young Ryan holding Lady Carnlough's hand, and as soon as Alice reached the trio, all four of them continued to the front door. Flynn must also have listened to the argument, because he was ready with coats and hats. Within a minute, Alice was gone.

Sam could do nothing more than stand there gaping for a moment. He had felt so certain of his decisions, certain of his love, just a few short hours before. Standing up with Alice and defying everything to marry her had been one of the proudest moments of his life. Now she was gone, vowing that she never wanted to see him again.

She wasn't who he'd thought she was. She wasn't some paragon of sensuality who also represented a perfect solution to the problems he'd found himself with. She was something else entirely. She was a strong, bold woman. She had married him despite misgivings. And while Sam couldn't believe that she was in any way ignorant of the scandal their marriage would cause, perhaps it had been a bit stupid of him to assume that she would glibly accept the fact that the inevitable scandal wouldn't bother her. He was in the wrong for not spelling the whole thing out, but he couldn't help but feel she was a bit in the wrong as well for not asking the obvious questions.

"Brother, are you well?" Francis asked, walking toward him from one of the parlors, Dean and Joseph with him.

Francis gestured for Sam to move back in the hall, which turned out to be a good plan, as the guests swiftly began to depart en masse. Sam wasn't certain what, if anything, had been said to them, but they all seemed to know that the party was most definitely over.

"We should retire to our parlor," Dean said when one of the guests tried to break away to say a goodbye to Sam—or perhaps issue his condolences. "It would be easier for all."

Sam nodded, stunned, and let his brothers usher him back to their private parlor.

"What exactly has transpired?" Joseph asked when the four of them were alone. "I was too busy being vexed by that strange American woman to notice much of what was going on."

"You seemed quite taken with Miss Ellen Garrett," Dean said, his mouth twitching as he smirked at Joseph.

Joe sighed. "There are more important matters at hand, Dean." He turned to Sam. "I saw Montrose speaking to your bride, and then she and her friends left."

"You missed the bit in between where Alice and I quarreled," Sam said in a small, hoarse voice.

"What did you quarrel about?" Joseph asked, approaching Sam with far more sympathy than Sam would have expected from his youngest brother.

Unlike their father, Sam accepted Joe's sympathy, letting his brother pat his back, then rest a hand on his shoulder. "Montrose told Alice that I only married her for her money and because marrying her would humiliate Father. She did not take it well, particularly when she discovered the journalists were at the wedding deliberately." He scowled at Dean.

Dean appeared shocked. "I told them not to come."

"You shouldn't have invited them in the first place," Francis grumbled.

"How was I to know—" Dean began, but was silenced when Sam held up a hand.

"It does not matter what happened and why," he said. "All that matters is that we have botched this entire thing, and now the woman I love has vowed never to see me again. My *wife* has vowed never to see me again."

Describing Alice in such an intimate term only twisted the pain deeper into Sam's heart.

Before he could do anything about it, a loud bark of laughter sounded from Lord Vegas, who now stood in the doorway.

"You ridiculous fool," Lord Vegas said with a snort and a sneer. "I told you you'd regret marrying that trollop."

"I will not have you speak of Alice in such a way," Sam roared—louder than was necessary, thanks to the overflowing emotion coursing through him.

Lord Vegas snapped back, as though Sam were diseased and had sneezed on him. "You are the one who married a whore, not I. Do not take your weakness and pitifulness out on me."

"I married the woman I love," Sam insisted, striding across the room to face his father toe-to-toe. "And I stand by my decision."

Lord Vegas laughed again and shook his head. "I've half a mind to banish you from my house for such insolence."

"But you won't," Francis said, stepping forward, a shrewd look on his face. He came to stand shoulder to shoulder with Sam as they confronted their father. "You won't because you know that any further action on your part, any extended attention that you draw to Samuel's marriage, will only damage your reputation further."

Lord Vegas narrowed his eyes in resentment. "You would allow your miscreant brother to drag you down as well?"

Sam sent Francis a sideways look. It was true that every move he made would not only damage their father's reputation, it could hurt Francis, Dean, and Joseph as well. He loved his brothers, and hurting more of the people he loved was the very last thing he wanted to do.

But instead of answering Lord Vegas directly, Francis said, "Your part in our affairs is done, old man. Go back up to your room and pretend to pray for forgiveness on your own. Leave our happiness in our own hands."

Sam's brow shot up. He glanced between his father and Francis in awe, wondering which of them would have the upper hand in the end. Up until that point, Lord Vegas had always been the undisputed king of the castle, in spite of Francis's strength, but now Sam wasn't so certain.

"Mark my words," Lord Vegas said, retreating a step and seeming to prove Francis was well on his way to becoming the more powerful of the two of them. "You will regret your petty games, my boy." He flashed a look to Sam, then on to the others. "You all will regret them."

Dean and Joseph moved forward to solidify the line of brothers standing against Lord Vegas. None of them had to say a single thing more. Lord Vegas glared at all of them, then turned and walked out of the room, muttering.

"Well, that appears to be the end of that," Dean said with a shrug as soon as the brothers were left alone.

"I have to win her back," Sam burst out a moment later. He pivoted to face his brothers. "This was all my fault. I should have been more honest with Alice from the start."

"Perhaps," Francis said, rubbing his chin, his thoughts seeming to wander off to something else.

"I cannot let the woman I love simply walk away from me because of my own rash misunderstandings," Sam went on.

"I do rather like Alice," Dean said, venturing a smile.

"Even if she is—" Joseph cleared his throat, his cheeks going pink, "—inappropriate."

"There must be something I can do to make things right and win her back," Sam went on, pacing across the room, suddenly filled with nervous energy. "I can woo her. I can apologize. I can find a way to beg her forgiveness and make her see that all of this unpleasantness is just a result of ridiculous rashness on my part."

"You've always been ridiculous," Dean said, his smile widening. "As long as I've known you."

"You'll have your work cut out for you," Joseph said with a pessimistic sigh.

"That may be the case," Sam said, turning to face his brothers, determination coursing through him, "but I intend to try."

Chapter Eleven

She had been a fool to hope, and Alice hated feeling like a fool. She'd been a fool when Michael Feeney had turned her head and seduced her—even if she did have her wonderful boy as a result of that foolishness—and she had been even more of a fool to think she could improve her standing in the world by lowering herself for even more men. And now there she was, faced with the prospect of becoming a courtesan again as a married woman, simply because she'd put far too much faith in the wrong person.

"I'm certain the situation can be salvaged," Maeve said in an unconvincing voice as she watched Alice stomp around her professional flat, packing up the things that genuinely belonged to her and sorting through the bits of furniture and artwork that were rented. "Mr. Rathborne-Paxton did have a certain degree of contriteness about him when we left his home yesterday."

Alice glanced up from where she was packing linens into a box and made an ironic sound. "Mr. Rathborne-Paxton was false with me from the start," she said, though deep in her heart, she wasn't entirely convinced of that. She was angry, and anger often smothered the truth.

"He's been so helpful to you over these last two years," Maeve argued carefully, echoing the feelings Alice had but was in no mood to nurture. "I may not entirely approve of his methods of helping you, but the man has been your friend. And both legally and in the eyes of the church, he is your husband now."

Alice threw a handful of pillowcases into the box, then let out a frustrated sigh. She rubbed her temples to stave off the pounding headache that had threatened her since Montrose's revelations the day before. "I suppose I shall have to do something about that," she sighed. "I cannot stay married to the man. For one thing, Lord Vegas will not allow it. He will force Sam to divorce me."

"Even if he does, I am not certain he could remarry as easily as that," Maeve said, chewing her lip in thought.

"I do not know," Alice said, staring at her box of linens. "I am not well-versed in divorce law."

But she might have to learn now. The prospect had her pinching her face, teetering on the edge of a sob. How could things between her and Sam go from the heights of bliss and defiance of social convention to such misery and disappointment so swiftly? She and Sam had been happy together, even if their association was less than savory. How could she still love him as much as she did when he'd been so deceptive and false with her?

She must have appeared closer to tears than she realized, because Maeve stepped over from where she'd been observing and rested a hand on Alice's back. "There, there," she said in her most compassionate, motherly voice. "I have known you since we were girls, and I've known Mr. Rathborne-Paxton for years. I have seen the two of you together, and I cannot help but think this is all just a misunderstanding that has come at a time of great distress for both of you. Perhaps with a bit of time—"

"He married me as a means of humiliation," Alice burst, not quite ready to hear Sam spoken of kindly yet. "He thought he was marrying me for money. And he invited journalists to our wedding to make the humiliation as public as possible."

"If I understand the situation, his reasons for marrying you have more to do with his father than you, dearest," Maeve said quietly, rubbing Alice's back.

"But it will damage me as much, if not more than Lord Vegas," Alice said. She pulled restlessly away from Maeve and marched into the main room of the flat, plopping into the velvet settee, which was now covered with canvas so that the outfit that rented it to her could take it back.

"Let us not forget that you were the one who suggested marriage to him," Maeve said judiciously.

It irritated Alice to know Maeve was right, that she'd set her own trap. But Sam was the one who made the jaws snap shut on her.

"Why do I still love him when he has been so horrible to me?" she wailed, sinking onto the settee in what was, admittedly, a dramatic pose on the settee with her hand covering her face.

Maeve followed her into the room and sat gingerly on the settee beside her. "You love him because he is what your heart wants," she said. "And because, you must admit, he is quite loveable. You love him because he is the man for you."

Alice pried her eyes open and gaped at her friend. "Are you taking Sam's side after everything he's done?"

Maeve winced and tilted her head to the side. "I am attempting to take the side of reason. Sam was not the only one entering your marriage with an ulterior motive. I think you can at least own up to that."

Alice sighed and sat straighter, though her shoulders slumped with a hint of guilt. "Marrying a man because he might be able to improve one's social standing and resolve the problem of keeping a roof over one's head is something women have done for generations."

"As is men marrying women for money," Maeve argued.

Alice pursed her lips and wrestled with her inner indignation for a moment before blowing out a breath and saying, "That is not the part of this fiasco that hurts me the most."

"I know, dear," Maeve said, patting Alice's knee.

They were interrupted a moment later by a soft knock on the flat's door. Alice stiffened, wondering what new disaster awaited her. She forced herself to stand and cross to open the door, glad that Maeve stayed right with her.

"Good morning, Mrs. Wood—er, Mrs. Rathborne-Paxton," Mrs. Knox greeted her once the door was open. The landlady wore an uneasy smile.

Alice's already depressed spirits took another blow. "Mrs. Knox," she said, attempting to be brave. "I can only assume you are here about the rent. I am doing the best I can, and I will be vacating this flat soon, but I am very sorry to say—"

"Oh, no, it's not that," Mrs. Knox said. The woman actually brightened a bit before going on with, "The rent has been paid, actually. Just this morning, just now."

Alice's breath caught in her throat. She blinked at Mrs. Knox, uncertain she'd heard the woman correctly. "I beg your pardon?" she asked.

"The rent on both of your flats has been paid, so there is no need to worry about that now," Mrs. Knox said.

"But...but how?" Alice asked.

"I am terribly sorry to interrupt this important discussion," a male voice sounded from the hall, sending Alice's heart back down to her feet, "but there are matters of great importance that I have come to see Mrs. Rathborne-Paxton about."

Alice stepped partially out into the hallway as Mrs. Knox moved to allow Montrose to come forward. Alice's breath caught in her throat at the sight of the tall, ominous man. He had likely been standing in the hallway with Mrs. Knox the entire time, listening to everything that had been said.

"Good morning, Mrs. Rathborne-Paxton," Montrose said, smiling. "May I come in?"

Alice's mouth dropped open, but for a moment she had no idea what to say, or even what sound to make. The man had audacity if he thought it was appropriate to show up on her doorstep the morning after the greatest humiliation of her life.

"I'll just leave you to your guest," Mrs. Knox whispered, then hurried down the hall, as though she had no interest in being around Montrose.

Alice snapped her mouth shut as she watched the landlady's retreat. From there, she had no choice but to take a small step back into the flat. Montrose boldly followed her in, just like any number of gentlemen callers she'd had in the past. The very idea of that turned Alice's stomach. She was eternally grateful that Maeve was there to act as a buffer, and that the partially covered furniture and boxes scattered about the flat indicated that she was in no way ready to entertain guests.

"Good morning, Lady Carnlough," Montrose greeted Maeve once the three of them were alone in the flat.

Sense returned to Alice quickly, and before Maeve could return any sort of greeting, she faced Montrose and asked, "Are you the one who paid my rent?"

Montrose smiled sheepishly and said, "No, Mrs. Rathborne-Paxton, I am not. But I do believe I would have, had I thought of the idea before whoever did pay it took action."

Alice's eyes went wide, and she exchanged a baffled look

with Maeve. She in no way liked the mystery that her day had become.

"Why are you here, Mr. Montrose?" Maeve asked on Alice's behalf.

"Why, I have come to express my condolences, Mrs. Rathborne-Paxton," Montrose said. He peeked at one of the chairs that flanked the settee, as if hinting they should all sit down.

Alice was too overcome to resist, particularly since she could have done with a sit-down herself. She moved to the settee, Maeve moving with her, and sat. Montrose took one of the other chairs stiffly.

"I have no need for your condolences, Montrose," Alice said, keeping her chin up and her shoulders squared. "You may have been the messenger that hastened the ruination of my marriage, but you are not the one responsible." She wouldn't give the bastard the power to think he had any control over her life whatsoever.

"I understand fully, and I agree," Montrose said.

Alice blinked. That was the last thing she had expected him to say. Montrose was a notorious villain and destroyer of lives. Perhaps he was responsible for her downfall indirectly, since he was the one who had utterly thwarted Lord Vegas. Though one could also argue that Lord Vegas brought about his own downfall through his hypocritical ways, and Montrose merely sped the process along.

"I can see that you are perplexed," Montrose said before Alice could think of anything to say in reply. "Let me explain myself," he said, shifting slightly in his chair to face her with a look of complete sympathy.

Alice exchanged another look with Maeve, who reached for her hand in solidarity as the two of them sat side by side. The air in the room seemed to vibrate with the sort of energy that preceded a long, devilish aria sung by the bass in a tragic opera.

"I do not like the aristocracy, Mrs. Rathborne-Paxton," Montrose began, meeting Alice's eyes and holding them in a way that hinted he believed that she, too, held a grudge against noblemen. "I have not liked them since I was a child employed as a hall boy in the London house of a certain duke, who shall remain nameless."

"I did not know you were in service," Alice said. She wriggled slightly with uncertainty. There was a great deal she didn't know about her enemy, and that was never a good thing.

"I was," Montrose said, anger just beneath the surface of his placid demeanor. "It was not a pleasant experience. I was abused by the butler and the housekeeper, and when I grew bold enough to slip up to the duke's study to bring the tale of my abuse to his attention, I was shouted at and sacked for my efforts."

"Oh, no," Maeve said, pressing her hand to her mouth for a moment. "How old were you? Did you have any family?"

"I was a mere eight years of age, my lady," Montrose explained, inclining his head to her. "And I did have an uncle. He secured me another position, with a marquess this time. But it was more of the same. Neglect, abuse, harsh words, overwork."

Montrose paused, as though he expected Maeve to make another expression of sympathy. Both Alice and Maeve were too stunned by the story to interrupt.

Montrose continued, "I had no choice but to continue on in the position, regardless of how I was treated. I was never shown an ounce of kindness by any employer I had the misfortune to work for throughout my childhood and adolescence. When I reached an age where I could have left service to attend school, the aristocrat I was employed with at the time moved heaven and earth to keep me in my position and to sabotage every chance I might have had to get out and improve myself. The man had developed a particular fondness for me, you see."

For the briefest of moments, Montrose's eyes were downcast and the color left his face. Alice swallowed, wishing she had a cup of tea to steady her nerves. The hair on the back of her neck stood up at the implications of Montrose's story.

"I did manage to leave that situation eventually," Montrose went on after a brief pause. "I worked my fingers to the bone attempting to build a place for myself in business. But again, at every turn, my ambitions were thwarted by men with titles, men who thought I was not worth the price of their shoelaces.

"It was not until I discovered and bought up the untoward debt of one of my former employers that I realized revenge is as sweet as success," he continued, sitting a bit straighter.

"How did you find the money to buy up a nobleman's debt?" Alice asked, her voice weak.

Montrose shook his head. "Unimportant. All that matters is that I was able to do it. And I think you will understand the delicious sense of satisfaction I felt in utterly ruining the man who had wronged me so grievously. Not just the one, but others as well, once I figured out the way of it. Noblemen are nothing more than paper figures, Mrs. Rathborne-Paxton, as I am certain you will agree. Their loftiness and security is an illusion, and I have dedicated myself to blasting away that illusion to expose evil men for what they truly are."

Alice's mind and emotions felt as though they had been scrambled. Blast him, but she truly could understand Montrose's motivations. At least to a degree. Perhaps a stronger man would have been satisfied with achievement and wouldn't have needed to tear down those who had wronged him along with that achievement.

Then again, when it came to men like Lord Vegas, perhaps they deserved it.

"I can see you understand," Montrose said after watching Alice for a long time. "I have been made out to be the blackest of devils, but I am merely taking back what was forcibly wrenched from me."

Alice wasn't certain she would go that far, but Montrose certainly believed his own story.

"What do I have to do with any of this?" she asked, as baffled about Montrose's presence as ever.

Montrose smiled. The gesture sent chills through her. "We are alike, Mrs. Rathborne-Paxton," he said. "We have both been wronged by the aristocracy. Present company excluded," he said, nodding to Maeve. "Though as I understand it, Lady Carnlough, you were not born into the upper class."

"I wasn't," Maeve said in a wispy voice.

"Then perhaps you, too, can understand the brutality of the aristocracy and how they treat those they do not see as on the inside."

Maeve pressed her lips together and stared at her hands in her lap. Alice knew enough to know that not every fine lady Maeve had attempted to befriend or entertain in the last two years had been open to accepting a middle-class woman into her circles.

"This still doesn't explain why you are here," Alice said, drawing Montrose's attention away from Maeve.

Montrose turned back to her with one of his smiles that chilled Alice to the bone. "I wish to help you, Mrs. Rathborne-Paxton."

"Help me?" Alice was deeply suspicious of what that meant.

"Yes, of course," Montrose said. "My mission is greater than simply tearing down those who should not be on pedestals to begin with. I wish to use the resources I have to enable you to live comfortably, now that London society has reared its ugly head to denigrate you."

Alice narrowed her eyes slightly. Had London society

denigrated her? She'd been humiliated at her wedding, to be sure, but did Montrose know something she didn't know?

She kept quiet, deciding to let Montrose give himself all the rope he needed to hang himself.

"I am aware that life requires money to be lived," Montrose went on, picking up a bit of energy, as though he'd come to the crux of the matter. "Though I cannot simply give you money as though you were a charity case, I can relieve you of some of your investments."

Alice frowned. "I do not understand."

Montrose shrugged. "As I understand it, you have an investment portfolio. I wish to purchase some of those investments from you. I am particularly interested in your railroad shares, your shares in the defunct diamond mine, and shares I believe you have in a paint manufacturer in Leeds."

Alice's suspicions flared even hotter. "How do you know what investments I have?" she asked.

Montrose smiled like a fox and shrugged. "I have my means. Would you be amenable to selling those assets to me?"

Maeve squeezed Alice's hand, which she hadn't let go of since the odd visit began, but Alice didn't need her friend's gentle warning. Something was most definitely not right about Montrose's offer. If only she could put her finger on it.

"To be perfectly honest, Montrose," she said with a sigh of pretend exhaustion, "I am not certain I have the energy to think about these things at the moment. I cannot give you an immediate answer."

"Understood." Montrose inclined his head to her, but Alice had the feeling he was annoyed that she hadn't immediately jumped at the offer. "Perhaps if I drafted a more formal proposal, we could—"

A knock sounded on the door before Montrose could finish, and a moment later, Sam burst through, a massive bouquet of colorful flowers in his arms.

"Alice, my darling," he began in a passionate voice, "please forgive me for my—"

He got no further than that. The moment he set eyes on Montrose, his mouth dropped open, and his face went red with fury.

Chapter Twelve

The only way Sam knew to win Alice back after the Gordian knot of misunderstandings that blocked the way between them was to approach his beloved wife on her own territory and to make certain she knew that he only wanted what was best for her. He left his family home early in the morning after the wedding—barely saying good morning to his brothers and refusing to say a single word to his father—and headed up to Marylebone with hope and determination in his heart.

However, his plans for spilling his heart out to Alice and making things right between them took an unexpected turn right from the start.

"Oh! Good morning, Mr. Rathborne-Paxton," Mrs. Knox, Alice's landlady, met him at the door of the building as she swept the front stoop. The harried-looking woman eyed him nervously, and for a moment, Sam wasn't certain she would let him pass. "What brings you here this morning?" she asked, as though playing gatekeeper for her tenants.

Sam put on the humblest smile he could manage. "Good morning, Mrs. Knox," he said, showing the woman more respect than he needed to. He winced slightly, then said, "I take it you heard about the events of yesterday?"

Mrs. Knox planted her broom and leaned against it. "After the sort of proposal you made in front of my building, how could I not take an interest in it?"

Sam could tell from the pucker of her lips and the lines of her brow just what the woman thought of him. He let out a sigh, removed his hat to push a hand through his hair, then said, "I made a terrible mistake, Mrs. Knox. So many things went wrong yesterday. But I love Alice dearly. You must know that. You've seen the devotion with which I've attended her these last few years. I want the best for her."

That seemed to soften the landlady a little. "I suppose every man deserves a second chance."

"That is precisely what I am here for," Sam said, heart lifting with hope. "In fact, I wanted to start out that second chance with a gesture of good faith. What do you think I could do to make amends to my beloved?" He figured it was as good a start as any to ask a woman who knew Alice what his bride might need.

Sam wasn't disappointed. Mrs. Knox's face lit up at once. "You could pay her rent," she said. "That's what the poor bird needs most right now."

Sam sucked in a breath as a twist of guilt shot through him. Had Alice struggled to pay the rent on her two flats? But, of course, if she was bankrupt, as Montrose had suggested she was, that would be one of her deepest concerns. The logic of the situation fit together like a puzzle, but it also squeezed his heart with worry. If Alice truly had been in such dire straits, she shouldn't have hidden as much from him.

"I can pay you right now," he said, reaching into the interior pocket of his jacket for his wallet. "How much is owed?"

Mrs. Knox gave him a sum. It was so high that Sam nearly fumbled his wallet once he had it out of his pocket.

"That is for more than one month, of course," Mrs. Knox said, seeing his shock. "But if you wish to pay only the amount that is in arrears...."

"No, no, I will pay the entire sum," he said, handing several bills to Mrs. Knox. It probably appeared to her as though he had a money tree in his back garden, what with being able to produce such a sum immediately. In fact, the amount Sam handed over represented the bulk of the ready money he had to his name. With only a few pounds remaining, he would have to think fast and dive into untapped resources to have enough to pay his tailor.

"You know what else you might try?" Mrs. Knox suggested as Sam made a move to walk past her. When he lifted his brow in inquiry, Mrs. Knox said, "Flowers."

"Flowers?" Sam nodded consideringly.

"Whenever Mr. Knox put a foot wrong with me, he always softened the blow by bringing me a fresh bouquet," Mrs. Knox went on. "There's nothing like a few roses or daisies to show a woman how much you care for her and how sorry you are."

Sam smiled. "Flowers it is, then. Thank you, Mrs. Knox."

He tipped his hat to the woman, then turned to march off down the street in search of a florist.

Of course, having just handed over most of his ready money, the florist shop where he'd bought the bouquets for the proposal was out of the question. He was forced to venture farther afield, in search of a flower girl who might sell him something pretty at a lower price. There were plenty along Oxford Street, and as soon as he was able to purchase a charming little burst of daisies and wildflowers, he headed back to Alice's building, only half an hour behind his original schedule.

It seemed as though half an hour was all that Alice needed to tip his heart completely upside down and frustrate his hopes of an easy reconciliation, though. He headed straight to her professional flat, knocked, and let himself in with all the hope in the world, only to find his beloved in the process of entertaining none other than the devil himself.

"Alice, my darling," he said as he burst into Alice's flat, ready to play the lover, "please forgive me for my—"

Sam's heart stopped at the sight of Montrose, and his jaw dropped in indignation. He didn't have the slightest idea what was going on in front of him, but if Alice could stoop so low as to entertain the man who was at the heart of every problem that had crashed into his life, like a cannonball into a ship, in the last few weeks, then perhaps she was crueler than he'd originally thought her capable of being.

"What is the meaning of this?" Sam demanded, stepping farther into the room. He clutched the stems of the flowers he carried so tightly that he wouldn't have been surprised if the entire bouquet had withered in his grip.

"Sam." Alice shot to her feet, eyes wide. Her cheeks splashed a shade of rose red that Sam would have found irresistibly attractive at any other moment. "What are you doing here?" she asked, pressing a hand to her stomach. Her expression shifted to angry disapproval. "And what makes you think you have the right to march straight into my flat without announcing yourself first?"

"You are my wife," Sam said, sounding far firmer than he felt. Every part of him began to second-guess every decision he'd made in the last fortnight. He glared at Montrose for a moment, then met Alice's eyes again. "You are my wife," he repeated, "but it seems as though not even a full day after our wedding, you are entertaining other men." He was close enough to throw the bouquet down on a nearby table.

He felt like a mouse who had set off a trap a moment later when Alice balled her hands into fists at her sides, pursed her lips, and glowered at him for a moment before saying, "Montrose called on me, you impetuous fool. And you cannot think for a moment that I would engage in any untoward activity with Maeve present." She thrust out a hand toward Lady Carnlough.

Sam sent Lady Carnlough the briefest look, which turned into an appeal for help. Alice was exactly right that she would never do anything salacious with Montrose while her dearest friend was around. But the sight of the villain bypassed his good sense.

"I do not see why you should care whether Montrose has come to visit me or not," Alice went on without allowing him to get a word in. Sam had a bad feeling about what she would say, based on the sharpness of her expression, and he was not disappointed when she flung out, "Perhaps you should inform the press so that they can write a story about that scandalous whore, Mrs. Samuel Rathborne-Paxton, who allows gentlemen to call on her the day after her wedding?"

"Alice, I'm sorry," Sam said, hopelessness flooding him.

Simultaneously, Montrose said, "I think it is time that I leave you." The great monster had risen from his chair during the argument and now walked toward the door. "It would appear you have unfinished marital business to attend to before you can consider my offer."

Sam narrowed his eyes at the blackguard, but turned to Alice to ask, "What offer?"

Neither Alice nor Montrose answered. Montrose merely swept the hat he'd been holding onto his head, nodded to Alice, and said, "My offer stands, Mrs. Rathborne-Paxton. I would relish the opportunity to help out a like-minded soul."

More confused than ever, Sam watched Alice stiffen and nod slightly to Montrose. He didn't like the fact that his bride and the man who had ruined so much of his life already had something between them that he didn't know about.

The moment Montrose let himself out of the flat and shut

the door behind him, Sam whirled to face Alice and demanded, "What offer? What is that bastard talking about?"

Alice let out a heavy breath, her entire demeanor sinking. "Montrose claims he wishes to help me out," she said, taking a step toward Sam, then appeared to change her mind and paced instead. "He offered to purchase some of my investments from me, some stocks and my shares in the diamond mine."

"Why would he care to do that?" Sam demanded. His question came out angry, but that anger was fueled by the pain of another man stepping in to help the woman he loved when the only thing he could do was pay her rent. His help was temporary, and he wouldn't be able to give much of it. Montrose's offer was far more useful in the long run.

"I do not know, Samuel," Alice snapped as she paced the room, rubbing her temples as though her head ached.

"What did he mean by like-minded souls?" If Alice was going to be peevish and cold, then he would be too. He crossed his arms and glared at her until she came to a stop near him.

"He spun a sad tale of how he has been wronged by members of the aristocracy," she said, huffing out a breath and letting her arms fall uselessly to her sides. "And to be honest, I believe I know what he was talking about." The way she glared at him could have pierced holes through his body.

"I have not wronged you." Sam jumped immediately to the defensive, once again letting his guilt and hurt express itself as anger and indignation. "I married you because I loved you."

"You married me to make a spectacle of me," Alice all but shouted in return. "And because you thought I was wealthy."

"You never told me you were in a dire position financially," Sam shouted right back. "You led me on and let me believe that you were as rich as Croesus."

"I never said anything about my financial state." Alice raised her voice even further, gesturing in frustration.

"We spoke of investments all the time." Sam let himself go and shouted in earnest. It felt good, if he were honest with himself.

"As a hobby," Alice argued back. Her shoulders loosened a bit, as though she, too, found catharsis in truly letting her fury fly. "I was too embarrassed by the precariousness of things and the means through which I'd obtained some of my investments to speak of them so bluntly."

"But you could have told me," Sam insisted. "You could have told me everything. You *should* have told me everything. We were lovers. Now we're married, and...and I demand you tell me everything." It didn't feel particularly wise to say as much, but he didn't know how else to hold Alice to him.

Of course, Alice's eyes flared wide. "I am not the sort of milquetoast wife who will bow her head meekly and obey your every word," she said, then sent a brief, guilty glance to Lady Carnlough. "If you wanted one of those, you should have pursued Lady Heloise."

"I never wanted Lady Heloise, or any other woman," Sam shouted. "I've only ever wanted you. You are the woman I love, and you are my wife."

"Then why did you marry me under such duplicitous circumstances?" Alice demanded, taking a step toward him. "Why did you drag me through the mud by inviting journalists to the wedding instead of simply telling me you loved me and marrying me because of that?"

"I would have." Sam's heart squeezed in his chest. "But this goes beyond just me. My family is in tatters. And don't go blaming me for the journalists. They were Dean's idea, but when I found out about it, I ordered him to disinvite every one. That they showed up regardless is not my fault," he added on a sheepish note.

Alice blinked at him. "Is that supposed to quell my anger?

That Dean was responsible? That you tried to call them off and they came anyhow?"

"Because I—because Francis has a plan for us all to marry unsuitable brides as a way of getting back at Father for his hypocrisy and misdeeds," Sam shouted, feeling as though he should whisper the truth instead.

Alice looked as though she would erupt like Krakatoa, but before she could do more than open her mouth, Lady Carnlough stepped in.

"Please, please," Lady Carnlough said, holding up both of her hands. "I cannot stand by and watch the two of you argue so fruitlessly for another moment."

Sam had never seen the fine lady look so distressed, or so determined to step in and take charge of the situation. He pivoted to face her fully, and noted that when Alice did the same, his bride ended up standing by his side.

"There," Lady Carnlough said, lowering her hands and taking a breath. "I cannot watch the two of you tear away at each other this way. The two of you love each other. You always have. And while I can appreciate the pain and the upset of the situation, you will only make it worse if you continue to hurl accusations at each other without pausing to examine the underlying truths of the matter."

Sam flinched slightly, both impressed by Lady Carnlough's sagacity and puzzled by what she might mean by the truth.

Alice seemed to share his confusion. "What truth is there beyond the fact that Sam married me under false pretenses with the intention of humiliating me?" she asked, chin tilted up indignantly.

Lady Carnlough frowned. "Alice, you were the one to suggest marriage first."

Alice's cheeks pinked, and she lowered her chin. "I did," she said, sending a covert glance to Sam.

"And Mr. Rathborne-Paxton, you say you explicitly disinvited the journalists to the wedding?" Lady Carnlough asked on.

"I did," Sam said. "And then they came anyhow."

Lady Carnlough seemed satisfied with that explanation, though Sam couldn't tell if Alice was. "And is it not true that you would not have pursued marriage to begin with if your father had not insisted upon it?" she asked.

"That is true." Sam turned to Alice. "I would have been perfectly content to continue on as we'd been, loving you fully, passionately, and discreetly, for as long as I lived."

Alice softened by a hair. Instead of anger, sentiment filled her eyes. She remained silent, though.

"Then it strikes me," Lady Carnlough went on, "that a great deal of fuss is being made over things that are not important when the true villain is obvious."

"Montrose," Sam and Alice answered in unison. They snapped to look at each other when their answer came out in harmony.

"Precisely," Lady Carnlough said. "And it also strikes me that instead of arguing, the two of you should be asking questions."

"What sort of questions?" Alice asked.

"The right questions," Lady Carnlough answered. "Questions such as why was Montrose at your reception yesterday when he was not invited and must have known he would be ousted the moment he was discovered."

Sam exchanged another look with Alice. "He was there to sow discord between us, obviously."

"He told you I was poor, and he told me you had married me for money and humiliation," Alice said.

"And why would Mr. Montrose feel as though your wedding reception was the correct time to make those revelations?" Lady Carnlough continued. "What does he stand to gain by the revelation? Why did he come here today, and why does he think you would be amenable to accepting his help? What is it about the particular investments he wished to purchase that makes them appealing to him?"

Sam blinked, completely breathless. He stared at Lady Carnlough as though seeing her for the first time. She was such a sweet, lovely woman, but only now did he realize how clever Avery O'Shea was in his choice of wife and how fortunate Alice was in her choice of a friend. Lady Carnlough was as sharp as they came.

Alice seemed to feel it as well. She sent Sam a look, then let out a breath. "Perhaps we should retire to the other flat for tea so that we can ponder these matters," she said wearily.

"Tea sounds like an excellent idea, my love," Sam said attempting to offer an olive branch. He offered his arm along with his words, hoping to escort Alice to the other flat.

"I can go on my own," Alice insisted, starting forward. There weren't as many prickles in her tone as there had been earlier.

As Sam followed Alice and Lady Carnlough down the hall to the other flat, hope buzzed within him. He could make this situation right, he was certain, but it would take some time. Whatever he did, he needed to tread carefully and pay attention to Alice's needs first and foremost.

As soon as they entered the domestic flat, a whole other concern burst at him in the form of young Ryan.

"Mama!" the cheery boy shouted, leaping up from where he'd been constructing some sort of tower out of blocks with Harriett. "And Sam!" The boy's smile brightened even more, and he raced at Sam, shocking him by throwing himself at Sam and hugging him. "I thought you were going to come live with us and be my papa now. Are you going to be my papa?"

Sam's heart melted into a gooey puddle of treacle at his

feet. "I don't know, my boy," he said, glancing to Alice. "That's rather up to your mama at the moment."

Ryan smiled. "Mama will let me keep you," he said with utmost confidence. He took Sam's hand and led him toward the table with the blocks. "Come help me build the Tower of London."

Sam let himself be dragged along, sending Alice a helpless, apologetic look as he went.

"Harriett, could we have tea?" Alice asked her maid, following Sam and Ryan to the table, Lady Carnlough coming with her. "I believe we are about to have a long and involved conversation, and tea will most definitely be in order."

"Yes, ma'am," Harriett said with a short curtsy. She sent Sam an optimistic smile before disappearing into the kitchen.

Sam couldn't help but feel optimistic as well, though nothing about the morning had unfolded the way he'd expected it to. Whatever Alice wanted to do about Montrose, whatever plans she and Lady Carnlough came up with, he would go along with them. The only thing that mattered to him at that point was winning Alice's forgiveness and continuing his life with her.

Chapter Thirteen

Reigning in her temper had always been something Alice was only able to achieve with great difficulty. As she, Maeve, and Sam took their tea together, pretending for Ryan and Harriett's sake that nothing was particularly out of the ordinary, it was all she could do to pretend serenity. Her heart screamed one thing at her—that Sam was just as much a victim of Montrose's nefarious deeds, and that his brothers had not helped the situation—and that he should be forgiven, but her pride continued to insist that she should be furious with him. He could have been honest with her from the start instead of allowing their situation to boil over into the public. Her suspicions were that she had not heard the last of the spectacle that was their wedding.

On the other hand, Maeve had proven herself to be the saint that she was by asking the right questions, both to dampen the initial heat of the argument and later, as Harriett took Ryan out for a walk so that Alice, Maeve, and Sam could discuss the matter further.

"It all comes down to the question of what Mr. Montrose stands to gain by everything he's done," Maeve said, sighing as if the lengthy conversation had taxed her and standing to take some of the tea things from the table to Alice's kitchen.

"He said that his motivation is revenge against the noblemen who wronged him," Alice said, feeling equally weary.

"There is always more to Montrose's actions than meets the eye," Sam said, standing and helping Maeve to clear the table.

"Undoubtedly," Alice said, staring at a spot on the table instead of looking at him. Her thoughts were all muddled together and wrapped in exhaustion that ran all the way to her bones. She needed to find a way to untie the knot of her life in the last few days and Montrose's influence in it.

"I'll just be going, then," Maeve said, shaking Alice out of her thoughts several minutes later. She hadn't realized she'd been so distracted until she saw Maeve already had her coat and hat on. "Unless you require further assistance?" Maeve went on, sending a querying look Sam's way.

Alice shifted her gaze to Sam—who was pretending to busy himself in the kitchen, straightening the dishes. She glanced back to Maeve and said, "No, dearest." She stood and crossed to the door, kissing Maeve's cheek goodbye. "I will wrestle with this particular dragon on my own."

Maeve smiled encouragingly, then headed out of the apartment.

That left Alice alone with Sam for the first time since everything had fallen apart. Unsurprisingly, Sam abandoned all pretense of being busy in the kitchen to join her in the main room.

"And here we are," he said with a small shrug, spreading his hands. "How would you like to proceed?"

Alice's brow shot up. She supposed it was a good thing that Sam would ask what she wanted instead of dictating terms to her, which he could have very well done. He was legally her husband, after all.

She weighed her words carefully, eyes downcast, before saying, "I should like to resolve things with Montrose before making any lasting decisions." As she finished, she raised her eyes to meet Sam's, praying he could see the strength of her determination not to be keelhauled by the conundrum they were in.

Sam held his breath for a moment, then let it out with a sad, disappointed sound. "I take it I cannot convince you to return home with me as my wife, then?"

There was something so earnest about Sam. So much so that a large part of her wanted to go with him, despite the way he'd betrayed her and the offense she still felt because of it. She bit her lip, then stepped away from the door to approach him.

"I love you dearly, Sam," she said when she was standing within reach of him.

"And I love you, my darling." Sam reached for her, vibrating with need.

Alice stepped back just enough to avoid his reach. "I am still angry with you for everything that happened," she said, not quite able to meet his eyes. "I will most likely forgive you in time, but my pride has been severely damaged." She lifted her eyes to meet his. "You know that."

"I do," he said with a sigh. "And I understand your wish to put distance between us for now. But Alice, I do love you so."

His entire mien took on a warm but defeated tenor. He truly was the sweetest man she'd ever known, particularly in the way he simply took a step forward, kissed her cheek, then walked on to retrieve his coat and hat from the rack where they'd been put earlier.

"When you are ready," he said softly.

He sent her one last, lingering look before leaving the flat.

As soon as he was gone, Alice's shoulders dropped, and

she let out a sob before she could stop herself. Nothing about the situation she found herself in was remotely how she thought a marriage to the man she loved would start.

It was all Montrose's fault, she thought as she marched into the kitchen to slice herself another piece of the chocolate tart Harriett had made for Ryan that morning. Montrose was the devil at the heart of everything. She didn't believe for a moment that the man's intentions were pure. Montrose wanted something from her. He wanted something specific. Maeve was right in her insistence that that was the most important question. But what could a man like Montrose, a man with a grudge against the aristocracy, want with her?

She contemplated the question as she ate her piece of tart while leaning against the edge of the counter. She was not aristocratic herself, but perhaps Montrose believed that he could further damage Lord Vegas through her. But then, the marriage itself was precisely the sort of damage that Montrose would have approved of. And that had been all Sam's doing, Sam's and his brothers'. What part could Montrose possibly hope to play in her domestic drama? Unless he hoped to further tarnish the Rathborne-Paxton family by seducing away the bride of his enemy's son.

The idea repulsed her, but it wouldn't leave her alone as she ruminated on the whole conundrum for the rest of the day and through the night. Men were forever thinking they could seduce her, and up until very recently, they'd been correct in assuming that they could. It didn't make sense to her that seduction was Montrose's aim, though.

By morning, there seemed to be only one solution to the mystery. She would have to seek Montrose out and ask him bluntly what it was he wanted from her. Other women might not have taken the direct approach, but Alice had no interest whatsoever in prolonging her misery. If she was going to have enough vitality to repair her fractured love affair, she needed to remove the arrow that had pierced her before treating the wound.

Which was how she found herself striding up the steps of Harvey's Gentleman's Club in a quiet corner of Mayfair late morning the next day.

"I am here to see Montrose," she told the man at the club's front desk, her expression implacable.

The concierge smiled tightly at her, as though she were a rat that had crawled in off the street. "Women are not admitted to Harvey's," he said in terse tones.

"Then tell Montrose to come out to the street to speak to me," Alice demanded, eyes flaring.

The concierge narrowed his eyes at her. "Madam, I am afraid I must ask you to leave at once."

"Not until I see Montrose." Alice tipped her chin up and held her ground.

"Impossible," the concierge clipped. "The rules of this club—"

"I'll take it from here, Penworth," a deep, unfamiliar voice spoke from behind Alice.

Given the circumstances, being addressed by a man she didn't know had Alice immediately on the alert. She turned to the stranger, attempting to keep a gracious smile in place.

"Are you to be my hero and have Montrose fetched for me?" she asked the unfamiliar man, sweeping him with a quick, assessing gaze.

The man was likely in his fifties, had probably once been handsome, and had a definite predatory gleam in his eyes. "But of course, Mrs. Rathborne-Paxton," he said.

Deeper dread swirled through Alice, even though the man gestured to a young man passing through the entrance hall, snapped his fingers, and said, "Rudy, fetch Montrose at once. I believe he is in his private office."

Not only did the man know who she was, the fact that he

addressed her by her married name then immediately raked her with a lascivious gaze did not bode well at all.

"Thank you for your help, sir," Alice said, moving away from the concierge's desk in an attempt to position herself for a quick escape, if one was needed.

"Lord Hornby," the man corrected her. "But I believe you can call me Albert," he said, lowering his voice and approaching her like a lion stalking a gazelle.

"Thank you, Lord Hornby," Alice said deliberately. The dread pooling in her stomach expanded to make her hands and feet numb.

A year ago, she would have explored the obvious interest Lord Hornby was showing her to determine if he was a potential client. Everything had changed now, though. But Lord Hornby evidently didn't think so.

"I must ask, madam," he said, stalking slowly closer to her. "Why pursue a cold fish like Montrose? Clearly, he is not the sort of man who can satisfy your particular tastes."

He came close enough that Alice had to dodge when he reached out as if he would brush a lock of hair from her face.

"I beg your pardon, my lord, but there appears to be a misunderstanding," she said, genuine fear curling in her gut. "I am here to see Mr. Montrose on a matter of business."

"Of course you are," Lord Hornby growled, fire in his eyes. "I read the papers, you know," he added. "I know all about it."

If Alice had been walking, she would have tripped over her own feet. Something was definitely amiss, and with Lord Hornby's mention of the papers, she had a horrible idea she knew what that could be.

"You are most definitely mistaken, sir," she said in firm tones. "I am a married woman now."

"Hornby, leave the poor woman alone," Montrose said,

suddenly striding into the hall from one of the side corridors. "She has suffered enough for one week."

Bittersweet feelings of relief and deepening dread lashed at Alice. Of all people who might have come to her rescue in a moment like that, it had to be Montrose.

"Montrose, you old dog," Lord Hornby laughed, as though the whole thing were a mere joke to him. He winked at Alice, then moved away, heading for the corridor that would take him deeper into the club. "Please do call on me at your earliest possible convenience, Mrs. Rathborne-Paxton," he said before disappearing entirely. "I can very much make it worth your while."

Alice shivered at the sound of the man's laughter as he left her alone in the hall with Montrose.

To her surprise, Montrose made a sound of disgust and gestured for Alice to go with him to what looked like a small sitting room just off the entry hall. "Aristocrats," he grumbled once he was certain Alice had followed him. "Now do you see why I have made it my mission to crush as many of them as I can?"

Alice's jaw dropped as she entered the sitting room, but she was at a loss for what to say. It irritated her to no end that Montrose was right about a certain breed of aristocrat and that he had been the one to come to her rescue. She did not, under any circumstances, want to admit that he was correct in his assumption that the two of them had things in common.

Montrose also saw that she was at a loss and graciously began the conversation for her, "I suppose you have sought me out today to question my motivations for helping you once again, Mrs. Rathborne-Paxton."

The way he bluntly named her exact reasons for being there, coupled with the kind way he gestured to one of the leather-upholstered chairs in the room and called for the attendant, Rudy, to fetch them tea, had Alice as much off-balance as she'd ever been.

"You have no reason to help me," she said, hoping that would provide an opening for her to ask even more questions. "I am no one to you. I cannot believe your hatred of the nobility would be motivation enough for you to offer me the kind of help that you have."

"But it is, I swear it," Montrose said with what seemed like complete sincerity. He was not a handsome man, so the innocent expression he put on did nothing to charm Alice over to his side. In fact, the wan appearance of his face and the paleness of his skin made him look nearly feeble as he blinked innocently at her. "I have many enemies, it is true, but that is why I value my friends all the more."

"I am not your friend, Montrose," Alice told him. She tried to scowl, but all she managed was a confused frown. "Unless this is all a ruse to lure me into becoming your *particular* friend." She arched one eyebrow at him, testing to see if his interest in her was, in fact, no different than Lord Hornby's.

But Montrose merely shook his head. "You mistake me entirely if you think my aim is anything remotely carnal," he said bluntly. "I can assure you, Mrs. Rathborne-Paxton, I have no interest whatsoever in the activities that other men ruin themselves over. In fact, to be candid, I find those sorts of relations completely abhorrent. I would rather share my bed with worms than another person of any persuasion."

Alice flinched back in her chair slightly. The trouble was, she believed him when he said as much. She knew there were people out there who hadn't the slightest interest in anything sexual, but she rarely encountered them in her former profession. And Montrose's asexuality only confused her further when it came to his interest in her.

"I can see I have baffled you," Montrose said, once again

telling her what she thought before she was able to find a way to express it.

"I cannot imagine there is anything I have that you might want, sir," she said, letting her guard down just a little. "Therefore, I am both baffled and suspicious of your continued interest in me." If he was going to pretend to be honest with her, she would pretend to be honest with him.

"Your investments, of course," Montrose said with a slight shrug, as if it was of no consequence. "I am after your investments."

"But why?" Alice shook her head. "As I understand it, you are a man of great financial worth. Why would a few failed investments appeal to you in any way?"

"I will be frank with you," Montrose said, sitting slightly forward in his chair and looking grave. "I wish to purchase a few of your investments because I am highly cognizant of the fact that you will soon need the money those purchases will provide."

When Alice merely narrowed her eyes slightly in response, Montrose went on.

"You may wish to depart London sometime soon," he said. "Once certain things are made public. It is my sincerest wish that you and your son be able to flee the maelstrom that is coming and that you are able to lead a peaceful life away from gossip."

"Again, why?" Alice scooted forward on her chair as well. Coming from practically anyone else, she would have found the offer of kindness touching. From Montrose, it chilled her blood.

"I have told you about my past, Mrs. Rathborne-Paxton," Montrose said. "I would not wish a young man like your son to be forced to repeat the horrors that befell me."

Alice's suspicions flared higher than ever. Montrose had changed his story. Now it was Ryan he was concerned about?

She was about to reply when a short man with avaricious eyes who was dressed impeccably appeared in the sitting room doorway.

"I beg your pardon," he said to Montrose, then turned his greedy gaze on Alice, "but I heard Mrs. Rathborne-Paxton was here, and I was hoping to have a word."

Alice flinched, wishing she had a shawl she could drape over her head to hide herself. "I do not know you, sir, and I am not inclined to converse with men I do not know at the moment."

"Oh, I see," the man said, as though Alice had revealed far more than she thought she had. "Who should I appeal to for a formal introduction, then?"

"A formal introduction?" Alice had a terrible feeling she knew what that meant.

"Yes," the man said. "To arrange a meeting. I did not realize you were working with a pim—er, a facilitator."

Alice gasped in offense. "Sir, you are mistaken," she hissed.

"Go away, Dawson," Montrose spoke out in Alice's defense. "Mrs. Rathborne-Paxton is an honest woman."

"Are you quite certain of that?" Dawson asked with a smirk.

Before either Alice or Montrose could assure him she was, another, slightly older gentlemen stepped into the doorframe beside Dawson.

"I heard Mrs. Rathborne-Paxton was here seeking clientele," the new man said with a broad smile. "That's a list I would relish being on. I always did love a lively red-head bouncing on my balls."

"This is insufferable," Alice shouted, standing so abruptly her head swam. "Gentlemen, I am not a whore, and I take the greatest possible offense to your insinuations that I am."

Dawson and his new companion jerked back as though Alice were the one who had offended them.

"Beggars cannot be choosers, Mrs. Rathborne-Paxton," Dawson said.

"I read the gossip columns just like any other man," the other one said. "I saw it right there in print. Do not blame me for your choices, madam."

Dawson and his friend nodded to each other as though they were completely in the right, then left, muttering to each other.

Alice's blood had started to run cold as soon as the gossip column was mentioned. She turned to Montrose. "To what are they referring?" she said, her voice as wispy as it was formal.

Montrose rose from the chair where he'd watched the entire exchange with a pitying look. He drew out a folded sheet of *The Times* from the inner pocket of his jacket and handed it to her.

"I am afraid the journalists who were invited to your nuptials did their job a little too well," he said, clasping his hands behind his back as Alice sped through the long and lurid article about herself, her past, her marriage to Sam, and speculation about her intentions going forward. "So you see?" he went on. "After this and several other articles that have been printed about you in the last two days, I imagine you will want to vacate London at once. I only wish to help you by purchasing your investments. If compiling an entire portfolio is too much, I would happily be willing to pay you five hundred pounds for your shares in the South African diamond mine."

Alice was so busy tearing through the article that she barely heard him. If *The Times* was printing salacious speculation about her triumphant return to the dark corners and secret meeting rooms of London high society, if they were broadcasting that she wished to establish herself as the queen of courtesans, now that she had the Rathborne-Paxton family name to protect her, then heaven only knew what some of the less reputable newspapers were printing.

"Mrs. Rathborne-Paxton?" Montrose asked. "The diamond mine? I could return to my private office to draw up transfer paperwork immediately." He gestured toward the door and even started walking in that direction.

"I have to go," Alice said, rushing past him into the front hall. She had just enough presence of mind to find it curious that Montrose had a private office within his club. "I have to speak to Sam," she said, crushing the slip of newspaper in one hand and heading for the door. "This is a complete disaster."

"Is that Mrs. Rathborne-Paxton?" yet another male voice called out as Alice reached the door. "I say, the two of us should get to know each other better. Much better."

Alice turned just enough to make a rude gesture at the man, then burst out of the club and onto the street. She'd been a fool to think things couldn't get any worse than they already were. Even if the journalists hadn't been Sam's idea, she had half a mind to make her dear husband pay for it. Although, judging by the article, Sam's name was being dragged through the mud as much as hers, as he'd been made to look like a buffoon. Something had to be done to save both of them before it was entirely too late.

Chapter Fourteen

Sam slept well, secure in the knowledge that his marriage to Alice was reparable, and that if the two of them had more honest conversations, like the one they'd had in Alice's flat, with Lady Carnlough's help, they could return to the way things had been between the two of them. He longed for that return more than anything, and kicked himself every time he paused to ponder how he'd allowed things to sail so far off course to begin with.

His buoyant mood stayed with him as he washed and dressed in the morning, spinning through ideas for ways to make amends to Alice, but the moment he set foot in the breakfast room and came face to face with his father, his spirits sank all over again.

"I've contacted my solicitor about obtaining an annulment," Lord Vegas said as soon as Sam crossed the threshold, without any greeting or any show of kindness. "This entire, ridiculous farce will be over within a fortnight.

Sam steeled his soul and walked to the sideboard to fix himself a plate. "I've no wish for it to be over, Father," he said without looking at the man. He was certain that the longer he stared at the hypocritical old bastard's face, the less of an appetite he would have. "I love Alice, and once the two of us puzzle through a few things, we will be happy together."

Lord Vegas snorted and opened his mouth, likely to say something irredeemably cruel, as Sam took his plate to the table.

Francis intervened before Lord Vegas could say anything. "That's the spirit, Sam. You'll woo your lady love back to you in no time, I'd wager."

Lord Vegas looked as though Francis had spit in his eggs. "How dare you encourage this fool in his misdeeds?" he demanded of Francis. "That woman is a whore, and I will not have a whore bearing my name."

"That woman is a fine and jolly bird," Dean argued, looking more upset than Sam would have figured he'd look so early in the morning while discussing Alice. "She...she doesn't deserve what she's gotten."

Sam narrowed his eyes at his brother. Something was off. Dean defended Alice staunchly, but there was a deeper sort of guilt that hung about him. He barely managed to look to their father, and as much as Sam stared at him, Dean most definitely would not glance up and meet his eyes.

"Is something amiss?" he asked, staring intently at Dean.

"Everything is amiss," Lord Vegas shouted, banging his fist on the table. Sam jumped in surprise. "Every damnable thing that has happened within the last month is amiss. Devil take that blackguard, Montrose."

Sam's eyes went wide, and he exchanged a look with Francis, who sat across from him.

"You made your own bed, Father." Joseph surprised them all even more as he spoke up from his seat at Francis's side. "You are the one who acquired years of gambling debt and lost bad investments to Montrose and God knows what else you've done."

Sam gaped at his youngest brother, as did Francis and Dean. Up until then, Joseph had been their father's last remaining champion.

Lord Vegas seemed to feel the venom of Joseph's words as well. "Shut your gob, you ungrateful whelp," he snapped. "You're as bad as the rest of them."

"And you are worse than all of us combined," Joseph shouted right back. He stood, threw down his serviette, and stormed sullenly from the room.

Sam peeked at Francis again, both of them wary and on edge.

"This is insufferable," Lord Vegas growled, pushing back his chair and standing as well. "I have been reduced to being insulted by my own flesh and blood. The lot of you are a mutinous gang of reprobates. If it were up to me, I would disown each and every one of you forthwith."

"You cannot disown us because you no longer have anything that you own," Dean grumbled into his plate.

"Insolent imp!" Lord Vegas hissed. "You will pay for this, mark my words." He stepped away from his chair, heading out of the room, but paused when he was across the table from Sam, behind Francis's shoulder. "And you will rid yourself of your whore immediately, do you hear me? It is bad enough that you sullied yourself in that woman's bed, but now all of London knows just how well-traveled that bed is."

"I beg your pardon?" Sam sat up straighter, blinking at his father.

Lord Vegas had nothing more to say. He grumbled under his breath, marching out of the room in a reflection of Joseph that would have been humorous under other circumstances.

As soon as he was gone, Sam focused on Francis and asked, "What is the old blighter talking about?"

Suddenly the mood in the room was tense. Francis turned to Dean, sitting back in his chair slightly and crossing his arms, as though Dean had a great deal of explaining to do.

Dean, in turn, cleared his throat and reached sheepishly for the pile of newspaper pages beside his place. Sam had noticed them when he'd entered the room, but he'd assumed it was that morning's copy of *The Times*, already parceled out so that everyone in the family could read a page.

What Dean gingerly set beside Sam's place was akin to Sam's worst nightmare. Several pages from various newspapers and gossip rags were stacked together, and all of them bore the name Alice Rathborne-Paxton within their headlines or first paragraphs.

Alarm rang through Sam as he picked up the first one and scanned through it. "Oh, Dean, what have you done?" he gasped as he read accusations and insinuations about Alice's character and speculation about her intentions in London society after marrying into the Rathborne-Paxton family.

"I didn't do anything, I swear," Dean insisted. "Look at the names on the articles. They're entirely different journalists than the few I contacted."

Dean was right, but it hardly mattered. It was worse than Sam could have imagined it to be. Not only had the gossip columns reported on the scandalous wedding, they made every sort of untoward assumption about Alice's ruthlessness and greed, not to mention his own weak-headedness and stupidity. Column after column announced Alice's intent to become the queen of courtesans in London—though how they had drawn that conclusion from his and Alice's marriage was an utter mystery, not to mention an incredible stretch of belief. Every one of the articles painted him as an ignorant, soppy boob who had been cuckolded as well.

As soon as Sam finished the last article, he slammed it down on the table, then pushed his barely-touched plate of

MERRY FARMER

food aside. "This is an unmitigated disaster," he said, his voice hoarse. "How did these worthless rags ever come up with the idea of suggesting Alice has designs on renewing her former profession?"

"Newspapers print what sells," Francis said with an uneasy pinch of his face. "More likely than not, one paper invented the most ridiculous, sensational story they could, and when the others saw those false stories sold copies, they followed suit."

Sam grunted, but he wasn't convinced. Nothing of what he'd read seemed like an accident. And of late, anything bad that happened to him or those he loved had Montrose's name written all over it.

"I'm not going to stand for this," Sam said, shoving his chair back and standing. "Montrose will not get away with whatever new evil he has concocted."

"I'm sorry, brother," Dean said, reaching out to grasp Sam's sleeve for a moment as Sam passed his chair. "Truly, I did not intend for this to happen when I invited those journalists."

Sam glared at him. "Perhaps when your turn comes to nab an unsuitable bride you will remember this fiasco and behave better."

He didn't stay to see how Dean would react to his admonishment, though he thought he saw his brother look duly solemn as he left the room. All Sam could think about was that Alice needed him, now more than ever.

He grabbed his coat and hat and flew out of the house as quickly as he could. He was in too much of a hurry to have the family carriage prepared or to walk all the way to Marylebone, so as soon as he reached the first busy street corner, he flagged down a cab and paid extra for the driver to deliver him to Alice's street as fast as possible.

As luck would have it—on a number of levels—he

alighted from the carriage just as Alice appeared to be returning from some sort of errand. Not only that, a gentlemen in a passingly fine suit seemed to be accompanying her, and not with Alice's consent.

"Come on, love," the man was in the middle of saying as Sam strode away from the cab, straight to Alice's side. "We all know what you are. I might not be the poshest fellow in London, but I've got the blunt to pay and pay well."

"Stay away from her, you bastard," Sam roared at the man. "This woman is my wife, not some two-bit strumpet."

Instead of taking the hint, the man laughed. "More like two-pound strumpet, if what the papers say is right. I never had me an expensive whore before. Thought I'd give it a try."

"Go away," Alice said. Only then did Sam realize his beloved was near tears.

"You heard the woman," Sam growled. "Begone before I call for the police to remove you."

He didn't wait to see if the man obeyed him. He slipped one arm around Alice's waist and hurried her off the street and into her building.

"I saw the papers," Sam said in a quiet, tender voice once they were sheltered inside. "Something nefarious is going on here. But not to worry, my love. I am here now, and I will—"

"Mr. and Mrs. Rathborne-Paxton," Mrs. Knox said, stepping out of the front room that served as her office. "I'm so glad to catch you."

The landlady looked anything but glad. She looked near to tears herself and far more frazzled than Sam had ever known her to be.

"Now is not a good time for a visit," Sam told the woman as kindly as he could, ushering Alice on to the stairs that would take her up to her flat. "My wife has had a bit of an upset."

Alice laughed ironically and sent Sam a wary look. "Upset does not begin to describe it."

Mrs. Knox kept after them. "I am afraid I must speak to you on a matter of urgent importance," she said.

"Can it wait, please, Mrs. Knox?" Sam asked.

"No, it cannot, sir." Mrs. Knox's tone grew firmer.

"After a cup of tea perhaps," Sam insisted, starting up the stairs with Alice. "It's been—"

"You have to go, Mrs. Rathborne-Paxton," Mrs. Knox said loudly.

That was enough to freeze both Sam and Alice in their steps. They both turned back to the landlady.

"You have to go," Mrs. Knox repeated, wringing her hands and looking moments away from sobbing. "I dearly wish there was more I could do for you, Alice." The way she addressed Alice by her given name was as sure a sign of friendship as the distress in the woman's face, despite her words. "It was so kind of Mr. Rathborne-Paxton to pay your rent the way he did, and if I could keep you on as a tenant, I would, but I simply cannot."

"You were the one who paid my rent?" Alice asked Sam in a soft, though defeated, voice.

"I was." Sam tightened his grip on her waist.

"It's just that the police were around this morning," Mrs. Knox went on, a tear escaping her eye. Sam could see now that fear was as much a part of the woman's emotions as regret. "I insisted to them that I run a clean and respectable boarding house, which you know full well is a bit of a fib." She glanced down sheepishly. "But they've got me marked now, you see. After what the papers said, they're suspicious of me. I told them you were a respectable married woman, but they threatened to bring me up on charges of running a brothel all the same." The woman's eyes went downright glassy with fear. "I cannot go to prison, I cannot."

Alice let out a breath and broke away from Sam to go to her landlady. "You will not go to prison, Mrs. Knox," she said, taking the distressed woman's hands. "I would not let that happen to you. I will move out by the end of the month, sooner if I can."

"I'm so sorry, Mrs. Rathborne-Paxton." Mrs. Knox broke into a sob in earnest. Alice tried to hug her, but the woman was too distraught. She covered her face with her hands and rushed back into her office.

Alice turned to Sam, her expression drawn and miserable. "I suppose that is the end of that," she said in heavy tones as she joined Sam on the stairs. The two of them continued up together.

"You will come stay with me at the family townhouse," Sam said, taking charge of the situation as he should have from the start. "Or we will set out on our own in a flat somewhere."

Alice shook her head and sent him a mournful look. "Neither of us has the money for that, I'm afraid."

No sooner had the words left her lips than she gasped and paused on the landing between two floors.

"What is the matter, my darling?" Sam asked, his heart bleeding for her.

Alice suddenly turned angry. She pursed her lips and continued up the stairs at a faster pace. Sam thought he'd done something wrong by addressing her by a term of endearment until she said, "Money. That is what it all comes down to. That is what the bastard meant by suggesting I will need money immediately."

Sam knew in an instant whom she was talking about. "Montrose," he said.

As they reached the door to Alice's domestic flat, she turned to him with a slightly guilty look and said, "I went to visit Montrose this morning at his club."

Sam waited for anger and jealousy to swoop in and rile

him up, but it never came. He was at the point where mention of Montrose only made him numb. "What did that devil have to say?"

"More of the same," Alice said with a sigh, letting them into the apartment.

As soon as they were inside, Sam searched around for Ryan and Harriett, the maid. Judging by the way the door to Ryan's room was cracked open and the sounds of Harriett puttering around in the kitchen, the boy was napping and the maid was preparing luncheon.

Alice removed her hat and coat, and Sam did the same. As she moved to slump into the sofa, Alice said, "I wanted to ascertain Montrose's true motivations for offering to help me. I do not believe for an instant that it is some altruistic part of his nature—"

"He has none," Sam agreed.

"—or that it is all a part of this grudge against the aristocracy that he holds," Alice finished.

"I do believe in that," Sam said with a wince, sitting on the sofa with Alice.

"The man insists on helping me, and it is unnerving," Alice said. "And now, just now, now that Mrs. Knox has given me notice, Montrose's insistence on purchasing my investments because I will soon need money makes all the more sense."

"I would be willing to wager what little I have left that he somehow managed to put Mrs. Knox up to evicting you," Sam said, chewing on his lip and on the mountain of furious thoughts about Montrose that raged through him. His scowl deepened and he went on to say, "I would be willing to wager that Montrose had something to do with the nature of the articles that were printed about us. Dean noticed they were all written by different journalists than the ones he alerted about our wedding."

Alice sent Sam a flat look. "I don't know if you are being kind or stupid to say the articles are about *us*. They are about *me*."

Sam shook his head. "They were most certainly about us, whether it appeared so on the surface or not." When Alice sent him a look as though she would argue the point, Sam went on with, "The Rathborne-Paxton family has been Montrose's chief target all along. By destroying your reputation in the gossip columns, he has also painted me as an incompetent and blind ninny. That will affect every one of my social relationships and business ventures. The bastard has effectively neutered me."

Alice blinked and sat up straighter. "I hadn't thought of that. I am sorry, Sam." She reached across to pat his hand.

Sam grasped her hand and held it as though it were the only thing tethering him to sense. "Montrose is cleverer than I thought he was," he said with a frown. "He set out to destroy Father, and now he has his sights set on my brothers and I. And here Francis thought we could pip him at the post by ruining ourselves."

"There must be a reason for all of this," Alice said sitting even straighter, frustration lacing her voice. "Revenge is one thing, but this goes beyond that. Why has Montrose made me a target as much as your family?"

"Because he is a petty bastard?" Sam suggested.

Alice shook her head. "There must be more to it than that. He suggested I take the money he is offering me for my investments and that I leave London. He wants me gone for some reason."

"To be honest," Sam said with a sigh, sinking against the back of the sofa, "I wouldn't mind leaving London at the moment myself."

Alice's shoulders drooped. "I'll have to go, since Mrs. Knox is evicting me."

A shiver of fear shot through Sam, but it resolved quickly into what seemed at first like a mad idea. "Let's go, then," he said. "Let's leave London, if only for one day."

"What do you mean?" Alice asked.

Sam sat up. "You, me, and Ryan. Let's leave London tomorrow. We'll have a picnic in the country. We'll escape from the gossip, from my father, and from the mess Montrose has created. Let's go out to Kent or Hampshire, or someplace like that, and simply be for a day."

For a moment, Alice looked surprised and defiant. Then she seemed to melt. "It would be nice to get a bit of distance," she sighed. "Perhaps then we can puzzle out what Montrose is up to and why he is pursuing us with such dogged determination."

Sam's spirits soared with sudden elation, not because of the talk of Montrose, but because Alice had referred to the two of them as "us". He had waited so long to be included as a part of her again that hearing those words came close to making everything better.

He scooted closer to her and took up both her hands. "We'll escape to the country tomorrow," he said, raising first one hand then the other to kiss her knuckles. "We'll give ourselves a day of reprieve. We'll sort through the messes that have been piled upon us, and we'll make it better."

Deep sentiment came to Alice's eyes. Enough so that Sam feared she was in serious danger of bursting into tears. "I just want it all to stop," she said in a broken voice. "I want us to go back to a time when we were happy just to be together without anyone knowing about it."

"So do I, my love." Sam leaned in and kissed her lips gently. Anything more would have been too much. He needed to show her love and support now, not overwhelm her with passion. If they could work through the mess Montrose had created, there would be time for passion later. "We will get through this and triumph," he told her. "We will beat Montrose, because our love is stronger than any hate that bastard harbors. And once we have defeated him, I promise you, Alice, we will be happy."

Chapter Fifteen

Alice considered it a mad risk to appear in public while salacious articles were still being printed about her in every gossip rag in London. After her miserable outing the day before, she had just about made up her mind never to leave her flat again. Staying home wouldn't have done any good, however, as a few horrifically bold gentlemen who had called on her in the past showed up at Mrs. Knox's building inquiring after her. Mrs. Knox dutifully turned the villains away, saying Alice no longer lived there, but one gentlemen—a new industrialist whom Alice had entertained briefly over a year before—managed to make his way up to Alice's professional flat.

She'd spied him striding down the hall with a bouquet of hothouse flowers through the keyhole of her domestic flat and watched as the man knocked repeatedly on the other flat's door, then gave up and departed. Alice had never been so happy to have let two apartments from Mrs. Knox or to have kept the domestic one a secret from her former clients.

She might have stayed home despite Sam's invitation to spend the day in the country, but for that incident. It was enough to frighten her into dressing for travel the next morning, helping Ryan into a suit he could play in once they were in the country, and donning her wide-brimmed hat before fleeing the flat in the cool hours of dawn, before any of the sort of man who would pursue her had even thought of rising from bed.

There was a certain amount of comfort in the anonymity of Paddington Station, even though it was crowded with commuters in the early morning. None of them were the sort who would accost her. At least, not in that way.

"*The Daily Mail*, madam," one of the adolescent newspaper barkers shouted at her as she walked past his station, holding Ryan's hand as her son glanced around in wonder. "Conflict looming in South Africa." When that story didn't seem to catch Alice's attention, he went on with, "London laundresses' strike continues." And when Alice failed to stop for that, he tried, "Mrs. Rathborne-Paxton takes a new lover. Find out who on page three."

That tidbit stopped Alice dead in her tracks. She pulled Ryan to a stop with her, then turned back to approach the grinning newspaper boy.

"I knew that would tickle your fancy, madam," the cheeky lad said as Alice silently handed him a coin, then snatched the newspaper from him. "God bless," he called after her as she and Ryan marched away.

As swiftly as she could with Ryan in tow, Alice made her way to a bench out of the flow of traffic, then sat, opening the newspaper to page three.

"Mama," Ryan asked, leaning against her arm and scanning the page along with her, though he wouldn't glean much since he'd only just begun to learn to read. "Are you Mrs. Rathborne-Paxton now?" he asked, turning his sweet gaze up to her.

"Yes, sweetheart," she said with a distracted sigh, finding

the article about herself and reading it quickly, her jaw set. Fortunately, everything in the article was blatant speculation, and the journalist had enough sense to state that the gentlemen who had spent the better part of the day yesterday with her might, in fact, have been her husband. But it was only mentioned as an afterthought when several other names were mentioned.

"Is Sam your new lover?" Ryan asked on, all innocence and confusion.

"No, darling," she answered, folding up the paper and discarding it on the bench beside her. "Sam is my husband."

"But you love him, right?" Ryan sat a bit straighter, staring earnestly at her.

"I do," Alice sighed, then added in a mutter, "More than I should."

"Then if you love him, isn't he your lover?" Ryan asked.

Before Alice could answer, Sam himself approached them, saying, "Out of the mouths of babes."

Alice's heart fluttered far more than she would have wanted it to as she tilted her head up to smile at Sam in greeting. She should still be furious with him for everything that had blown into her life like a storm, ruining the relative calm she now longed for. But Sam looked surprisingly fetching in his summer suit, a straw boater hat placed jauntily on his head. His outfit was a newer style of summer dress, but he wore it well.

Alice stood, preferring to look Sam straight in the eye instead of gazing up at him in a way which would quickly turn adoring, if she let it. "I do not have the constitution to love anyone at the moment," she said, trying to be firm, but sounding weary instead. "Not until this damnable mess is sorted and I am no longer the center of inappropriate speculation."

Sam's impish grin melted into genuine sympathy and care. He turned so that he could offer Alice his elbow, winking at Ryan as he did. "Come on, then. I believe our train is boarding. The sooner we get out of this cesspit of salaciousness the better."

Alice couldn't help but send him a small grin for his alliteration as she took his arm and let him escort her and Ryan to the train platforms. All he had told her was to meet him at Paddington at the ridiculous hour of seven o'clock and that he had already arranged everything. Alice was only mildly curious as he handed a porter their tickets, then helped her and Ryan into a private, first-class compartment. How he could afford the luxury, she had no idea. As the train made its way out of the station and out of London, she breathed a sigh of relief.

"Where are we going?" Ryan asked, kneeling on the seat beside Alice so that he could gaze out the window at the countryside.

"To Winchester," Sam said, looking at Alice as though she were more beautiful than any countryside. "I figured it was close enough for a day trip," he explained, "but far enough that London gossip might not have reached the place. And besides, there are several lovely shops and restaurants along the high street, and the grounds of Winchester Cathedral are perfect for strolling and untangling knots tied by devilish villains."

The peace that had started to settle in Alice's heart as she escaped from London rushed away from her. "I have thought about it and thought about it, and I simply do not understand why Montrose is both vexing us into the ground and offering to help, as though he is the sole savior in this drama," she said with emotion.

Sam sighed and rubbed a hand over his face. "Montrose has his own designs in everything," he said.

"Those designs must extend further than a desire to tear down noblemen," Alice figured, thinking aloud. "I cannot think that something so vague would be his sole driving factor."

"I have to admit," Sam said. "My father is enough of an arse that I would have relished bringing him down myself at this point."

Alice's gut tightened, and she arched an eyebrow at Sam. "Is that not what you and your brothers are doing by bringing whores and heaven only knows what else into the family?"

Sam's puzzled look flashed to contrition. "Darling, you know that was not my primary motivation in marrying you." He had the good sense to pause and wince for a moment before going on with, "Though, yes, I will admit that was part of the game."

Satisfied that he would, at least, not deny it, Alice asked, "What else does Montrose want or need that ruining your father alone wouldn't bring him?"

They debated the issue for the remaining half hour of the trip, considering everything from sheer madness to espionage of some sort to financial necessity. The trouble was that they knew so little about Montrose to begin with that anything might have been possible.

By the time the train pulled into the Winchester station, Alice was exhausted all over again.

"Let's put the matter aside for the moment and simply enjoy a walk on a lovely June day," Sam said, offering his arm again once they were outside of the station.

Alice sent him a long, lingering look. She was no fool. The outing wasn't just so that they could contemplate Montrose's motivations and escape the gossip of London for a day. Sam had taken her away from the scene of her disgrace so that he could woo her and win her back into his arms.

As much as part of her would have loved nothing more than to let bygones be bygones and to fold herself into Sam's embrace, her pride wouldn't let his foolishness and the chaos it had caused go so easily. She had spent the last seven years of her life, since the mess with Michael Feeney that had given her Ryan, trying to prove that she was strong enough to stand on her own, despite social convention, and that she would not slip quietly into the role of a pitiable, fallen woman. She would not be locked away, out of sight of those hypocrites who considered themselves better than a woman who had done nothing more than follow her heart, foolish though it had been. The danger of forgiving Sam too quickly was that she could end up as his disgraceful wife, hidden from society, and perhaps that Sam would even come to resent her someday as the albatross she might be.

It would have been so much easier to hold onto her own, though, if she didn't love her handsome fool so much.

"A walk would be lovely," she said with a sigh, accepting his arm.

They headed along the cross street until they reached the top of the high street. Winchester was a quaint old town with buildings that dated back to the Plantagenets. There was something to look at around every corner and down the sloping hill that made up the central street.

Ryan thought so as well.

"Mama, look!" he gasped, pointing to a shop window display of toy trains. "They're so perfect!" He let go of Alice's hand and dashed to the window, pressing his hands and face against the glass as he looked in.

Alice laughed despite the tightness in her soul. "Boys and their trains," she said, shaking her head.

"I was never one for toy trains," Sam said, grinning at her as they walked slowly to join Ryan at the shop window. "I was far more interested in toy soldiers."

"Were you?" That was a bit of information that didn't seem to fit with what she knew of Sam.

"Oh, yes." He grinned at her. "Dean and I both had legions of soldiers. I preferred Roman ones, but Dean had a collection of cavaliers and loyalist soldiers. We would line them up on the nursery table and stage epic battles between them."

"Cavaliers and Roman soldiers?" Alice laughed. Come to think of it, she could imagine that after all.

"Absolutely," Sam smiled broadly. "And the Romans always won, of course. The Romans always won everything."

"Until they didn't," Alice laughed.

"And yet, Latin is still the language of the scholars," Sam pointed out with a smug grin.

Alice had to give him that much. She laughed and shook her head. "Ryan has adored his farm animals so far, but I can see his interests are turning toward more citified things now."

She nodded to her son as he practically salivated over not only the trains, but the small buildings and miniature shops that had been set up to create a world for the trains to run through. A child inside the store stood by the table where the trains were set up, pushing the metal engine along a set of tracks. Alice could practically see Ryan vibrating with jealousy.

She sighed and said, "To be honest, as much as I adore London, after less than an hour here, I am beginning to crave the solace of the country."

Sam hummed, moving his hand to the small of her back as he, too, watched the other child playing with the trains. "I understand completely. London is hostile territory right now." He glanced to Alice and went on with, "Perhaps we should retire to the country for a year or two after the initial storm has blown over."

Alice's heart caught in her chest. The way he spoke of the two of them making a life together was so confident. He was so certain that the two of them could mend the hurts between them and carry on. She wished she was as certain.

"Come along, Ryan," she said, stepping away from Sam and taking her son's hand. "Let's find a bit of lunch first, and we can come back and consider trains later."

"But Mama," Ryan whined.

Judging by the look on Sam's face, he was probably whining on the inside as well as she walked away from him.

"I'm rather fond of this pasty shop right here," Sam said, his tone cheerier than the regret in his eyes, as they walked down a few buildings from the toy store.

"You've been to Winchester before?" Alice asked.

"Several times, yes," Sam admitted. "Francis's country house, Chilcomb Park, the one that came with the title of Viscount Cathraiche, is two or three miles south of here."

"Oh." Alice lit up a bit, and her rebellious heart immediately conjured up dreams of Francis allowing her and Sam and Ryan to live in his Hampshire house for a time.

She shook those thoughts away. She could not entertain her future until she had resolved the present.

"I want the biggest pasty there is," Ryan declared as he rushed ahead to peer at the wares on display inside a glass-encased counter.

"Well, I want one bigger than yours," Sam said, teasing Ryan and ruffling his hair.

Alice hung back for a moment, watching her son and her husband together. A pang filled her heart. More than anything, she wanted the peaceful, domestic picture that the two of them together hinted she could have. That sort of happiness seemed so close and so real, but for the moment, it was only an illusion.

A sudden sense of desperation and anxiety filled her. She couldn't go back to London and expect to live peacefully. As long as the newspapers printed gossip about her, men would pursue her as if she were a shiny bauble they could possess. At the moment, it was merely inconvenient. How long would it be until those men presented a dangerous threat to her? How long until she was forced to leave London, with Sam or without him?

Montrose had to be behind it—the gossip columns and the men. There was no question in Alice's mind. But how? What did the bastard stand to gain by tormenting her, then forcing her to give up and flee?

She bit her lip and glanced around at the shops and pedestrians of Winchester, racking her brain for some kind of answer. Nothing made sense at present. Perhaps that was the answer, though. Perhaps Montrose was simply cruel and enjoyed dangling his prey over the fire. He claimed to be a friend, but the only thing he'd offered to help the situation was to buy up her investments. He could have had the power to tell the newspapers to stop printing stories about her. He could have left the Rathborne-Paxton family alone entirely. He could have—

The cycle of her increasingly-frantic thoughts stopped as she found herself staring at a jeweler's shop near the top of the high street. It was as if something clicked in her mind.

"The diamond mine," she said aloud, just as Sam and Ryan returned to her.

"I beg your pardon?" Sam asked, handing her a pasty.

Alice took it, but continued staring at the jeweler's shop rather than biting into it, like Ryan and Sam were. "The diamond mine," she repeated. "That has to be what Montrose is after. In fact, he more or less told me as much to my face when he said he was after my investments."

Sam frowned, finished chewing his bite, then asked, "Why would Montrose want shares in a failed diamond mine?"

"What if it hasn't failed?" Alice turned to Sam, her mind

working faster than ever. "What if the reports I've received are false and the mine is still profitable?"

Sam shook his head, looking a bit too sympathetic for Alice's liking. He steered the three of them to walk on, to the archway that would take them into the park on the cathedral grounds. "The mine might very well still be profitable, but it is well known that Cecil Rhodes and his company have rearranged the laws in South Africa so that Rhodes controls the entire industry. Even if the mine was still profitable, they cannot work it."

"Perhaps there are plans to sell to De Beers?" Alice suggested as they crossed onto the grass and made their way to a bench under a spreading tree. Ryan ran ahead, securing their spots.

Sam rubbed his face with one hand while holding the paper-wrapped pasty in the other. "Have you been given any indication that the owners of the mine plan to sell?" he asked.

Alice winced. "No," she said. "In fact, they seem determined not to sell, as if they want to fight Rhodes."

"If they do, they will lose," Sam said as the reached the bench and sat.

"Then what could Montrose possibly want with a defunct mine?" Alice burst with frustration. "I cannot think of anything else that he wants from me or any other reason he has offered his help, but it does not make sense that the mine would help him in any way."

"Right," Sam said, as if taking charge. "We must assume that there is some value in the mine, or in one of the other investments Montrose had made an offer for, that we currently cannot see."

"But what?" Alice said with a flustered shrug. "Montrose has more money than the Queen. He doesn't need to take on bad investments." She growled out her frustration, then took a large bite of her pasty, chewing vigorously.

Sam was silent for a moment before tilting his head to the side and asking, "What if Montrose is not as rich as we all think he is? What if he is simply very clever about pretending he has money when he hasn't."

Alice sat straighter, entertaining the idea for a moment, before deflating again. "The man has his own private office at Harvey's. He has a residence in Mayfair as well, does he not?"

"He does." Sam deflated as well. "I only know of a few lucky blighters with enough cash to have their own private office at their club."

"So if it's not money he's after and it's not...me," she sent Sam a significant look, then peeked at Ryan—who was swiftly losing interest in his pasty and becoming interested in a group of ducks waddling across the grass several yards away.

"Are you certain it's not you?" Sam asked with a cheeky grin. "I cannot imagine anyone not being interested in you."

Alice's cheeks heated despite herself. Why did Sam have to be so damnably charming when all of her defenses were up? "He told me himself that he is not interested in that side of life at all, and I believe him."

Sam furrowed his brow. "What an odd egg." He sent her a look of such blatant sensuality and invitation that a squiggle of desire shot through her, resting in all of the most inconvenient places.

Sam must have seen her reaction to his flirting. His expression grew more serious and more amorous. "Alice, you know that I love you like you are the blood in my veins and the breath in my lungs." He inched closer to her on the bench, setting aside the remainder of his pasty. "You know that I regret the last few days more than I've ever regretted anything in my life, and that if I could make everything better with a kiss and a promise, I would."

"Oh, Sam," Alice sighed, her heart beating heavily against

her ribs. "I wish that things were that easy to resolve between us."

"But they could be," he said, moving closer still. He plucked the half-eaten pasty from her hand, then went on with, "They could be, if we let them be."

He leaned in, his gaze focusing on her lips. Alice drew in a breath, frantically trying to decide if she wanted Sam to kiss her—yes, she did—and whether it would ruin her resolve to remain strong and independent if she did—very likely. Sam seemed intent on kissing her, though, no matter how tumultuous her thoughts were. The closer he swayed to her, the more she was inclined to let him. She could feel the heat of his mouth a breath away from hers, and it was irresistible. Even her hat couldn't get in the way of what seemed inevitable between them.

"Mama! They're off!" Ryan shouted suddenly, breaking the mood between Alice and Sam as the two of them separated from their near kiss. Alice's hat brim smacked Sam in the face as she turned to her son. Ryan leapt off the bench and tore after the ducks, which had picked up speed and started to take flight. "They're off, they're off!"

Alice burst into a laugh for her darling boy, and Sam dissolved into laughter as well. The intensity of the moment was broken.

"Oh, dear," Sam said, sending her an impish look. "We've been foiled by ducks."

"We'd better chase after him," Alice said, standing and adjusting her hat, her heart suddenly light. "There's no telling what sort of mischief he'll get himself into if left to his own devices."

"Like mother, like son," Sam said, standing with her and starting across the grass to where Ryan was flapping his arms wildly at the ducks.

Alice moved with him, her steps somehow lighter. Perhaps

there was hope for them after all. Perhaps there was a way for them to leave London and start a life in the country without calling it a defeat or bowing to Montrose's whims.

But no, if she and Sam and Ryan were going to enjoy any sort of prolonged happiness without losing the battle, Montrose's motivations had to be exposed, and the man most definitely needed to be thwarted.

Chapter Sixteen

W hat had started out as a necessity to get Alice and Ryan away from the horrible consequences of his and his brothers' ill-conceived actions and Montrose's villainy, somehow turned into one of the most pleasant days of Sam's life. Alice relaxed inch by inch as they walked around the sunny grounds of Winchester Cathedral— or rather, chased after Ryan as he dashed off in one direction or another, disturbing birds, attempting to pluck the flowers in the cathedral's gardens, or simply running across the lush, green lawns of the park surrounding the cathedral.

More than once, Sam found himself regretting the fact that Alice's lively and intelligent son lived in the city—a place with a dearth of lawns to run through. Perhaps it was his age, or maybe it was his heritage and early upbringing, but Ryan struck Sam as the kind of boy who needed to live in a place of open spaces, where he could ramble over hills and explore dales. He was tempted to leave Winchester proper to take Alice and Ryan on a side excursion to Chilcomb Park. He was also tempted to remain there once they'd arrived, forgetting all else and starting life anew with his bride and her son.

"We could never get away with it, Sam," Alice sighed with regret when Sam expressed his thoughts to her.

They stood on the train platform in the late afternoon, waiting for the train that would take them back to London and their problems. Ryan had fallen asleep with his arms and legs wrapped around Sam, and the way that Alice stared at the two of them, her heart on her sleeve as sentiment filled her eyes, had Sam's heart beating desperately.

"I don't see why not," Sam said. He tried to keep his tone light, as though they were joking rather than discussing one of the most crucial topics of their lives, but he was certain the longing in his soul shone through. "Francis wouldn't mind if we took up residence at Chilcomb Park," he said. "In fact, I'd wager he would be thrilled to have someone in residence there to give the staff he pays too much for something to do."

Alice smiled warmly at him for a moment before regret pinched her face. "You know we cannot consider any future, domestic situation at all until we manage the mountain of problems in front of us," she said as a train whistle sounded a short distance down the track and activity on the platform picked up. Alice stepped closer to him and said, "If Montrose believes we've simply retreated, he will continue to pursue us with his villainy until he gets whatever it is he wants."

Sam sighed in agreement. "You're right. We need to beat the bastard at his own game before we can consider ourselves in the clear."

There wasn't time to say more as the train chugged into the station, whistle blowing and steam hissing, but Sam's thoughts continued. Montrose was slippery and clever. He was undoubtedly behind every nasty thing that had happened to Alice and to him in the last week, even if his fingerprints were not directly on the pens of the journalists who had turned Alice's life into a nightmare. Unless they determined the motivations behind Montrose's actions and came up with a way to force him to stop, he and Alice would never find a moment's peace.

That thought seemed to hang over them on the train journey home. Every bit of relaxation Sam had watched come over Alice vanished the closer they came to London. It hurt to observe her smiles disappear and her face grow pale and wan again. Night descended around them as the train sped through the countryside, and when the distant lights of the city made the horizon glow with the yellow-orange of too much lamp-light, there was a moment when Sam thought Alice might burst into tears.

Whatever he did, whatever Alice thought of him and his part in her ruination, he would move heaven and earth to make certain she smiled again and that her path going forward was as smooth and beautiful as possible.

Paddington Station was just dim enough when they stepped down from the train, and Alice's ridiculous hat was enough of a shield, that no one approached her or even looked askance at them as they made their way from the train plat-form through the station and out to the street. Sam hailed one of the many cabs waiting to convey passengers home rather than forcing them all to take a public conveyance or walk the long distance back to Marylebone.

"You don't have to, Sam," Alice told him, her voice wearier than ever, as Sam pulled out his wallet to pay the driver. "I...I know you don't have the spare money for cab fare."

"Maybe not," Sam said, managing a brave smile all the same, "but I feel as though our fortunes are changing."

It was clear she didn't believe him, but she smiled all the same and helped her half-asleep son into the cab.

It took a moment for the three of them to adjust into the cramped interior of the cab. Ryan seemed to be all arms and legs as he sprawled across the seat by Alice's side, trying to settle his head on her lap, but also stretch out his well-worn legs. Alice had her massive hat to deal with. It blocked her from sitting comfortably and shed copious amounts of feathers every time she moved or tried to bend the brim so that she could lean back. Sam leaned over to help her adjust it at one point, and as he did, the cab hit a rut in the road, sending him spilling into her lap.

The result was that both of them ended up laughing ridiculously, and since exhaustion played a major role in that laughter, they could not stop. Alice finally reached up and pulled enough pins from her hat to be able to wrench the massive thing off and toss it to the floor. Her hair came out of its style in the process, and while some might have thought she looked a mess because of it, Sam thought she was the most beautiful thing he'd ever seen.

The only dark spot on their ride home was when they arrived at Alice's building and Sam spotted a gentlemen dressed too finely for the neighborhood loitering near the doorway. The blighter almost looked like he belonged there as he leaned against the wall, enjoying a cigarette in the lamplight, but when the man's face lit up at the sight of Alice, it was clear to Sam who and what he was. One fierce look from Sam, though, coupled with the way Alice lifted Ryan into her arms with a maternal smile for her boy, sent the bastard on his way.

They were lucky not to encounter any more interference as they made their way up to Alice's domestic flat. Mrs. Knox must have imposed some sort of rule about gentlemen callers being banned from the building, for which Sam was grateful. And there was a chance that Alice had been so busy with Ryan that she hadn't even noticed her potential caller.

"Can we go back to the cathedral again?" Ryan asked sleepily as both Alice and Sam helped him through his bedtime rituals.

"I'll take you back any time you'd like, my boy," Sam told

him as he shimmied Ryan's shirt off over his head, then helped him to sit on the bed. He knelt to untie Ryan's shoes while Alice fetched her son's nightshirt from the wardrobe. Evidently, Harriett had been given the entire day off and had gone to visit her sister in Fitzrovia.

Ryan lit up a bit. "I want a boat to push through the river, like that other boy had," he said, wriggling out of his trousers on his own as Alice brought his nightshirt over.

It took Sam a moment to remember the boy with a toy boat on a string playing in the narrow canal that cut through the lower part of the town. He remembered Ryan playing with his boat in the Serpentine a few weeks ago—it felt like years after everything that had happened—and made a note to supply Ryan with a whole fleet of sailing ships, once his fortunes were restored.

"I'll see to it you have one," Sam told him with a wink, helping him into his nightshirt.

"You already have a boat, dearest," Alice reminded her son, peeling down the bedcovers so that Ryan could settle himself in for the night. "There's no need to be greedy when some boys have no boats at all."

"Yes, Mama," Ryan said with a sleepy sigh, wriggling against his pillow as Alice tucked him in. "But I don't have a train, so I'll need one of those."

Sam laughed, then leaned over and kissed Ryan's forehead. "I'll get you the finest train in England, mate," he said before straightening.

Alice sent him a look of affection mixed with censure over her shoulder, then finished tucking her son in. "Sleep well, love," she told him, kissed his cheek, then straightened.

Sam and Alice headed out of the room, but before they could shut the door behind them, Ryan said, "I like goodnight kisses from two people."

Something gripped Sam's heart that felt as new and

185

exciting as the start of an adventure. As soon as he and Alice shut Ryan's door and were alone in the main room of the flat, he let out a heavy breath and said, "As God is my witness, I will do anything and everything it takes to defeat Montrose so that the three of us can be a family."

Alice blinked, startled over the vehemence of his words, then her eyes went glassy. "I can't do this, Sam," she said, surprising him by turning and marching away from him, one hand covering her mouth as if to stifle a sob.

It was absolutely not the reaction he would have expected from her.

"What can't you do, my love?" he asked, trying to keep his voice tender when what he really wanted to do was shout and rail over how unfair things had become.

He tried to rest a hand on Alice's shoulder once he reached her, but she shrugged it away and took a few more steps to avoid him. "I can't lead Ryan into hoping that everything will be sweet and wonderful," she said, turning to face him at last. "He's been through too much already. He deserves a calm, settled life."

"That's what I wish to give him," Sam said, desperation bubbling within him.

"But can you?" Alice asked. "Can you promise him peace and deliver when you and I and your entire family have an enemy like Montrose set against us?"

"Montrose cannot touch us and what we have," Sam insisted. In fact, he was well aware that what they had between them was still damaged and fragile, but he would pretend all was well until all actually was well.

"Oh, but he can," Alice said, moving restlessly around the room, putting her jacket and reticule away and tidying up a few things that had been left out during the day. "He has proven mercilessly that he can interrupt the course of our lives. He has ruined everything."

"And I will fix it," Sam insisted, following Alice around the room. "Montrose wants the diamond mine, I'm certain. I will discover why and—"

"And give it to him?" Alice stopped, turning to him. "How can you win a battle by capitulating?"

Frustration lashed Sam. "He will only want more once he has what he's after," he agreed with a sigh.

Alice kept moving about the apartment, but instead of sinking into despair with her, as he could see she was doing, a different sort of inspiration hit him.

"I still say that the key to thwarting Montrose is to discover what he truly wants, what his deeper motivation is," he said.

"I agree," Alice said, irritation lacing her voice as she came to a stop in front of him, "but we've been round and round on this carousel for days. What does Montrose truly want and why does he believe a failed mine will provide him with that?"

"I don't know," Sam said with a shrug. Just as Alice began to sigh with defeat, a second wave of inspiration hit him. "I don't know," he repeated, "but I will find out." Before Alice could question him again, he pressed on with, "If you were a nefarious villain with grudges against the aristocracy and ulterior motives that you were attempting to hide from your enemies, where would you store all of your secrets?"

"Sam," Alice began with a sigh, rubbing her forehead, "I don't have the vitality left to play these games. I am exhausted, overwrought, harassed, pitiful—"

She stopped abruptly, her eyes going wide. It was the antithesis of every word she'd just used to describe herself.

"Yes?" Sam asked, hope and expectation pulsing through him. Alice had come up with an idea.

Alice blinked, then confirmed his suspicion by saying, "His private office at that club of his."

Sam caught on without her having to say another word.

"You're right. If Montrose has secrets, they will be hidden in his private office."

"And a club like that would be an ideal place to store things, because not only is it not his personal residence, the club is likely guarded day and night by its staff," Alice went on. "Gentlemen's clubs put a great deal of emphasis on discretion and security, do they not?"

"Some of them," Sam said with a shrug, thinking about the club that he and his brothers belonged to. That one put more emphasis on showing its members a damn good time. He took a step closer to Alice, and this time she didn't move away. "How do you propose we find our way into a club like that and all the way up to Montrose's private office without being stopped or even arrested?"

Alice's mouth hung open and her eyes had a far-away look for a moment before she closed her mouth and blew out a heavy breath. "I have no idea. It might be impossible."

"Aren't the two of us experts in achieving the impossible?" Sam asked, reaching for her hands and sliding their fingers together. Alice's eyes took on an entirely different, softer, longing look as Sam gazed into them. "Isn't everything about us impossible? And yet, here we are." He shrugged, taking a risk and sliding one arm around her to pull her close. "We are husband and wife despite impossible odds. We've defied social convention and societal norms to be together, and even though there have been a few bumps in our road, we are together."

"Sam," Alice whispered his name, the emotion behind the single word as fraught and heated as anything he'd ever heard.

Alice was on the brink, worn out from her troubles, but in desperate need of comfort. Sam knew her well enough to see all of that. He knew her far better than most men knew their wives after decades of marriage, and he wouldn't let a black-guard like Montrose steal that from him. Montrose could have everything else—his money, his name, and his pride—but he could not steal the love he and Alice had for each other.

Risking everything, he pulled Alice closer and slanted his mouth over hers. There was an even chance that she was still too furious with him to reconcile and that she would push him away and slap his face. But after an initial brush of their lips, she was still in his arms. He tried for more, parting her lips with his and deepening their kiss to explore the familiar warmth and taste of her.

By some miracle, she let him in. The faintest whimper sounded from deep within her as she relaxed and let Sam kiss her. Gradually, as Sam worshiped her mouth with his own, she kissed him back. It was as if the wall she'd erected between them was slowly crumbling under the calm, steady force of the love that they shared. That love might have been dented, but it would never be broken.

Sam nearly shouted in victory when Alice gave up the last of the tension holding her back and sagged into him, resting her arms over his shoulders and threading her fingers through his hair. She was his again, and no one could take that away. His passion instantly flared, and he clasped her close, making no secret of the way his cock responded to their kiss and their proximity.

"Take me to your bed," he said between kisses, more as an entreaty than a demand.

He waited for a few, precarious seconds of doubt before Alice dragged her heavy-lidded glance from his mouth to his eyes and nodded.

Triumph and hope and desire surged through Sam. He kissed Alice once more, long and lingeringly. Then, with all the energy pulsing within him, he swept Alice off her feet and headed for her bedroom.

Alice's bedroom in that flat was worlds away from the large, ornate affair in the flat down the hall. It was small and tidy, with few furnishings and a surprisingly narrow bed. Sam lay her on the bed all the same—it was plenty big enough for what he had in mind—then shifted to remove her traveling boots. Instead of rushing to undress as he did, Alice simply watched him, her thoughts seemingly miles away. Sam respected the reverence of those thoughts and of the moment. He didn't say a word as he removed her boots and stockings, then paused to slip off his own shoes, hurrying through tossing off the rest of his clothes while he was at it. There was something right and proper about him being naked and serving her while Alice reclined on the bed, watching him.

"I love you, my darling," he said, sitting on the bed with her once he was undressed and starting on the buttons of her blouse. "Never doubt that, no matter what happens. I love you, and I would give my life for you if I needed to."

"Oh, Sam," Alice sighed, clasping the sides of his face and kissing him soundly. "I love you too. I shouldn't. I tried not to. But I do. Even when I am angry with you."

"You have every right to be furious with me, my love." He pulled her blouse off with her help and tossed it aside, then set to work unhooking her corset. "And you have every right to punish and chastise me in any way you see fit."

A sultry, impish grin flittered across her lips. "I may just have to take you up on that offer," she said, eyes flashing as she wriggled enough to unfasten her skirts in the back. As Sam helped her free herself from the rest of her clothes and pull back the bedcovers, she said, "I have a few rather interesting items in the other flat, including a rather attractive paddle that makes a delightful sound when applied to the backsides of husbands in need of discipline."

"Yes, please," Sam said in a hoarse, voice, settling into bed with her, nestled between her parted legs. His cock thickened at the idea of Alice tanning his hide until his arse smarted. "But not tonight," he went on, molding their bodies together in a more sensual dance. "Tonight, I want to make love to my wife for the first time."

Alice caught her breath, gazing up at him with hope and expectation in her eyes. "I want that too," she said, her voice filled with sentiment. "Because I love you, Sam. And I don't want to let anyone or anything come between us ever again."

"Neither do I, love."

It was a wish and a promise. Enough messes had been made. The time had come to fix things instead of letting them disintegrate further. Sam wouldn't stop until every day was as glorious and filled with love as that day had been.

Chapter Seventeen

Alice didn't want to wake up from the beautiful dream she found herself in the next morning. In that dream, Sam was with her, the world was at peace, and nothing at all nipped at her heels, trying to drag her down. It was heaven, and she wanted to hold onto it for as long as possible.

She drew in a breath and shifted from her side, with Sam spooning her from behind, to her other side, nudging Sam to his back so that she could nestle against him. The scent of his skin and the lingering hint of musk from their activities the night before filled her nose. She reveled in the feeling of Sam's naked body against hers, the heat and softness of his skin. How wonderful would it be if this could be her life?

But it couldn't, she remembered with a disappointed sigh. Not until Montrose and the threat he presented were eliminated.

She spread her arm farther across Sam's chest, feeling the gentle rise and fall of his breath as he slept on. There had to be a way to defeat Montrose at whatever game he was playing.

There had to be a way to determine what that game was. She was certain beyond a shadow of a doubt that the answers to everything were hidden in Montrose's private office at his club, and that if they could just find their way inside, all would be revealed and the information needed to end her nightmare by throwing Montrose off his game could be discovered.

But how? The club didn't allow women inside, for one. There was no way to sneak past the concierge manning the front hall. And there were too many other club members roaming the hallways. They likely all knew who the members were, and if she and Sam so much as peered in through a window, they would know the two of them didn't belong. Harvey's club was akin to an impenetrable fortress, as far as Alice was concerned. Montrose's office might as well have been a bank vault.

As Alice's thoughts turned over and over, she found herself playing idly with one of Sam's nipples, rolling it between her fingers and rubbing her thumb over it until it was a taut point. As soon as she realized what she was doing, she sucked in a small breath and stopped.

"No," Sam groaned, far more awake than she thought he was. "Don't stop. That was a lovely way to awaken."

Alice laughed low in her throat at his silliness. It was ridiculously good to wake up with him in her arms, even if none of their problems had been resolved.

"I would have thought you'd rather wake up to me playing with something else," she said in a sultry voice, sliding her hand across his abdomen to brush his half-hard cock, demonstrating her words.

Sam growled languidly as she closed her hand around his girth and stroked him lazily. "Yes, that is a much better way to wake up," he said.

Alice giggled and continued to pleasure him, teasing her

fingertips around his foreskin and pulling it back to rub his sensitive tip and slit until moisture leaked out.

"Dear God, woman," Sam gasped, "how I missed having you in my bed."

Alice managed to prop herself on one arm while still stroking him. "Might I remind you, this is my bed," she said. "And it has only been a few days."

Sam opened his eyes and grinned at her. "It feels like it's been an eternity," he said.

He reached for her face and drew her down for a long kiss, in spite of less than fresh breath for both of them. Alice continued fondling him, reaching down to cup his balls, as they kissed. She was moments away from straddling him and riding him hard until they were both spent with passion when the door to her bedroom flew open.

"Oh!" Harriett exclaimed as soon as she saw the two of them. She had a load of linens in her arms that she nearly dropped. "I beg your pardon, ma'am. I am so sorry. Mr. Rath-borne-Paxton." She nodded, beet-red, and bobbed a curtsy before dashing out of the room and shutting the door behind her so loudly it rattled.

Sam burst into a laugh, his tension draining as he sprawled across the bed.

Alice had exactly the opposite reaction.

"Servants!" she gasped, letting go of Sam and sitting up straight, eyes wide. That was the answer to everything.

"Yes, they can be a bit intrusive," Sam laughed, misunder-standing her.

"No," Alice said, grabbing his arm as inspiration formed an entire plan in her head in an instant. "Servants can go wher-ever they please, and most of the time we don't even see them."

Sam frowned slightly, shifting so that he could sit with the pillows and his back against the head of her bed. "What ideas are forming in that beautiful mind of yours?" he asked. The bedcovers tented over his arousal, but Alice was far too distracted to continue with those games.

Alice moved to sit up fully beside him on the narrow bed, not caring that she was exposed from the waist up as she did. "We need to get into Montrose's private office at his club to discover what is motivating him and what he wants."

"I think it's clear he wants your diamond mine," Sam said, a bit too languidly to be fully engaged in plotting along with her.

"But why, when it is clearly a wasted asset?" she asked, then answered herself immediately with, "The answer to that and every other question is contained in Montrose's office, I simply know it. And the way we can obtain access to that office is by posing as servants in the club."

Sam froze, staring at her as though she were half mad. "I am not saying it is a bad idea," he began slowly, "but staff in clubs such as that are generally male, and always deeply vetted. Besides, the other members of staff would know in an instant we are not who we say we are."

"Do we have enough money to bribe them to silence?" Alice asked, climbing out of bed and heading to her wardrobe to fetch a robe. "And would the night staff be as dedicated and discreet as the day staff?"

Sam sat even straighter, gaping at Alice. "My darling, are you proposing that we infiltrate Harvey's club in the middle of the night, disguised as servants, and that we invade Montrose's private office to search for clues about his motivations for ruining us and what might convince him to give up his plans?"

Alice finished shrugging her robe on and tying the sash. "Yes," she said, bursting into a smile. "That is precisely what I am suggesting."

She rather enjoyed the way Sam stared at her. She could tell that he was tempted by the idea, mad as it was. Only fools would attempt something so wildly risky. Fools or people who were at the very end of their rope and had nothing left to lose.

"Think of it," she said, returning to the bed and sitting by Sam's side. "If we succeed, we may find more information than we ever could have dreamed of. We might be able to bring Montrose's reign of terror to an end. If we fail—"

"We could be arrested and thrown in prison," Sam finished for her, though the spark of mischief in his eyes didn't match the doom of his words.

Alice shrugged. "Was it not your and your brothers' aim to destroy your own family name so that there is nothing left for Montrose to destroy? What better way to accomplish that than by ending up in prison for breaking and entering?"

Sam barked a laugh, as though every word Alice spoke was ridiculous. Because, in fact, it was.

"I could not bear to see you imprisoned as well, though, my darling wife," he said, resting a hand on the side of her face, then leaning in for a kiss.

Alice accepted the kiss, then pulled away. "My life has become a prison in the last two days," she said with all seriousness. "I can only imagine that actual prison would bring some sort of a respite with it, since I would no longer be accosted by arrogant gentlemen with salacious aims every time I leave the house."

Sam frowned, though Alice didn't have the feeling he was angry with her. "Part of me wonders if, like we suspect about the gossip items in the newspaper, Montrose has also somehow arranged for those men to accost you."

Alice's brow shot up. "I hadn't thought of that, but do you know, I think you might be right." She rose from the bed again, starting toward the door. "Which is all the more reason that we must infiltrate Montrose's inner sanctum to discover the truth of the man. And if we happen to find something to dangle over his head the way he has dangled so much over ours, then perhaps we could do your entire family a favor by warding the bastard off in the process."

Sam grinned from ear to ear as he watched her reach for the doorhandle. "You do beat all, Mrs. Rathborne-Paxton. This plan of yours is insane and likely to fail, but I will indulge you in it and be right by your side through the entire thing, because I love you."

Alice smiled, warming to the tips of her toes. Perhaps things would work out between them after all.

She blew him a kiss, then left the bedroom. The second she stepped into the main room of her flat, however, she was faced with the unexpected sight of Mrs. Knox speaking to Harriett across the threshold of the flat's main door.

"Mrs. Knox," she said, approaching the woman, even though she was dressed in only a robe. States of undress had long since ceased to bother Alice at all. "What can I do for you this morning?"

Mrs. Knox seemed to be thrown off by Alice's cheerful mood. Harriett stepped aside so that the landlady could enter the room fully, then shut the door behind her.

"I've brought you a letter that was delivered this morning," Mrs. Knox said, presenting an envelope in Maeve's light green stationary. Alice stepped forward to take it from her, uncertain whether she should be delighted by her friend's missive or wary of it. "And I am afraid that I must reiterate my need for you to move out as soon as you can, Mrs. Rathborne-Paxton," Mrs. Knox went on.

Alice's smile dropped. "Oh dear," she said. "Was there more trouble yesterday?"

Mrs. Knox's face pinched. "Several kinds, I'm afraid. No fewer than half a dozen gentlemen showed up inquiring after you," she said, clearly distressed about it. "And the police came around with their own inquiries as well. And...and...."

Something was most definitely wrong.

"What is it, Mrs. Knox." Alice stepped closer to her, lowering her voice. "You can tell me. In fact, perhaps I could start by suggesting what might have happened. Was Mr. Montrose involved?"

Mrs. Knox breathed out as though she might burst into tears. "He said he would buy up my mortgage and bankrupt me if I didn't evict you by the end of the week," she whispered, as though Montrose were hiding behind the curtains and might pounce if he heard her. "And that he will have me arrested for running a bawdy house as well."

"Mr. Montrose has a grudge against me," Alice said plainly. "He is a villain for involving so many of my friends. I will not let him ruin one more soul."

"He said that I should encourage you to sell him your diamond mine, as he asked of you," Mrs. Knox went on in a whisper.

So that was it, then. Irrefutable, tangible proof that Montrose wanted the mine shares. Even though they were worthless.

Which, of course, meant they weren't worthless.

Alice rested a hand on Mrs. Knox's shoulder. "Do not worry yourself, Mrs. Knox. My husband and I are on the verge of discovering what is truly happening here, and we are very close to eliminating all problems."

It was a blatant lie, of course, but one that would put Mrs. Knox at ease.

"All the same, madam," Mrs. Knox said, wringing her hands in front of her. "Would you mind if I started having some of my boys remove the furnishings from the other flat so that it at least looks as though I've done what has been asked of me?"

A pang filled Alice's heart, but she knew it was a necessary action. "Of course, Mrs. Knox. Do what you must."

Mrs. Knox thanked Alice and said her goodbyes. Alice hoped that would be the only major turmoil of the day, but as she moved to the table to sit while Harriett brought her tea, she opened Maeve's letter and found another bout of trouble waiting for her.

"*Dearest Alice*," the letter began. "*I would have called yesterday, but I knew you and Sam were out of London. Avery has made the decision that now is not the best time for us to be in London. The situation with Montrose has begun to seep in his direction, and he wishes to avoid it entirely by returning to Ireland. We've been meaning to go back for some time, and Avery has decided that the time is now.*

"*We would both very much like for you to come with us, of course*," the letter went on. "*I, for one, believe you would be much safer in Ireland at present. As far as Avery has been able to determine, Montrose has no influence there, and you would be safe from his meddling at home. Sam is, of course, welcome to come as well, but I urge you to depart with us. We will be leaving first thing on Friday morning. I understand that gives you hardly any time at all to prepare, but please, my friend, leave London and this chapter of your life behind and come home.*"

Alice let out a heavy breath as she finished the letter and dropped it to the table. Friday morning was only two days away. True to what Maeve had written, it was barely any time at all.

"What is that you have there?" Sam asked, coming out of the bedroom, fully dressed, washed, and groomed.

Alice gathered up the letter and stuffed it back into the envelope before Sam could catch a glimpse of Maeve's plans. She smiled and said, "Just a letter from Maeve, inquiring how things went yesterday."

Sam closed the distance between them and bent down to

capture Alice's lips in a kiss. "I would say things went well," he said with an amorous purr.

Alice smiled in return, but despite the glorious pleasure they'd shared the night before, there were still a thousand, deep concerns that held her back from giving in and putting all of her trust in Sam.

"Was that all?" Sam asked, sitting across the table from her as Harriett brought him a cup of tea, and a plate of scones for the table as well. "I thought I heard voices while I was dressing."

Alice hesitated, then said, "Mrs. Knox came by to reiterate her desire that I move out as soon as possible." She felt a visceral need to withhold the rest of the conversation from Sam. There was no point in worrying him more than he was already worried.

"Not a problem," Sam said, smiling as he sipped his tea. "I'll have you moved into our Mayfair house as soon as possible. In fact, we should head there right away to go over the room arrangements and figure out the best place for Ryan, and for Harriett."

"Me, sir?" Harriett asked as she headed across the room to Ryan's door.

"Of course, Harriett," Sam called to her. "I expect that you'll be a regular member of our household now."

Harriett's whole face lit up. "I would love a live-in arrangement, sir," she said, stars in her eyes. "Especially in a grand house." She paused, then sent Alice a guilty look and went on with, "Not that I haven't been perfectly happy with the arrangement we have, Mrs. Rathborne-Paxton."

Alice sent her a kind smile. "I have always wished I could employ you more fully, Harriett."

She would have to leave it at that, as there were sounds from the other side of Ryan's door indicating he was awake. In truth, everything seemed to be moving too fast for Alice, and at a time when she wasn't entirely certain what her future held to begin with.

"I've given your mischievous plan some thought," Sam said as the two of them continued with breakfast. "I believe we have enough old clothes in storage at home that both of us could dress up quite convincingly as servants. I also believe we would be able to disguise you as a boy." He winked as he spoke. "And if we are careful, it should be the easiest thing in the world to sneak into Harvey's through the kitchens late at night. Perhaps we could even pretend to be making a delivery."

Sam continued to spin out ideas of all the ways they could avoid other servants in the club, how they could navigate the hallways to locate Montrose's office, even though neither of them had ever stepped foot in the building before, and how they could search the office once they found it to discover the information they needed.

The more animated Sam grew, the warier Alice felt. The plan was ludicrous. There was no way at all they could slip in and out of a highly-guarded club and the private office of a member—an office that could have been anywhere within the club, that could even have been locked—without disaster befalling them.

At the same time, there was something warm and wonderful about watching Sam spin the plan, especially when Ryan came out to join them at the table for breakfast. Ryan thought Sam was discussing some sort of game and came up with his own, childish suggestions. He made Sam laugh, and Sam made Ryan laugh in return. It was all a beautiful dream again.

But dreams ended. Maeve and Avery, her staunchest supporters and perhaps her only true friends, were returning to Ireland. Mrs. Knox's livelihood and life were in danger now because of her. Sam had more danger hanging over him than he knew, as did his brothers. Raiding the club was ridiculous and dangerous, and the whole thing might very well end in disaster, but it was the only thing Alice could think of that represented a drastic enough response to everything Montrose had put them through. She could only hope that they'd be able to find what they needed in the bastard's office and that they could escape from the club without even more disaster raining down on them.

Chapter Eighteen

There were times when Sam became convinced that optimism and a penchant for mad risks were his best friends. He never would have befriended and seduced Alice—if it could even be called seduction when she'd been so willing—if he hadn't been completely convinced that things would work out between the two of them. He never would have taken her up on her suggestion of marriage if he hadn't been a little bit mad. And he never would have found himself creeping through the mews behind Harvey's club after midnight, dressed in the livery his family's servants wore, attempting to break into the club.

"Are you certain the door will even be open?" Alice whispered in the darkness, clutching his arm as the two of them inched closer to the club's kitchen door. Alice, too, was dressed in male livery, her thick, ginger hair braided tightly around her head and concealed with a cap. She made quite an impressive, but utterly unconvincing, boy.

"Institutions such as this sometimes receive deliveries at night," Sam whispered back to her, his eyes trained on the closed kitchen door. "And even if they don't, members of staff will still be up, cleaning the place and tossing out rubbish, now that the members are all at home in their beds."

Alice made a sound that might have been approval, but might have been doubt. Sam reached back for her hand, and when she slipped hers into his, he gave hers a reassuring squeeze.

Things weren't entirely where he wanted them to be between the two of them, even though they'd spent a peaceful day together and a glorious evening the night before. Sam wasn't green enough to believe that just because Alice had been willing to give her body to him, it didn't mean her heart was unfettered or that her worries had been alleviated. In the morning, she'd been more withdrawn than he'd expected her to be, and that guardedness had continued throughout the day. Especially when they'd gone to his family's house to search for disguises for the night's mission.

His father had been horrible to her the moment he saw her, of course. He'd railed against Alice, Sam, and their marriage, then gone out to visit whatever friends the black-guard had left. Francis and Dean had been far kinder to her, and Joseph probably would have been too, if he, too, hadn't been away on some visit or errand. But the entire time that Sam had plotted with Francis and Dean and solidified their plans for the nighttime raid, Alice had remained withdrawn.

She didn't fully trust him. That was all there was to it. Their current mission felt like a last resort to prove to her that he had never intended her any harm, and that he would give everything he had to make things right between them and the world again.

"Look," he hissed suddenly when the kitchen door cracked open, revealing a sliver of golden light in the darkness.

The door opened all the way as a portly man in a stained and wrinkled cook's uniform elbowed it and carried a large pot out into the cobblestones behind the club. He walked it to the far end of the space and dumped it onto what looked like some sort of midden bin, then headed back into the house, snorting and wiping his nose on his sleeve. After the cook shut the door behind him, Sam waited to hear the sound of a lock clicking, but he heard nothing.

"We should be able to get in," he whispered, pulling Alice forward. "I don't think the door is locked."

"It might not be," Alice said with a trace of alarm in her voice, "but what if that cook is just on the other side of the door?"

"We'll check to be sure," Sam said.

He slowed his steps as they reached the door, then let go of Alice's hand to crack the door just enough to peer inside. He was met with the sight of a long, dim hallway. There were lights on still in the kitchen off to the left, but the rooms on the right were shadowy and empty.

"We can get in as long as we speed silently past the kitchen entrance," he whispered to Alice. "Pray that no one is looking in this direction."

"Sam, no, this is far too dangerous to—"

Sam silenced Alice's second thoughts about the whole adventure by pulling the door open wide enough for the two of them to slip inside and dragging her along with him as he entered the club. She was forced to stay silent out of necessity as he hurried her along the hallway, dashing past the kitchen door. He barely had time to peer inside to see how many people were still there and whether they might be suspicious that they'd just been invaded.

They made it past the kitchen and to a staircase at the end of the hall without incident. As much as Sam wanted to shout in victory and tell Alice that everything would be just fine from that point on, it was imperative that they remain completely silent. Still holding Alice's hand, they crept up the stairs, trying hard not to make the old things creak.

At the top of the stairs, they found themselves in another long, dark hallway.

"This must be the main part of the club," Sam whispered, squinting in the darkness. The walls were paneled with rich wood and hung with fine paintings of pastoral scenes and hunting dogs. The marble floor was covered with a long, narrow carpet. It would be perfect for muffling their footsteps as they searched for Montrose's private office.

But therein lay their bigger problem.

"Where is Montrose's office located?" Sam asked, still whispering, even though they were alone and the paneled walls absorbed sound.

Alice straightened from her protective hunch and glanced around. "I haven't the foggiest idea," she said, disappointment in her voice. "Not on this floor, I would assume. These appear to be parlors for meeting guests and whatnot."

"Agreed," Sam said, walking on through the darkness. "So our first order of business is finding a staircase to take us—ah! There it is."

Part of Sam felt ridiculous for bumbling around a darkened gentleman's club after midnight, no idea where he was going. There were very few sources of light in the hallways, particularly upstairs, though a few windows at the end of the upstairs hallway and an occasional fireplace with glowing embers gave them just enough light that they were not literally wandering blind and in danger of bumping into things. The club wasn't particularly large, so it wasn't as though they had three dozen rooms to search through in order to find Montrose's, but there were at least a dozen rooms that needed investigating.

"Where do you think Montrose—" Alice started, but was immediately cut off when the glow of a lantern shone from one of the rooms several paces ahead of them.

Sam grabbed Alice's arm and dashed through the nearest

door with her, sending up a quick prayer of thanks that the door opened in the first place. He shut the door behind them as quietly as he could, then sank to a crouch so that he could peek through the keyhole into the hall.

A moment later, he had a brief, obstructed view of a young man in work clothes carrying a lantern in one hand and a bucket with cleaning cloths and brushes in another walking past. Judging by the sound of things, the man entered one of the other rooms, likely to clean it.

Sam waited until he heard the sound of a door opening and closing before standing and glancing to Alice. To his surprise, she'd moved away from him toward a desk at the far end of the room, near a moonlit window.

"Don't tell me we hit a streak of luck on our first attempt and found Montrose's office," he whispered.

Alice shook her head as she searched a few of the papers on top of the desk. "No, none of this is Montrose's. But it is an office," she said. When she glanced up at him, her pale face rimmed in blue-white light from the window, she smiled. "Do you suppose this club specializes in providing its members with offices?"

Sam shrugged. "Could be. Although that would mean every room on this floor is an office that might or might not be Montrose's."

"We'll simply have to check," Alice said, stepping away from the desk and heading toward him.

"There's the cleaner to consider," Sam pointed out as he put his hand on the doorhandle, ready to venture out into the hall again.

Alice bit her lip in an enticing gesture of thought, then said, "Do you remember which room he came out of? We can start by searching the ones he's already cleaned."

"One can only hope he began at the far end of the hall and is working his way toward the stairs," Sam said. If the lad had some other, topsy-turvy system that saw him flitting from one random room to another, they'd be in trouble. "With any luck, he spends quite a bit of time in each room."

Alice nodded, looking wary. Sam took a deep breath, then eased open the door so that they could sneak out into the hallway again.

Knowing someone else was on the same hallway as them made the whole, mad endeavor hair-raising. As soon as they were in the hall with the door shut, they sped as quietly as they could to the room Sam had seen the cleaner come out of. Only, that room turned out to be another parlor of some sort and not an office at all. Disappointed that the mission was not turning out to be quick and simple, they slipped across the hall and tried the door opposite the parlor.

To Sam's great distress, that door was locked. His heart began to thump against his ribs in earnest as Alice spoke exactly what he was thinking in a whisper. "What if Montrose's office is locked?"

Sam shrugged and shook his head. He didn't know what they would do. There wasn't time to think about it either, as the door to the room the cleaning lad had entered a few moments before swung open and the light of his lantern shone into the hallway. Sam grabbed Alice's wrist again and dashed back into the parlor they'd just come out of to avoid being caught.

The cleaning lad did not make an appearance where Sam could spot him before entering another room. Worse still, there was no sound of a door opening and shutting. At first, Sam hoped the lad had finished his duties and gone downstairs, but when he and Alice poked their heads into the hall, they discovered that the young man had left the door to the room he was cleaning open. His lamplight shone into the hall, and if Sam wasn't mistaken, he could hear the lad humming a popular tune.

There was nothing for it but to hurry on to try the next door. That one led to an office, but in short order they determined that it wasn't Montrose's. The door across the hall from that one wasn't Montrose's office either. They were forced to move down the hall in a way that brought them closer to the cleaning lad and discovery.

The next office they tried wasn't Montrose's either, and after that, they came across another locked door. The next set of rooms was closer still to where the cleaning lad was working. Every angel in heaven must have been working at double intensity to bring him and Alice the miracle of not being discovered as they tried more door handles and crept into more rooms. It seemed utterly implausible that they wouldn't be caught and dragged off to prison for breaking and entering within a few seconds.

"This is it!" Alice gasped suddenly, shaking Sam from his thoughts of impending doom, as they slipped into the office directly adjacent to the room the cleaning lad was working in. Even though Sam had shut the door behind him when they entered the room, he was acutely aware of how close they were to discovery. But Alice's further whisper of, "These are Montrose's papers. They have his name all over them," as she pored over the large desk at the far end of the room filled Sam with an awkward relief.

"Are you certain?" he asked, rushing to join her.

"As much as I can be," Alice said, lifting a paper from the desk and taking it to the moonlit window to squint at it. "Yes," she went on. "This letter is addressed to Montrose from some sort of solicitor."

"What does it say?" Sam joined Alice by the window, pressing closer to her—so close that he could breathe in the scent of her and feel warmth radiating from her. It was the most inconvenient time imaginable for him to hum with desire for his bride, but he supposed that there would never be a time when being close to Alice didn't result in him wanting her.

"It has to do with some other poor soul that Montrose is vexing, apparently," Alice said as she skimmed the letter. "Someone who is nearly bankrupt. The solicitor is urging Montrose to pay off about three different sorts of debt for—hang on." Alice stopped and blinked at the letter, holding it almost all the way to her nose. She squinted harder, then sighed and pulled the letter away from her face. "I need a lantern. It's too hard to read in the dark."

Sam peeled away from her and set about searching the room. There were lamps aplenty, but finding a box of matches took a little more searching. It should have been on the mantel of the fireplace, where any ordinary person would keep their matches, but the mantle was lined with porcelain figures or small brass sculptures—bits of stuff and nonsense, as his mother liked to call them.

He did a double-take when he recognized a particular porcelain shepherdess. It belonged to him, or to his family, at least. Sam would have known it anywhere. It had graced the mantel of their private, family parlor for as long as he could remember. He picked it up and turned it over, studying its details to be certain, then put it back.

"That bastard," he hissed.

"What is it?" Alice asked from the desk.

"This statuette belongs to us." He glanced at the busy row of ornaments across the mantel. "Dammit, but I think this is Montrose's trophy case."

"His what?" Alice asked, stepping away from the desk to join him. She happened to find a box of matches on a small table she passed as she came, and before joining Sam, she lit the lamp on the same table.

Immediately, the room was illuminated. It wasn't as bright as day or as it would have been if more lamps were lit, but with

Sam's eyes used to darkness, it seemed very bright indeed. Which made it easier to see the dozen or so statuettes, clocks, vases, and other sundries on the mantel. He was particularly struck by something that looked like a golden statue of an Indian goddess, the sort with several dozen arms, and a music box with a ballerina in some sort of silk tutu posed on top. There was even a taxidermized frog with a sword and cavalier's hat that looked quite dashing. They were only some of Montrose's prizes.

"I think the bastard must take something from everyone he's interfered with," Sam said as Alice joined him by the cold fireplace. "All of these things must be items he gloats over every time he comes in here. Proof of his victory over people he despises."

Alice hummed low in her throat. The sound was downright menacing. "It's even more proof that we've found the room we were looking for."

That gentle reminder brought Sam back to their mission. "And what, precisely, are we looking for in this room?" he asked.

Alice turned a half-circle, surveying the contents of the room. There wasn't as much in it as Sam would have thought. The bookshelves weren't full, and the desk was neatly organized. The only clutter in the room were the trophies atop the mantel.

"I'm not precisely certain what we need to find," she said, heading back to the desk with the lamp. "Something that would indicate why he has targeted me. Why he's targeted you and your family as well. And something that might help us figure out how to turn him away to some other pursuit."

"I don't think you're going to find that sort of thing easily," Sam said, following her to the desk.

Of course, the moment he reached the desk, he spotted a miniature photographic portrait, about the size of the palm of his hand, and picked it up to take a look. The photograph was of a young man, perhaps a bit younger than Sam himself, who looked eerily familiar. Familiar, and yet Sam didn't have the first idea who the man was. The name "Petrus" was etched into the frame at the bottom of the portrait.

"Do you supposed Montrose has a love child he hasn't told anyone about?" Sam asked.

When he set the portrait back on the desk, he found Alice reading the letter she'd been trying to make out before. "I doubt it," she said distractedly. "He made it quite clear to me that he isn't interested in—" Her following gasp was so loud and so sudden that it made the hair on the back of Sam's neck stand up. "This is it," she blurted, snapping her shining eyes up to him and smiling. "This is it, Sam, this is the answer."

"What is?" Sam raced around the edge of the desk to see what Alice had seen.

In the process, his thigh brushed up against a pile of newspaper clippings and loose papers, sending the lot spilling to the carpet.

"Dammit," he hissed, crouching to gather the papers up.

"Sam," Alice scolded, putting the letter down and joining him in picking up the mess. "Do be careful."

"I thought I was being careful," Sam said.

There was no way to know what order the papers and newspaper bits had been in, so he could only just stack them in whatever way he grabbed them. He started doing so without looking, then stopped when he saw that one of the clippings was printed in a language he'd never seen before.

"What language do you suppose this is?" he asked, showing the newspaper to Alice.

For a moment, Alice looked at him in irritation, as though they didn't have time for nonsense. But then her expression popped to surprise, and she answered, "It's Afrikaans."

"Is it?" Sam glanced down at some of the clippings he'd gathered, wondering if there would be more in that language.

Instead, he found himself in possession of several articles from South African newspapers. All of them were about the discovery of gold in places with unusual names that he'd never heard of. They were enough to make him raise his eyebrows. Apparently, quite a bit of gold had just been discovered in the central part of South Africa. Which explained why Her Majesty and the government were so determined to wrestle the area away from the Afrikaners and other non-English encroachers in the territory.

"Look at this one," Alice said, standing once they'd gathered all the papers from the floor and put them back on the desk. "It's about investments in American steel mills."

"All of these appear to be about investments of some sort or another," Sam said, disappointment spreading through him. "Montrose is an investor, after all. None of this is unusual."

"But it is," Alice said, her eyes alight again. She reached for the letter she'd been reading earlier. "This letter from Montrose's solicitor isn't about the debt owed by whichever nobleman that bastard has his eyes set on now, it's about Montrose's own debt."

Sam started. "I beg your pardon?"

"Montrose's debt," Alice said.

"But Montrose is as rich as Croesus. That's why he's able to crush men like my father under his heel."

Alice shook her head, showing him the letter. "Montrose has speculated every step of the way in order to crush his opponents. In fact, according to this letter, his financial situation is as precarious as could be. He only pretends to be wealthy so that he can get back at his enemies."

"Impossible," Sam said, his doubt turning to incredulity, and that emotion turning to rage. "The bastard cannot have bluffed his way into destroying everyone whose life he has ruined. He cannot have faked his way into grinding my father and my family under the heel of his boot by leaving us penniless and desperate."

"But he did," Alice said. She moved to rifle through the other papers on the desk. "He bought up your father's debt, did he not? And your father doesn't have the means to pay for his gambling and other losses. But neither does Montrose. He's done the whole thing on speculation."

"Which means he needs some source of income in order to keep himself from sinking under along with my father and the other noblemen he's ruined," Sam said. He glanced to the pile of papers he and Alice had messily returned to the desk. Clippings about investments abroad, about South Africa.

Montrose truly was after Alice for her investments. He needed her money to keep afloat. But what did a failed diamond mine have to do with all the articles about gold being discovered in South Africa?

Unless—

His thoughts were cut short before he could do more than open his mouth to express them to Alice as the door to the office flew open. The cleaning lad was suddenly revealed, bucket of supplies and all, gaping at Sam and Alice in shock. Alice yelped in return at being discovered, and for a moment, the three of them stood where they were, staring at each other.

"Intruders!" the cleaning lad shouted, recovering first. "What are you lot doing here?"

"We're...we're new hires," Alice said, dashing out from behind the desk and approaching the cleaning lad with far more boldness than Sam ever could have mustered. "We're new staff, and we have no idea what we're doing."

"Like hell you are," the lad said, pinching his face in offense that Alice would lie to him. "You're a bird, for one."

"And I do believe it's time for this bird to fly," Sam said, striding up to Alice and taking her hand. The only thing he could think to do was to use his class and manners to intimidate the cleaner. He stood straight and squared his shoulders, as if addressing a duke, touched the brim of his cap, and said, "Good day, sir," before marching straight out of the room with Alice.

He was able to stun the lad long enough for him and Alice to make it to the hall. That was all the head start they got, though.

"Hang on a moment," the cleaner called after him. "You're robbers, you are."

"Run," Sam hissed to Alice, taking her hand and doing just that.

They dashed down the hall to the stairs, then tore down to the first floor, then along that hallway to the stairs that would take them down to the ground floor and the kitchen hallway. Silence and subterfuge were of no use to them now, so Sam simply ran, impressed that Alice could keep up with him.

He was so certain they would be able to dash right out the kitchen door into the chilly night when the exhausted-looking cook poked his head out of the doorway to the kitchen to see what the clatter was.

"Jimmy, are you—" he started before spotting Sam and Alice. His eyes went wide, and he shouted, "Oy! Who are you?" Worse still, he stepped into the hallway, blocking Sam and Alice's path.

"Get out of my way!" Sam shouted, attempting to push the massive man aside. The cook was like a rock, though. He wasn't going anywhere.

Panic poked at the edges of Sam's thoughts until Alice shouted, "Fire!" with all the fear and bombast of an actress performing a dramatic role. "There's a fire upstairs! We have to get out as quickly as possible!"

There was no telling whether the cook believed her or not,

but Alice's warning was enough to make the man let down his guard and shift slightly to the side, craning his neck to look toward the stairs. It was just enough of a slip to allow Sam and Alice to run past him and on toward the kitchen door.

"Hey! Stop them!" the cleaning lad's voice echoed in the hallway behind them just as Sam shoved the door open and pulled Alice out into the cool darkness of the yard behind the building.

Confidence filled Sam as soon as they were outside. The cook and the cleaning lad ran after them, but he and Alice had enough of a lead on them—and Alice was a surprisingly fast runner—that they were able to make it through the cluttered areas in back of the buildings, to the mews, and out to the street before either of their pursuers could catch up with them.

Once they were on the street, they continued to hurry, but without running so that they didn't raise the suspicions of the policeman patrolling the street nearby. Neither the cook nor the cleaning lad followed them.

"That was terrifying," Alice gasped, catching her breath, once they had rounded a corner and could walk more slowly.

"Terrifying, yes," Sam agreed, also winded. "But we discovered exactly what we needed to."

"We did." Alice paused, turning to him, her eyes bright with victory in the moonlight. "Montrose's weak point is the same as everyone else's. He doesn't have any money."

"And if we're lucky," Sam added, "we can use that to bring him down."

"Or at least to get him to leave us alone," she said, sagging a bit. A strange sort of realization seemed to dawn on her, as if her mind had whispered to her that Montrose would never leave her alone now because he couldn't afford to.

Sam's heart went out to Alice. He couldn't blame her for wanting nothing but peace after what Montrose had put her through. He was more determined than ever to bring her that peace, especially considering what they knew now. A plan to defeat Montrose felt as though it were right at the end of his fingertips.

"Come along, my love," he said, bending close to kiss Alice's parted, panting lips. "Let's go home and consult with my brothers about the best way to bring this ugly chapter of our lives to an end."

Chapter Nineteen

Alice had never been so glad to creep into the house of a man who hated her, exhausted from daring actions that could have seen her arrested, as she was to slip in through the kitchen door of the Rathborne-Paxton house. A nighttime calm had settled over Lord Vegas's house, but the entire place still had an air of upset and energy to it that kept Alice from falling asleep completely as Sam took her up to the private parlor he shared with his brothers.

"Stay right here and I'll fetch the others so we can tell them what we've discovered," Sam told her as he settled her into one of the room's sofas.

Alice barely had time to nod at Sam before he dashed out of the room with as much energy as if it were midday and he was about to run a race. Once he was gone, her shoulders slumped and every one of the aches and pains in her body from running and creeping and tension flared to her attention. She reached a hand around to rub her shoulder, but the motion brought little relief.

Discovering the secret to Montrose's ruthlessness brought

her no relief either. As they'd hurried through Mayfair in the dark, her initial excitement at uncovering the truth had slowly been replaced by the unsettling realization that Montrose's precarious financial state made it even less likely that he would call off his proverbial dogs and leave her or Sam and his family alone. Yes, they had discovered the man's weak point, but what good would that do? Montrose was as desperate as anyone else, and Alice was certain he would continue to come after her until she capitulated and sold him whichever of her investments he wanted.

Though, she still didn't understand entirely why Montrose thought those investments were worth anything. The newspaper articles that Sam had found from South Africa about the potential gold strike were fascinating, but the news had nothing to do with her shares in a defunct diamond mine. Diamonds and gold might look beautiful together when made into jewelry, but they didn't grow together in the earth, did they?

But what if they did? Montrose must have thought so, she concluded as she pushed herself up from the sofa to see if the Rathborne-Paxton brothers kept anything that might wet her throat and give her courage to face the rest of the night in the parlor. Fortunately, there was a small table with a variety of decanters in one corner. She helped herself to a modest glass of brandy and frowned as she tried to decipher what Montrose must be thinking. She doubted the man had ever traveled to South Africa himself, which meant he was merely speculating if he thought there was some sort of connection between the diamond mine and the newly struck gold. And if Montrose was merely guessing—but still confident enough to make her life miserable and turn her into the most scarlet of scarlet women in the press—then perhaps the bastard wasn't as intelligent as everyone believed him to be.

Nothing was more dangerous than an idiot who was clever

enough to make people think he was smart. Particularly an idiot with a grudge.

"...means that we have the ability to thwart him," the deep sound of Francis's voice sounded from the hallway.

Alice panicked for half a second, wondering if Sam's brothers would judge her harshly for helping herself to a drink in the middle of the night. She decided they wouldn't—they were all shamelessly on first-name bases, after all, thanks to the nature of her previous relationship with Sam—and she didn't have time to hide her tipple anyhow.

"We've proof that Montrose isn't what he seems, and we can exploit that," Francis finished his thought as he and Sam turned the corner and entered the room. Dean and Joseph walked in a step behind them.

Sam's three brothers were all in their nightshirts, wearing robes and slippers. Joseph's hair was a mess, and he looked as though he'd been woken from a sound sleep.

"So Montrose is teetering on the edge of financial ruin," Dean argued, raising a hand to greet Alice, even though he was deeply engaged in whatever conversation the brothers had already started to have. "That simply means he's in the same boat as half of London, the same boat we're all in."

"It means Montrose is in no position to undertake half the things he's undertaken," Sam argued with energy. "In attempting to ruin us, he has come close to ruining himself."

"I still don't see how that necessarily opens the door to our side doing away with him for good," Dean argued.

"It's a start," Francis said, his brow knit into a frown. "We know that we can outmaneuver him. We know that his resources for destruction only extend so far." He turned to Sam. "Did you happen to see who his creditors were specifically?"

Sam shrugged and turned to Alice. "Alice was the one who discovered most of the important information."

All eyes in the room suddenly turned to Alice. With the half-finished glass of brandy still in her hand, dressed as a boy the way she was, utterly worn out and filled with anxiety and doubt as to whether anything could actually be done, she was caught off guard.

"I...I did see the name of the solicitor who wrote the letter informing Montrose of his debts," she stammered. "Morgan something? Moriarty? Or, no, perhaps that was Montrose and the solicitor's name was something different." She frowned hard, forcing her exhausted brain to remember. "Sanderson?"

Francis let out a breath of disappointment and turned away from her. "There are likely hundreds of solicitors in London," he said. "And we can only speculate about what sort of assets and debts Montrose has acquired from the men he's ruined. We don't even have a full list of men he's destroyed."

When Francis turned away from her, the other brothers dismissed her as well. Even Sam. They mulled around the other end of the room, rubbing their stubbly chins and pressing their fingertips to their temples as they racked their brains, trying to come up with other noblemen who had been wronged. They'd listened to Alice for all of half a minute, then dismissed her as though she were useless. She was the one who had discovered they were in Montrose's office, though. She was the one who had scanned the papers on Montrose's desk with a keen eye while Sam had knocked everything to the floor. Francis had made one inquiry that she'd stumbled over because of exhaustion, and all four brothers had dismissed her out of hand as useless.

It stung, despite her attempt to tell herself everyone was rattled and no one was thinking clearly. It hurt because her whole life, men had discarded her once she'd fulfilled her use to them. And it was clear as day what use men thought she had. They'd never flocked to her because of her wit or her intellect or her ability to solve complex problems. Men had only ever wanted her for one thing.

The bitter ache in Alice's heart was not made any better when Francis said, "Our current plan is a solid one, then. The three of us will continue our pursuit of wealthy, if disreputable, brides. That way, we will have the financial power to go after Montrose and defeat him for good. It is only a shame that your choice of bride will be of no use in this endeavor, Sam."

Alice didn't know why, but Francis's words cut right to her core. He didn't even glance in her direction as he more or less branded her as a waste of time and effort. She had always liked Francis, liked all of Sam's brothers, but an insult like that could not be borne. She'd done more to help the brothers in their plans for retribution against Montrose than anyone, and yet they thought of her as a liability and a failure.

Men rarely changed their minds, particularly when it came to the opinions they formed about the women in their worlds. Alice knew that if she stayed where she was, her life would be nothing but disappointment and being shunted to the side. If she was lucky, the gentlemen who had accosted her for the last few days since her wedding would realize she wasn't on the market and leave her alone. But if they didn't, if she stayed in London, she would be harassed by lascivious arses every time she stepped outside, and she would be pushed aside as a failure if she stayed in.

Perhaps it was the late hour. Perhaps it was the effects of the brandy that she was beginning to feel. Perhaps it was the cumulation of anxiety and misery of the last few days. Alice couldn't bear it anymore. There was a solution in front of her, a solution offered by the one person who had always stayed by her side, through thick and thin, since they were girls. It was a solution she was going to take.

"I'm going back to Ireland," she said, setting her half-finished glass of brandy down and starting toward the parlor doorway without looking at anyone. "Goodbye."

"Alice, wait." Sam peeled away from his brothers and leapt after her. He caught her arm as she neared the doorway and held her to her place. "What do you mean, you're going back to Ireland?"

Alice shook herself free of his grasp. "I mean exactly that. Maeve and Avery are returning to Ireland, and they've invited me to go with them. They're leaving this morning, and I've decided to join them."

She took another step to the doorway, but Sam stopped her with, "Just like that? Without any warning or reason?"

Alice spun to face him, incredulous. "Without reason?" she snapped. "I have every reason imaginable. My life in London has been reduced to rubble."

"But we're on the verge of defeating Montrose," Sam argued.

Alice gaped at him. "Montrose isn't the only one who has destroyed my life." She sent a glance past Sam to his brothers. "You've all just dismissed me as useless while barely acknowledging me. You gave me hardly any time at all to recall the information I saw on Montrose's desk. I know how the minds of men work. None of you will ever give me the slightest bit of credit again. You've all decided already that I am a failure in your grand plan to marry money and use it as a weapon against your enemy. I am of no use to you, or so you have determined, and I will not stay where I will only ever be treated as an embarrassment and a failure."

She turned back to Sam. "I might not have much of a life waiting for me in Ireland, but what life I could have is a damn sight better than constantly living in the shadow of my past, fearful of going out, lest I be accosted by some arrogant gentleman who thinks I'll part my legs for him. How long until one of those men fails to take no for an answer? And from the sound of things, I will not be supported in any way by the family I've foolishly married into." She glanced to Sam's brothers again. "You are all just as bad as your father, whether you want to hear that or not. I'm going home now."

Alice turned and marched for the door, ignoring Sam's impassioned call of, "Alice, please wait," as she went. She thought she heard Sam take a step after her, but something or someone stopped him. It was all for the best, really. She'd come to London to try to make a new life for herself on her own, and she'd made every mistake that it was possible to make. The time had come to admit she was a failure and to return to her lowly, Irish home to live out the rest of her days in seclusion with her son.

Sam stood gaping at the parlor door, frozen with shock that Alice would walk out on him the way she had. No, he was not so concerned for himself or the feeling of panic and loss that welled within him. He was completely taken aback by the raw statements of painful fact that Alice had laid out for him before leaving.

His beloved's life truly had been ruined, and all because of mistakes that he had made. He could blame Montrose for attacking her as a way to hurt him and his family, and as a way to shore up his own fortunes. He could blame Francis for dismissing Alice the way he had just moments ago. He could blame his father for creating the mess in the first place. But the truth of the matter was that he had failed to protect the woman he loved when she was at her most vulnerable. Worse still, he wasn't certain that he could protect her the way she truly needed to be protected. Only Lady Carnlough could do that by whisking Alice away to Ireland.

"Sam," Francis said behind him, barely budging Sam out of his guilt-ridden thoughts. "Sam, pay attention."

Something about the coldness in his brother's voice sent a spike of fury through Sam. He whipped to face Francis, Dean, and Joseph, his emotions near the brink.

Francis evidently didn't see just how angry Sam was. "We need to concentrate on how we are going to use this new information to attack Montrose."

"Is that all you care about?" Sam demanded, taking a few steps toward his brothers. "You care about revenge and getting back at Montrose?"

All three brothers seemed startled by the vehemence of Sam's outburst.

"That is what we must necessarily care about," Francis said. "Montrose is the sort of enemy that will continue to fire and fire until we are all dead unless we can neutralize him first."

"Once Montrose is taken care of, everything else will fall into place," Dean argued as well.

"At what cost?" Sam asked, barely able to stand still and continue with the conversation. "What sort of a war have we gotten ourselves into, and what will the casualties of this war be if we are not careful?"

"We didn't start the war," Joseph grumbled, looking more miserable than angry over the whole thing.

"Montrose is the single, defining factor in this carnage," Francis said. "Unless and until we find a way to rob him of his ability to continue his attacks against noble families, against our family, more people will fall under his ax and more lives will be ruined."

"And what of Alice's life?" Sam demanded, taking a step closer to Francis. "Her life is already ruined, and it is all our fault. She lived a perfectly happy and content life, albeit not one that most of society would have accepted, until you hatched your mad scheme to marry unsuitable brides with money as a way to revenge ourselves on Father."

"Are you blaming me for giving you the courage to marry the woman you love?" Francis barked, eyes wide with incredulity. "Do you want me to beg your forgiveness for handing you the courage to defy social convention so that Alice could be yours for all time?"

Sam flinched, rocking back. "I love Alice, yes," he said. "I would gladly spend the rest of my life doing everything I can to make amends for the last few days. I would have stayed with her one way or another until our dying days, with or without your mad marriage scheme."

"But now you can be with her legally and above board," Dean pointed out, less confrontational than Francis. "And to be honest, the idea of marrying whom we wish to marry because they have money instead of attaching ourselves to heiresses that society deems fit, but with whom we would be miserable, isn't the horrific scheme you suddenly seem to think it is."

Sam clenched his jaw to stop himself from hurling some sort of unkind reply at his brother. He'd suspected for a while that Dean actually had a woman in mind to fulfill Francis's mad scheme, but he hadn't approached her or revealed her identity to the rest of them yet. He wondered if Dean was in love with that woman or if she was someone like Lady Heloise.

Whatever the case, before he could say a word about it, Francis let out a tight breath and rubbed a hand over his face. "I feel as though I've stuffed this whole thing up," he sighed.

That minute sign of contrition from his older brother threw Sam off-balance. He was more than prepared simply to be enraged at his brother. "You have offended my bride," he said in a cautious voice, "and therefore you have offended me. Alice is more than just a pawn in whatever game you're playing against Montrose."

"I know, of course," Francis said, spreading his arms to his sides in a shrug of defeat. "It is just that Montrose has spread his evil so effectively across everything that he touches that it's infected all of us as well. I had no intention to offend Alice. You know that I think very highly of her. But the truth of the matter remains. If any of us are going to find a moment of peace in the future, we have to defeat Montrose utterly and thoroughly. And as Alice so deftly discovered for us, the means of doing that might well be through money."

"Money is the root of all our problems," Joseph grumbled as he moved to flop into one of the room's chairs. "Money is the root of all evil. It's how Montrose crushed Father, and it's how he will end up crushing all of us, if we're not careful."

No one said it aloud, but Sam could hear the echo of Francis's plan and the idea that if the rest of them married wealthy women, they might still have a chance of winning the war.

"The rest of you can plot and plan and marry whomever you want," he said, starting toward the door. "I have only a few hours before the woman I love more than life itself flees England for Ireland. I refuse to let her go without a fight. So if you will excuse me, I need an hour or so of sleep, a good wash, a change of clothes, and then I intend to fight like mad to keep my bride from leaving me for good."

And if anyone or anything tried to get in his way, he would crush them in his path.

Chapter Twenty

lice didn't want to think about the danger she had likely put herself into as she made her way back to Marylebone along nearly empty streets in the small hours of the morning. Perhaps the fact that she was dressed as a boy and kept her head down helped her to make it home unscathed, or perhaps no one had the energy to accost her as the hours crept on toward dawn. She didn't have the energy for much herself, and when she finally did make it back to her flat at Mrs. Knox's, she peeled off her boy's clothes and fell into bed for a few hours of heavy sleep before she could do anything to prepare for her journey back to Ireland.

Once the rays of the morning sun seeping through her curtains woke her, she dragged herself out of bed and set to work packing the few things she and Ryan would need for the voyage to her old home.

"You're returning to Ireland?" Harriett gaped as soon as Alice informed her of her plans while Ryan ate his breakfast. "This very minute?"

"Lord and Lady Carnlough are departing this morning," Alice said, still rushing about the flat, packing a few mementos that she would rather not have left for anyone else to pack. "I don't have the train and ferry fare to make it home with Ryan on my own. I shall have to catch them at the train station and beg for their mercy to take us with them."

Of course, she knew Maeve would accept her flight home with open arms and that she would convince Avery to foot whatever bill there was for her and Ryan's passage. She didn't have time to send a note around to Maeve, however. They would have to meet at the train station, where she would explain everything once they were face to face.

"I'll pay you whatever wages I can until the end of the month," Alice told Harriett as she brought the two traveling bags she'd finished packing out to the main room of the flat. She crossed to where her purse sat on the small table near the door and searched through to see if she had any ready cash in it at all. "And I'll give you all the references you need to find future employment. I may need you and Mrs. Knox to work together packing up the remainder of my and Ryan's things so that they can be sent to me, though."

"But what about Mr. Rathborne-Paxton, ma'am?" Harriett asked, stepping away from the table, where she'd been helping Ryan with his tea. "What about your husband? I thought...I thought we were all going to be a household together."

For the first time in what felt like an hour, Alice stopped her incessant, nervous movement and simply stood where she was. She'd avoided thinking about Sam and what her flight back to Ireland might mean to him. She'd forced herself to think of him not as her husband, but as the dear friend she'd once been close to, but with whom things that should never have been had fallen apart.

It was no use. The more she thought of him, the more she saw his handsome, teasing smile in her mind, the more her heart throbbed at the thought of leaving him, the worse she felt. It wasn't Sam's fault that everything had fallen apart so spectacularly. The blame for all of that fell squarely on other people's shoulders. But Sam hadn't stopped her from leaving —though she hadn't been in a state of mind to let him stop her those few, painful hours ago—and he wasn't there to hold her back from what he must have known was best for her at that moment.

Alice let out a sigh and started moving again. "I will admit that I do not know what will happen between Sam and I. I would welcome him in Ireland—as I will welcome you, if you choose to come—but his duty and his family are here, and at present, his brothers might need him more than I do."

That felt a bit like a lie. If she were honest with herself, she needed Sam as desperately as she needed to get away from London and the ruined life that was all that remained for her in the city. It would have been heaven to take Sam with her somehow, but her first priority was for Ryan's safety and happiness, and for her own.

That priority was made even more clear half an hour later, as she and Ryan departed the flat, dressed for travel.

"Mrs. Rathborne-Paxton, might I have a word with you?" a man Alice had never seen before stepped forward from where he'd been leaning against the side of the building as soon as Alice and Ryan stepped out. He wasn't dressed in the same, fine manner as most of the men who had approached her in the last few days.

"No," Alice told the man firmly. "No, you may not. And I am damn well tired of being accosted every three seconds by men with salacious ideas about my worth and how low I would stoop to accommodate them. Get out of my sight."

She walked on at a fast pace, pulling Ryan along with her.

"I'm not one of them lot, I'm from *The Times*, Mrs. Rathborne-Paxton," the man called after her.

"Even worse," Alice called over her shoulder. It would be a

horrific expense, but she was intent to hail a cab as soon as she made it to the main street running perpendicular to Mrs. Knox's. Anything to stop herself from being harassed.

"We'd like to do a story about all the ways you've been maligned and misunderstood," the journalist continued to call after her. "About the slanderous way newspapers ruin the lives of innocent victims to sell a few copies."

A flicker of hope passed through Alice. Perhaps there was a way she could come out of the situation with her reputation improved.

A moment later, she decided it wasn't worth the risk. She'd reached the main street, and a cab pulled up close by, as if its driver knew she was waiting for a means of escape.

Euston Station was crowded for a Friday morning by the time Alice and Ryan arrived.

"I don't like it," Ryan said, clutching Alice's skirts, since she didn't have a free hand to hold his, not with two traveling bags. "I want to go home."

"We're going home, love," Alice reassured him. "As soon as we find Auntie Maeve and Uncle Avery."

Alice stood taller, trying to search the morning crowd to find her friends. She checked the departures board to find where the trains to Liverpool were departing, then headed across the station in the hopes that she might find them there.

She nearly stumbled over her own feet when she heard a newspaper boy call out, "Burglary at Harvey's Gentleman's Club! Middle of the night heist carried out! Suspects not found!"

The boy's shouted declaration nearly brought a smile to Alice's face. She was curious enough to veer off to the side so that she could catch a glimpse at the copy of the paper that the boy held up.

"Mayhem at Harvey's Club," the boy told her hopefully as

she leaned in to read as much of the article as she could. "The suspects haven't been found. We could all be in danger."

Alice smirked slightly. She doubted anyone was in danger. Those particular burglars had no intention of doing anything like that ever again.

She had started to straighten and turn back to the crowd to search for Maeve and Avery again, but another item on the front page of the newspaper caught her attention instead. She leaned in again to read.

"*Gold Discovered in South Africa*," the headline read. Alice's brow shot up as she read on. "*Landowners near Johannesburg are counting their blessings today as the announcement of not one, but several potentially profitable mines have been discovered in the area of the Witwatersrand Basin. Reports are that locals have known of the gold deposits for some time, but only now have enterprising mine owners, some of whom have, of late, lost their diamond-mining contracts to Rhodes's De Beers monopoly, set their minds to uncovering these rich gold deposits.*"

Alice sucked in a breath and stood straighter. It couldn't possibly be...could it? Diamond mines were not the same thing as gold mines. It seemed wildly improbable that gold could have been discovered anywhere near the mine Mr. Kalman ran. But if that were the case, it would certainly explain Montrose's unflagging interest in—

"Excuse me. Mrs. Rathborne-Paxton, I presume?"

Alice whipped around at the sound of the male voice behind her. Unlike the journalist near her flat, the gentlemen who stood a little too close to her, grinning a bit too broadly, his cheeks ruddy with interest as he swept her with a look from head to toe, most definitely had lascivious intentions toward her.

"I do not know you, sir," Alice barked at the man, so vehemently that the newspaper boy flinched. "I am with my son. You will move away from me at once."

Ryan clutched her skirts so tightly Alice thought he might disappear into them.

The man balked, looking at Alice as though he had slapped her. "You would speak to me like that?" he demanded. "A cheap strumpet like you?"

"How dare you insult my wife in such a manner?"

Alice nearly yelped in relief as she spotted Sam striding swiftly toward her, his face set with fury as he glared at the man who had accosted her. Her heart leapt to the heavens over the way he seemed intent on rescuing her. The reaction was so swift and unfettered that it blasted away any wariness or anxiety she might have had at seeing him.

"What is the meaning of this?" the man asked, turning to Sam with a look of confusion. "She don't have a husband, she's a whore."

Alice blinked. The man spoke with a fine, pronounced accent, as if he were a gentleman, but his phrasing was decidedly lower-class.

"Would you like proof that this fine, beautiful, intelligent, brave woman is my wife?" Sam asked, closing the distance between them. "I'll give it to you."

Without waiting for the man to say anything, Sam balled a fist and punched the blighter square across the jaw, sending him reeling.

The man cried out as his lip split, spilling blood across his chin. Several people who had been walking nearby and the newspaper boy gasped in shock at the sudden attack. That drew the attention of even more people in the station.

"I will thank you never to insult my wife in such an underhanded manner again," Sam said in a booming voice, as if speaking to the crowd—and perhaps all of London—as well. He shifted to stand by Alice's side, taking the traveling bags from her. "She is the most magnificent and precious creature in all the world, and I will not allow even a modicum of harm to come to her."

Alice smiled despite herself, her eyes growing watery. She told herself it was exhaustion and not bone-deep gratitude that Sam would stand up for her. But he was standing up for her. When it truly mattered, too.

A moment later, her emotions shifted entirely when the man who had accosted her burst out, "Oy! I did not agree to getting me face bashed in," in a decidedly cockney accent. "That's where I draw the line."

Both Alice and Sam gaped at the man. As finely dressed and groomed as he was, suddenly it was clear that he was an imposter.

Sam reacted swiftly, grabbing the man by the front of his jacket. "Who are you and why have you accosted my wife?"

The man had a hand to his jaw, and evidently, he didn't relish another blow. "He paid me to proposition her," he said. "I thought it were good money for a couple minutes' work. But it weren't. Not if it means getting my face bashed."

"Montrose," Sam said, shaking the bastard. "Montrose paid you to accost her, didn't he? I'd wager he's paid dozens of men to come after you," he told Alice over his shoulder.

"Don't tell him," the man said, suddenly looking shaken. "He'll have me hide, he will. Don't you tell him you know."

With that, the man wrenched himself free of Sam's grasp and dashed off.

Alice gaped in his wake. So Montrose had hired all of those men to proposition her after all. He'd likely done it to frighten her into selling her investments and leaving London.

As quick as she was to feel anger over that nefarious trick, the same sort of hopelessness that had overcome her earlier returned. When would Montrose stop? Would he ever stop, even if she sold him her not-so-worthless diamond mine shares?

"Sam, you're a darling for coming to my rescue," she said, pain and bitterness in her voice despite Sam's arrival, "but I cannot do this. I have to go, and you cannot stop me."

She took Ryan's hand and lifted to her toes, searching the station to reorient herself and remind herself which way she should go. By a twist of luck, she spotted Maeve and Avery, along with baby Alonzo and his nursemaid, across the sea of people crowding the station. Maeve caught sight of Alice, waved in surprise, and tugged Avery's sleeve as she started toward Alice.

Before Alice could take even a single step, Sam, grabbed her arm and spun her to face him.

"I love you, Alice," he declared for all to hear. "I love you more than anything."

"Oh, Sam," Alice felt herself starting to melt, but she couldn't do it. She couldn't put herself through the misery again. "I love you too, but—"

"No buts," Sam said, adjusting so that he held her hand. He'd put one of her traveling bags down to catch her, and now he put the other one down as well, taking up her free hand with both of his. Ryan stared up at him with wide, wary eyes as he clutched Alice's other hand. "I love you," Sam repeated, "and I am not going to let you go."

Alice opened her mouth to protest, but Sam cut her off with, "I know that I have done everything wrong at every step of the way in this last week, but no more. I have but one thought and one aim from here on out, and that is to make you happy. I will not let Montrose or my father or the machinations of my bothers stand in the way of me keeping you safe and protecting you from every danger that you face. You are my wife now, and I've never been happier. Whatever there is to face, we will face it together."

As much as part of Alice wanted to protest, wanted to assert her independence and her ability to take care of herself, there was something so just and so true in Sam's eyes. He was serious in a way she'd never seen him be before. And for perhaps the first time, she had true confidence in his ability to love her and take care of her.

"I cannot stay in London," she told him. It wasn't an ultimatum as much as it was a question of how far he was willing to go for her. Knowing that Montrose had paid the men who had been vexing her for the last few days—and guessing that he might very well be responsible for the cruel newspaper articles that had been printed about her as well—changed the intensity of her problems in London a bit, but it didn't alleviate them entirely.

But Sam surprised her by saying, "I have no wish to stay in London either, my love." A warm smile spread across his face. "Perhaps it is a defeat of some sort. Perhaps it means I am weak or somehow less of a man if I wish to flee Montrose's meddling with my family, to abandon my brothers to whatever plan they have against him. I would rather put all of my efforts into making the very best life I can with you. I do not care if people consider me a coward for retreating from the fight and leaving it to Francis and the others to solve. I just want to be with you, in peace." Sam sent a glance to Ryan, who smiled. "Don't you think that's a good idea, Ryan, my boy?"

Ryan's smile turned into full-fledged beaming. "Yes, I do!"

Alice's eyes stung with tears to see her son so happy, even if the adorable boy didn't know what he was agreeing with or what it would mean. Sam truly was the sort of father she'd always wanted for her son.

She noticed that Maeve and Avery had almost made their way through the crowd to join them, but Sam went on with, "I don't care whether Francis gives his permission or not, we're moving to Hampshire, to Chilcomb Park. He can try to stop me, but his estate has nothing to do with the lands and assets Montrose has seized from Father, so it has nothing to do with the mess in London. No one will bother us there. We were so happy in Winchester the other day."

"We were," Alice agreed breathlessly.

"It's settled, then," Sam said with a nod. "Our life awaits us in Hampshire." A sparkle came to his eyes, and he let go of Alice's hand long enough to reach into the inner pocket of his jacket. "Oh, and this might help," he said, drawing out an envelope.

He handed it over to Alice. Alice was surprised to find it was addressed to her at her flat, and that the postmark was from South Africa. She also noted that the envelope had been opened.

"Mrs. Knox gave that to me when I went to your flat first thing to find you," Sam explained. "I didn't catch you in time, it would appear. I also took the liberty of opening this correspondence. I hope you don't mind." He could barely contain the excited smile he wore.

Alice pretended to frown at him as she let go of Ryan's hand in order to take the letter out of the envelope. Ryan shifted to stand with Maeve and Avery as Alice read the letter.

"*Dear Mrs. Woodmont*," it read, addressing her by her unmarried name. "*I am beyond pleased and delighted to inform you that gold has been discovered on the property owned by Niemeer Mines. As you know, we were forced to cease our diamond mining operations earlier this year, but I can now inform you that the reason the company was not disbanded entirely and your shares were not canceled was because we had hope that gold was present within the vicinity of the original mines. Our suspicions were proven correct, and the company's focus has already shifted to gold mining. Below is a detailed outline of the projected profits of the new mining operation.*"

Alice glanced further down the letter, then let out a gasp at the numbers contained there. They were so large that she clapped a hand to her mouth to stop herself from squealing outright.

Samuel Rathborne-Paxton was a lucky man indeed. As it turned out, he'd married an extraordinarily wealthy woman after all.

"Isn't it grand?" Sam asked, beaming at her with a combination of giddiness and pride. "I thought...well, I thought you might like to come back to the house with me to break the news to Father and to my brothers."

Alice's joy thudded to her feet and her smile dropped. "You want me to hand all of this money over to your family?" she asked, disappointment already gripping her.

"Absolutely not," Sam said with a wide smile, restoring her hope again. "That money is yours and yours alone. I don't want a thing to do with it, and I most certainly don't want my family to touch a farthing of it. But won't it be fun to tell them how rich you are, then to deny them even a tiny share of it after all we've been through?"

She loved him. If she hadn't known before that, she would have known now. Samuel Rathborne-Paxton was a misfit and a joker, and she loved every single part of him more than she could possibly say.

She folded the letter back into its envelope, then turned to Maeve. "I was hoping to catch you at the station this morning so that I could beg you to take me back to Ireland with you," she said, stepping closer to Maeve to greet her—finally—with a kiss on each cheek. "But as it turns out, I don't think I'll return to Ireland after all. I think I have a whole life that waits for me in Hampshire."

"And I wouldn't hold you back from that for all the world," Maeve said, embracing Alice in return. She squealed, then went on with, "I always knew that everything would turn out for the best for you. Love truly does conquer all."

Alice still wasn't completely convinced of that, but she was more convinced that love might just win out for her in the end after all.

She took a step back, positioning herself at Sam's side after Sam finished shaking Avery's hand.

Ryan rushed to stand between Alice and Sam, taking their hands and beaming. "Are we really going to move to Winchester?" he asked, glancing first to Alice, then to Sam. "Can I have a train if we do? Like the one in the shop window? And can I have a boat too? And some ducks?"

Alice laughed, but it was Sam who answered, "I'm certain all of that can be arranged. And if I remember rightly, Uncle Francis has a delightful set of hunting dogs who live at Chilcomb Park, and I remember him saying that one of them has just had a litter of puppies."

Ryan's eyes went wide, and he gasped. "Mama, can I have a puppy?" he asked Alice, as though puppies trumped trains and boats and ducks all together.

"I believe that will be up to your *Uncle Francis*," she said, emphasizing the familial title Sam had given him. She sent Sam a sly look and shook her head slightly as she did.

"Uncle Francis owes me quite a bit," Sam said. "And he feels extraordinarily guilty for everything that has happened," he added in a quieter voice. "He said as much after you left this morning. I plan to rake him over the coals a bit more later as well." He added a wink for good measure.

"As long as he lets us live together as a family in peace and quiet, then I might just be able to forgive him anything," Alice said, leaning closer to Sam.

"I will forgive anyone anything as long as I can be with you," Sam said, his eyes shining with love.

Despite the crowd of the station and the number of people watching them, whether they should have been or not, Sam leaned closer and slanted his mouth over Alice's in a tender kiss. It was exactly the sort of thing Alice needed in that moment. It was sweet, loving, and filled with the promise that the two of them could be happy together, no matter what forces were set against them and no matter what people thought. At last, she'd found exactly the place where she belonged and where she could be happy.

Epilogue

Nothing made Dean Rathborne-Paxton happier than a night at the theater. He loved the hum and buzz of people taking their seats before the orchestra began the overture and before the curtain rose. He loved the scents of perfume and sweat and whatever the patrons of the theater had had for supper before arriving. And he loved the bits of gossip he could hear being discussed around him as he waited for the show to start.

"...left London, just like that," someone in the box next to his family box said. "Took that questionable bride of his and left for Hampshire, or so I heard, without a backward glance."

Dean grinned from ear to ear and kept himself concealed from the next box so that its occupants would keep talking. They could only be talking about Sam and Alice.

"Did you read all of those newspaper articles about her?" another, female, voice said. "The woman is downright scandalous. I cannot believe she married the son of a marquess."

"No, no," the other woman in the box said. "Didn't you read the most recent article about her in *The Times*? The one with all the retractions?"

"What is this?" a male voice asked.

"There was an article just last week," the other woman said. "It seems that someone had deliberately set out to ruin Mrs. Rathborne-Paxton's reputation. They'd paid a great deal of money to several prominent newspapers to print salacious stories about her. In fact, Mrs. Rathborne-Paxton is a fine, lovely woman. She's very good friends with the Earl and Countess of Carnlough."

"Is she really?" the first woman asked.

"Indeed. And she's on good terms with several other members of the aristocracy as well."

"No wonder she and Mr. Rathborne-Paxton left London behind for the country, then," the man said. "If I were them, I would sue all of those newspapers for slander."

"I've heard they might," the other woman said.

Dean covered his mouth with one hand to hide his laughter. Sam and Alice had no intention of suing anyone for slander. The only intention they had was living a peaceful life in Hampshire, begetting a few more children to spend Alice's considerable wealth on, and being happier than the rest of them could imagine.

His father was livid about the whole thing, of course. He'd demanded that Alice turn over her shares in the gold mine to Sam at once, and that Sam hand them over to him in turn. Both of them refused the demand, of course, and as much as Father railed against women owning investments and all of the damnable laws that had been passed in his youth that allowed women to maintain their property in their own name upon marriage, there wasn't a damn thing he could do about it. The old bastard was as stuck and desperate now as he'd been at the start of the whole fiasco.

Of course, that meant the rest of them were still in a bind as well. Sam might have escaped Montrose's trap, but the rest of them were still in it. In fact, Dean was as determined as

Francis was to figure out a way to exploit what they now knew about Montrose and to turn it against him.

And speaking of the devil, as soon as Dean turned his thoughts toward the man, he spotted Montrose entering a box on the opposite side of the balcony from where he sat. Montrose noticed him immediately, of course. Everyone in London knew whom the box where Dean sat belonged to. The Concord Theater was small enough that the two of them could see each other's faces clearly across the distance.

Montrose looked as though he was out for blood. The bastard had guessed exactly what the so-called burglary at Harvey's Club was all about. Alice and Sam hadn't taken anything from the man's private office, but from what Dean had heard through bits of gossip, Sam and Alice had left a mess in their wake when they'd been discovered and forced to flee the club. Montrose knew they had his number, and judging by the glare he sent Dean, the man was already plotting some new form of revenge.

Dean merely grinned back at the blackguard as if he and his brothers had already won the game and Montrose's days were numbered. They weren't, of course. There was still a long way to go until they had Montrose under their thumb where they wanted him.

All thoughts of Montrose and revenge vanished as soon as the lights in the theater began to dim and the orchestra started in on the overture of the latest Cristofori play. Immediately, Dean's heart began to beat faster. He moved from his spot near the back of the box, where he'd been listening to his neighbors, to take up a seat in the very first row. At last, it was time for the very thing that he had come to the theater to bask in that night: Nannette D'Argent.

He held his breath as the curtain rose, revealing the most beautiful woman in the entire world. The audience burst into applause, and Dean applauded along with them, his heart feeling as though it might burst from his chest.

Nannette stepped forward and began her glorious aria, the perfect way to start a show. Dean watched her, holding his breath and adoring her from afar. She was the most famous actress and dancer currently performing on the London stage. It was rumored that she'd amassed a large fortune through demanding exorbitant fees for her performances and through investments. She had legions of admirers who would meet her at the stage door every night. Her dressing room was over-flowing with flowers. But as she continued with her song, she glanced straight at Dean and smiled that secret smile of hers.

Dean blew her a kiss, his insides thrumming with excite-ment. If Sam could fulfill Francis's marriage plans for them all by marrying his mistress and scandalizing everyone, then Dean could make just the sort of splash that would embarrass their father and enrich the family coffers by marrying the most cele-brated actress London had seen in ages. All he had to do was figure out how to woo the woman and win her.

I hope you have enjoyed Alice and Sam's story! It was about time Alice had a happily ever after, considering everything she'd been through. And it was only fitting that she end up a wealthy woman as well.

Everything I've included in this story about diamond and gold mining in South Africa during the 1890s is accurate. It's true that the diamond mining industry was massively prof-itable at that time, and also true that Cecil Rhodes and De Beers Consolidated Mines ended up with a monopoly by the time this story takes place. They crushed almost all of the smaller mining operations—and don't get me started on working conditions in the mines and the way native-born

Africans were crushed by encroaching British imperialists—and men like Rhodes not only ended up ridiculously wealthy, they controlled the South African government as well. It is also true that gold was "discovered" around this time in many areas where diamond mines were already operational. Although, to say gold was discovered when native South Africans had known about its presence for generations and had mined it themselves is a bit of a stretch. So it is entirely possible that enterprising men, like the fictional Mr. Kalman, would have been able to turn a misfortune into profit by switching up the nature of their mining operations.

Also of note, newspapers and gossip columns in the 1890s were notoriously horrible. Many a life was ruined by salacious stories. But as long as people were rushing to buy papers to eat up the gossip, damaging stories continued to be printed. Several of the major events of the 1890s—like the Jack the Ripper case and Oscar Wilde's trial—were made a thousand times more sensational than they would have been otherwise because of the coverage newspapers gave them. So if you think that news stories today are just a bunch of nasty click-bait, well, that kind of journalism has a long history.

But what about the continued efforts of the Rathborne-Paxton family to fight back against Montrose? What about the brothers' plans to marry wealthy but unsuitable brides so that they can ruin their family name before Montrose can? What were those "trophies" sitting on Montrose's mantel, specifically the Indian goddess and the ballerina? And who was it in the photograph on Montrose's desk marked "Petrus"? You'll have to read the rest of *The Unsuitable Brides* series to find out! Next up is Dean's story, *Let's Face the Music and Dance*, as he attempts to woo and win Nannette D'Argent!

• • •

If you enjoyed this book and would like to hear more from me, please sign up for my newsletter! When you sign up, you'll get a free, full-length novella, *A Passionate Deception*. Victorian identity theft has never been so exciting in this story of hope, tricks, and starting over. Part of my West Meets East series, *A Passionate Deception* can be read as a stand-alone. Pick up your free copy today by signing up to receive my newsletter (which I only send out when I have a new release)!

Sign up here: http://eepurl.com/cbaVMH

Are you on social media? I am! Come and join the fun on Facebook: http://www.facebook.com/merryfarmerreaders

I'm also a huge fan of Instagram and post lots of original content there: https://www.instagram.com/merryfarmer/

ONE LAST THING! Do you crave historical romance filled with passion and red-hot chemistry? Come join me and my author friends in the Facebook group, Historical Harlots, for exclusive giveaways, chat with amazing HistRom authors, raunchy shenanigans, and more!

https://www.facebook.com/groups/2102138599813601

About the Author

I hope you have enjoyed *That's Why the Lady is a Tramp*. If you'd like to be the first to learn about when new books in the series come out and more, please sign up for my newsletter here: http://eepurl.com/cbaVMH And remember, Read it, Review it, Share it! For a complete list of works by Merry Farmer with links, please visit http://wp.me/P5ttjb-14F.

Merry Farmer is an award-winning novelist who lives in suburban Philadelphia with her cats, Torpedo, her grumpy old man, and Justine, her hyperactive new baby. She has been writing since she was ten years old and realized one day that she didn't have to wait for the teacher to assign a creative writing project to write something. It was the best day of her life. She then went on to earn not one but two degrees in History so that she would always have something to write about. Her books have reached the Top 100 at Amazon, iBooks, and Barnes & Noble, and have been named finalists in the prestigious RONE and Rom Com Reader's Crown awards.

Acknowledgments

I owe a huge debt of gratitude to my awesome beta-readers, Caroline Lee and Jolene Stewart, for their suggestions and advice. And double thanks to Julie Tague, for being a truly excellent editor and to Cindy Jackson for being an awesome assistant!

Click here for a complete list of other works by Merry Farmer.

Printed in Great Britain
by Amazon

79283198R00149